WAR BUNNY

CHRISTOPHER ST. JOHN

Harvest Oak Press

Published by Harvest Oak Press, July 2021

First Printing, 2021

ISBN: 978-1-7368857-0-3 (paperback)
ISBN: 978-1-7368857-1-0 (ebook)

Cover art by Belle McClain

Hi Marquetta + Bob,
Hope you enjoy it!.
-Christphr
Sr. John

For the animals

Chapter 1

The Loved One spake unto them, saying, "Glory to those that run. For I shall meet them in the jaws of the Blessed Ones, and we will be with Yah in Paradise."

—*Book of Fescue: 4:17-19*

ANASTASIA

The jaws of the fox snapped shut where Anastasia's head had just been, the right canine tooth catching the tip of her long left ear. A lick of pain raced down her ear and her heart banged against her ribs. The fear burn rushed through her, and her powerful legs hurled her forward. The fox's jaws closed again, so close to her neck that she could feel the hot breath.

Heart hammering, the brown yearling rabbit flung herself through the small bushes and over the dead leaves and twigs. The fox came behind, paws casting up a welter of leaves and dirt. His eyes were bright, his teeth shone. Anastasia heard his excited whine rising over his harsh breathing.

Why had she left the area near the warren, again? Why couldn't she be obedient and follow Warren Mother's commands? *I'm so stupid.*

She flashed past the ancient apple tree where she had stopped just a few minutes before. Her back legs drove her forward, her spine expanding and contracting like a steel spring, her front legs barely guiding her flight. Her golden eyes were wide, scanning the branches, stones, stumps, and grasses racing toward her, charting a path. And behind, she heard the fox's claws digging into the earth as he drove forward, the kill whimper already forming in his throat.

She knew she should pray now, and accept Glorification as Yah commanded, but somehow, she couldn't. She didn't love the fox enough, in spite of being taught to do so since the day she was born.

She veered left, felt a burning in her right flank, and turned her head to see the fox's canine rip down her right side, tearing open a gash. A spray of blood flicked outward. Pain arced along her right rear leg. She started to limp, slowing down, and the fox whined in the killing joy as he hurtled forward. She could not escape.

She felt the Giving start to come upon her. Her limbs began to weaken, her mind clouded. She stumbled. The fox yelped with pleasure. But one word drummed in her mind. The obstinate kernel of herself that would not give in: *No.*

Suddenly, Anastasia's wide eyes found the thing she was looking for: the southernmost hole in Bloody Thorn Warren. The sight of safety helped her throw off the Giving, and she plunged ahead, trying to shake the fog in her mind. The fox saw the hole, too, and angled toward it, trying to reach the hole before she did and cut her off.

Anastasia tensed the ropy muscles in her back legs and launched into the air, ignoring the pain, aiming right at the welcoming darkness of the burrow. The fox saw her shadow and looked up to see her airborne, just above him. He tried to push himself upward with his forelegs, jaws reaching for her soft belly. But the change in direction slowed his motion, and his teeth clicked shut on empty space.

An instant later, Anastasia's body crash-landed at the mouth of the burrow and tumbled inside. She hurtled down the slope, half running, half falling, leaving a smear of blood along the side of the entry passage. Behind her, the fox jammed his muzzle into the hole, his head filling the space and blocking out the light. His angry snarl echoed down the corridor. "Next time!"

Anastasia stumbled to a stop at the foot of the slope, staring up at the entryway, panting heavily. Once his shadow disappeared and the songbirds started singing again, she knew he was gone. She ran back to the entryway and touched the left side three times, then the right side three times, eyes darting around, looking for the fox.

Still panting, she hastily murmured a rhyme she had learned long ago:

"Two little bunnies went up a hill,
One came back and the other lay still."

Then she slapped the earth at the foot of the doorway twice, and an instant later she was bolting down the passage into the soothing smell of rabbit as fast as she could go. Within a few feet, she ran into a well-fed blue and white rabbit, and bowled her over. It was Sweet Leaf, an older sister. She nipped Anastasia's belly, hard.

"Why don't you watch where you're going?" she said crossly.

"Sorry," panted Anastasia. "Blessed One. Right on me."

"Oh, were you almost Glorified?" asked Sweet Leaf, her eyes warm and bright.

"Yes," said Anastasia.

"Poor thing," said Sweet Leaf, and nuzzled her. "Oh, and your side, too." She began to lick the wound. "Holy day," she murmured.

"Every one a gift," said Anastasia, automatically, her heart still hammering.

"Did you go beyond the Ring of Love?" asked Sweet Leaf.

Anastasia pulled her left ear down with her paws and licked the blood off the tip. She was starting to really feel the pain of her injuries now.

"Did you go past the Ring?" Sweet Leaf asked again.

"What difference does it make?" asked Anastasia. She was breathing hard, the smell of her fear loud in the close space.

Some other rabbits in the warren were attracted by the sound of talking and the smell of blood. "What happened? Someone get Glorified?" asked a tan tortoiseshell bunny with a slight limp.

"Warren Mother asked us not to go beyond the Ring a month ago," said Sweet Leaf. "She said from now on, stay close to the warren. Always stop at the acacia trees."

Anastasia's favorite little sister appeared. She was just two months old, too young to understand her relationship to Anastasia. "You hurt, auntie?" she asked, her green eyes huge against her golden fur. Without waiting for an answer, she immediately began licking Anastasia's ear.

"Thank you, Sunbeam," panted Anastasia. "You are a sweet baby girl."

Sweet Leaf turned in the passageway, pressing against Anastasia while she licked her flank. "What was it?"

"Fox," said Anastasia.

"This tear starts very high on your side. That Blessed must have been almost over you."

"It was close," said Anastasia, nuzzling against Sunbeam's shoulder.

"That was careless," said Sweet Leaf.

Anastasia stiffened. "Yes. I was stupid."

The tan tortoiseshell bunny scratched his ear. "And you led the fox back here?" *Tsk tsk.*

"Where should I have run?" asked Anastasia.

A handsome, cream-colored rabbit with black ears stepped out of the crowd. It was Aiden, the Rememberer of Bloody Thorn Warren, redolent of fresh radish tops. He spread his paws in a kindly way. "We run even when we don't need to run," he said gently. He kissed Anastasia's cheek. "There's no outrunning the mercy of Yah."

"There's no outrunning the mercy of Yah," repeated Sunbeam softly as she licked Anastasia's ear.

At the sound of Sunbeam's tiny infant's whisper, Anastasia felt her head get hot, and the streak of heat traveled down her back.

"Where is the mercy of Yah in this?" she asked Aiden.

Aiden smiled. "Yah's mercy is everywhere. It's here with you, right now. You're safe. You're alive."

"If I almost die, that shows Yah's mercy?" asked Anastasia.

A murmur ran through the crowd of furry faces surrounding her. She could smell their rising hostility.

Aiden looked at her sternly. "There's no call for that kind of language, my child," he said. Then he laid his forepaw on her shoulder and said, softly, "*Glory to those that run,* it says in the Word of Yah. Even when you run, Yah is with you." He looked out over the crowd. "He is with all of us."

Somewhere in the crowd, a rabbit stamped three times. Not the panicky, single, hard staccato stamp that says *alarm*! But rather, the slow and heavy triple-stamp of affirmation. Another rabbit took up the triple-stamp, then another, until the space was filled with the sound. Aiden's smooth and kindly voice continued, "Yah's mercy is in the dandelion leaf. His mercy is in the apple twig." Aiden sat up tall and spread his forepaws wide, gazing beneficently down at Anastasia. "Yah loves *you*. Yah has a plan for *you*. And that's so wonderful, since…" he broke off, awkwardly.

"Since what?" said Anastasia.

"Since … how you … are." Aiden looked embarrassed. Some rabbits were looking away.

"What do you mean, Honored Rememberer?" asked Anastasia. She knew very well what he meant.

Aiden was silent. He looked away. Sweet Leaf stopped licking for a moment. "You know. Without kittens," she said, blandly. "After four or five bucks have tried their luck..." She shrugged. "Warren starts talking." She snuggled in close to Anastasia's side. "But Yah still loves you. And so do I."

BRICABRAC

Bricabrac, a rather handsome young water rat with a copper earring in his left ear, grinned as he looked up at the tree and saw the magpie circling a nest. *Perfecto*. He approached the base of the tree carefully, moving a little more slowly than usual under the weight of his heavy backpack. It only took him a couple of minutes to find what he was looking for: the entrance to a burrow. He sniffed. Smelled like a mouse. He opened his pack and rummaged around inside. Then, he struck a lazy pose just outside the mouth of the burrow and started talking.

"So, if there was a wood mouse in this area, that would be good news for everyone, eh?"

Bricabrac fell silent and scratched his belly. He turned over on his back and looked up at the sky. "A smart mouse. A hardworking mouse. That's what makes the Million Acre Wood a great place to live. *And* raise a family."

A mouse's head appeared suddenly out of the darkness. "Oh, a rat." He looked grouchy. "What?"

"Oh, hey! What up? What up?" said Bricabrac. "A wood mouse? That's awesome! Cuz I've got some items that could be just perfect for a wood mouse." He rattled his pack. "Gifts of the Dead Gods. Rare tools. I brought these all the way from Oom."

He took out a curved piece of glass with jagged edges that said "*epsi*" on it. "Look at this here. Solid diamond. I'm sure you've heard of diamonds. The Dead Gods loved them." He held up the glass and looked through it at the wood mouse. "Two major uses here. One, it's a window. Set this in an opening in the outer wall of your passage, and you can see what's outside without the cold air coming in."

The wood mouse scoffed. "Pffft. Who cares?"

"Aaaaaand you can cut with it," said Bricabrac. "Sharp edge here: Perfect for a big root that you can't get your choppers around. Pretty sweet. Am I right? Here, take a feel. See how hard it is, eh? Heft it. Solid diamond."

The wood mouse squinted at the glass. "Eh, I don't know."

"Or, or, or," said Bricabrac, rummaging through his pack, "A very fine piece of workmanship by the Dead Gods: this burrow protector." He took out a large metal thumbtack. "Check it out, friend. Punch this up through a leaf to anchor it. Place it in the mouth of your burrow and cover it with a fine layer of dirt. You know where it is, but no one else does. Some no-goodnik comes up—maybe a weasel?— and thinks he's gonna sneak in and surprise you, right? That would be bad news! But he steps on this burrow protector and suddenly, he's got a metal thorn in his paw. Does he scream? You bet he does. Goodbye, surprise."

Bricabrac laid the thumbtack on the ground. The wood mouse sniffed it. "What are we talking about?"

"Now, that's a sharp wood mouse right there," said Bricabrac. "But I have to tell you, friend, for items like these, from the Dead Gods direct to you, I have to be paid in moneystones. No roots, no slugs, no favors."

The wood mouse looked at Bricabrac and chewed one of his whiskers. Up above, the magpie called loudly. "What's a moneystone?" asked the wood mouse.

"City thing," said Bricabrac. "Shiny disks. They love those things in Oom. Go figure. I'm a country boy, myself. I grew up around here, just a few miles south." Bricabrac looked through the trees. "My family's still there, bless their hearts."

The wood mouse looked at a small beetle crawling nearby.

"I see you have an upstairs neighbor who collects shiny things," said Bricabrac, hurriedly. "And I'm guessing sometimes she drops them. I used to live under a magpie, myself, as a youngster. So, I got a feeling you could have some moneystones in your burrow right now."

"Maybe," said the wood mouse.

Bricabrac smiled. "Just gathering dust, eh? You could trade them for something *pretty* useful."

The wood mouse stared at Bricabrac for a moment. Then, he went down into his burrow. A few moments later, he emerged, holding a coin in his teeth. On one side, it said, "10 CENTS" and "CANADA 2097" next to a beaver under a palm tree.

"There's that nickel I've been looking for!" chuckled Bricabrac. "And look at the beaver on there. Handsome devil, eh?" Bricabrac picked up the coin in his small, fine hands. "So, what can I do you for, buddy?"

"I'll take the diamond," said the wood mouse.

"Excellent choice!" said Bricabrac. "You'll get many long years of service from this, friend." Bricabrac picked up the *"epsi"* glass and presented it to the wood mouse with a flourish. Then he put the dime in his backpack and fastened it on his back again. "Now then," said Bricabrac, his copper earring shining in the sun, "Could I trouble you for the location of any other magpie nests in this area?"

ANASTASIA

Anastasia limped through the passages of Bloody Thorn Warren, trying to avoid running into anyone. It was well into twilight now, so most of the rabbits would be outside, feeding and playing near the many holes leading into the warren. The warm vanilla smell of rabbits surrounded her, but she could take no comfort in it. At the end of a long passage, she

11

found a small chamber, cluttered with objects. A latticework of roots in the upper part of the chamber allowed a small hole in the ceiling to exist without causing the ceiling to collapse. A single ray of light shone down, illuminating an old rabbit with dappled silver fur and a splash of white on his forehead, peering intently at a small pile of lichen.

Her heart leaped. "Nicodemus!" she cried. She limped toward him, and double-nose-bumped his flank. His tranquil scent calmed her. Then they touched noses, and the whole story of the fox came tumbling out. Nicodemus nuzzled her, pressing his face into the fur near her ear.

"I'm so sorry, dear one," he murmured. "It makes my heart hurt to think how close you came."

He pulled away and crept slowly across the chamber, past piles of twigs, flowers, leaves, moneystones, and a jumble of other items. Against the wall, five ancient, yellowed pages stood, carefully bracketed between fresh maple leaves. Along the bottom of one of the pages some text was visible: *Wilderness Survival in North America – 142*.

"I think I have something here for you," said Nicodemus. "Willow bark will help with the pain." He picked up a scrap of bark in his mouth and brought it over to Anastasia. "Chew on this for a bit, my dear."

Anastasia took the bark and chewed it for a few moments. Then she began trembling. "I was almost Glorified today," she said.

"We will all be with Yah in the end," said Nicodemus. "Even the lucky ones, like me." He settled down next to her, pressing against her unwounded left flank and calming her trembling. There was a small sound in the passage.

Anastasia leaned into him. "You know so much," she said.

Nicodemus shrugged. "I'm just an old Reader," he said. "But I've seen a few things."

"So how does this mean that Yah loves me?"

Nicodemus placed his paw upon hers. "Shhhh," he murmured.

They heard the sound in the passage again and looked up to see Sweet Leaf in the entrance to the chamber. A moment later, she had stepped back into the shadows.

"Do you want to come by tomorrow morning when the light is good?" asked Nicodemus.

"But—" began Anastasia.

Nicodemus smiled gently. "Best time of the day for reading."

Anastasia's eyes flicked toward the mouth of the chamber. "Fluffy's better than me," she said. "You've already said he'll be Reader of Bloody Thorn after ...." She trailed off.

"After my time," said Nicodemus. "Will you come and read?"

"I'm so bad with capital letters," she said.

"You have the hunger to learn," said Nicodemus. "And no matter what anyone says about you, your mind is strong." He looked up into the fading shaft of light. "Remember that, my dear."

Anastasia heard a large rabbit moving down the passageway. Then a sturdy buck with chestnut fur and a tan underbelly stepped into the light. It was Briar, one of the First Born. "Warren Mother requests your presence in her chamber."

Anastasia followed him, her heart skittering as they threaded through the many runs and passages of the warren. Briar said nothing. Soon, they were at the entryway to her mother's chambers. Briar gestured for her to enter. A trembling seized her. She froze.

"Go on, then," said Briar, stepping toward her.

"Yes, yes," said Anastasia. Shakily, she touched the left side of the entryway three times, then the right side three times. She quietly sang an ancient couplet.

"Hush little baby, don't you cry,
Fox won't hear and he'll pass right by."

Then she touched the floor twice.

"Go on!" hissed Briar, shoving her forward with his large chest. Anastasia stumbled into the chamber and came to a stop at the front paws of a stately, steel-gray rabbit with a slash of white across her face and down her back. It was Olympia, the Warren Mother of Bloody Thorn.

Olympia regarded her with her ocean-blue eyes, then she coolly laid her chin on the ground at Anastasia's feet. "Holy day," she said.

Anastasia obediently began to lick Olympia's forehead. "Every one a gift," she murmured.

After a few moments, Olympia lifted her head and sat up. "A fox came close to you today."

"Yes, Honored Mother," said Anastasia, turning so Olympia could see the wound. Olympia's eyes flicked along her side.

"A nasty scratch," she said. "Did you go beyond the Ring of Love?"

Anastasia hung her head. "Yes, Honored Mother."

Olympia settled into a relaxed pose and became still. "Beloved daughter," she said, "There are things that must be spoken." Anastasia was silent, even though her wound throbbed. "I'm worried about your illness."

"I'm getting better," Anastasia blurted. "I only have to say the entry spell once now."

Olympia looked at her without blinking. "One thing gets better, another gets worse," she said.

Anastasia looked at the raw, earthen floor. "No, I'm good ... pretty good ..."

Olympia sat upright, looming over Anastasia. "I dug the

first chamber of this warren by the light of a quarter-moon when I was a yearling doe like you are now. I peopled this city with my children and my children's children. What if you are contagious? Would you have me put them all at risk?"

"I would never do that," said Anastasia quickly, fighting down the urge to begin drawing a circle in the earth. "I'm not contagious. I love the warren. I love you, Honored Mother."

Darius, the Prime Buck, entered the chamber through a passage on the far side and sat beside Olympia. His tan fur was dappled with brown along his left side.

"We're worried that your mind is sick," said Darius. "Every day, a new problem. And today, you're questioning Yah? In the front passage? That's bad for the warren." He pulled his left ear down and cleaned it between his paws. "You're the runt of our fourth litter. We fought for you to live. We loved you—"

"*Love* you," said Olympia, sharply.

Darius let go of his ear. "We love you. But we can't keep looking away."

Anastasia felt Briar coming up behind her and she shifted uneasily.

Olympia advanced toward her, looked into her eyes, and then licked her forehead three times. "I'm so sorry, my love. But you know there is only one place for a sick rabbit to go."

"No," said Anastasia, her breath quickening.

"I'm sorry," said Olympia.

"No, mother," said Anastasia, pushing her face into Olympia's fur. "No, please."

Olympia's scent was cool, unengaged. She stepped away from her daughter.

"The good of the warren demands it," said Darius.

"No," said Anastasia, her heart pounding. She turned to him and tried to nuzzle against his side. "No, Daddy, please," she whimpered.

Darius moved away from her, and suddenly Briar heaved his bulk in front of Anastasia. "You heard Warren Mother. Out."

"Briar," Anastasia's voice came out in a tiny whine. "Second of the First Four. You're my oldest brother. You can't do this to me."

Briar shoved forward, pushing her backward out of the chamber. "Warren Mother has spoken."

"Mommy!" Her voice came out in a shriek. The other two First Born males appeared and stood shoulder to shoulder with Briar, steadily heaving her backward. Now they were in one of the main warren passageways. The runs on each side were filling up with rabbits. There was a jumble of voices. "What? What is it? Someone get Glorified today?"

Anastasia's powerful rear claws bit into the ground, but she could not gain any purchase and kept sliding backward.

The pain of her injury burned along her flank. The cacophony of voices rose. "Someone's getting unwarrened? Who? The crazy one? The barren one? Poor little thing. Let's hope it's quick."

She caught sight of Nicodemus' sad face and gray whiskers off to one side. Just as the First Born were about to shove her past, she darted toward him and pushed her face next to his, sobbing. For a moment, his mouth was next to her ear. "You are strong," he whispered. Then she was past him, and she could feel the cool of the night air on her back. The heavy chests and shoulders of the First Born were a moving wall, and behind them, there was a confused tumble of furry faces and long ears flicking in every direction.

She scrabbled to stand still for a moment, quickly reaching out and touching each side of the entryway three times, gasping her spell:

> *"Hold your breath by the light of the moon,*
> *Golden wolf is coming soon."*

Then she slapped the floor twice. The last thing she saw before she was shoved out through the entryway was Sweet Leaf and her warm, bright eyes in a side passage. "So sorry, dear sister. It's for the best, really."

A burst of rage rushed through her. "Why?" shouted Anastasia.

Sweet Leaf gazed at her kindly. "Just let the Giving do its work. They say you don't feel a thing."

And then Anastasia tumbled out into the night.

FREDDIE

Freddie was concentrating as hard as he could, his black and gray harlequin face a study in bunny fierceness.

"Again," said Rose, the Rememberer of Fallen Oak Warren. She lay sunning her tawny body in the warm sunlight.

Freddie nodded and started over. He was chubby, and his thick, gray and white fur was making him feel hot. *"And the Loved One busied himself among the root vegetables of the field. Soon, the seven rabbits fell to arguing about who would be greatest in the Kingdom of Yah. The Loved One set up seven carrots in a line—"*

"Seven carrots in a *row*," said Rose. Snowdrop, the other Remembering acolyte, snickered.

"Yes, of course," said Freddie. *"Seven carrots in a row, and looked upon them. Behold, quoth he. How many carrots do you see? We see seven, master, they said. No, said the Loved One. For one belongs to Yah. One belongs to the North Wind. One belongs to ... to, um ..."*

"Take a moment," said Rose. "Let the words rise up within you."

Freddie squirmed and looked out over the meadow. He had been farblind from birth, so everything more than a few feet away was a blur. The grass smelled sweet, with an undercurrent of wild lupine and calendula. *"One belongs to ... the ... fog."*

"Brother Worm," said Snowdrop.

"Don't interrupt," said Rose.

Freddie frowned at Snowdrop. "I was just about to get it."

"Totally," said Snowdrop. "You were *super*-close." She wiggled her nose, and her scent was spiky and aggressive. "Maybe you should spend less time hanging around with the Reader and more time on what really matters."

"Do you know the rest of the verse?" Rose asked Snowdrop.

"No," said Snowdrop. "I *feel* the rest of the verse. It's like fire in me."

Freddie rolled his eyes. The sound of a squirrel chittering on a tree branch above was loud in the warm air.

"Tell me," said Rose.

Snowdrop sat upright. *"One belongs to Brother Worm. One belongs to the summer sun. One belongs to Sister Crow. And one belongs to the earth. As the Loved One spake, he knocked the carrots down, one by one, until only one was left standing. Then, he asked them, How many carrots do you see? One, said the rabbits. Yes, said the Loved*

One, And that is why Yah created the Blessed Ones. He that hath an ear, let him hear."

"Perfect," said Rose, lazily.

Snowdrop batted her eyelashes at Freddie, clearly saying, *you can't catch me, you fat stupid doofus. I'm first acolyte, and always will be.* He looked down at his toes.

Rose noticed a lone figure coming across the meadow and sat up quickly. "It's the Lord Harmonizer!" she said. She swatted Freddie across the behind. "Run get some dill for our honored guest." Then to Snowdrop, "Go and make sure his chamber is ready."

The rabbit approaching through the grass was lean and rangy, with huge ears, ropy muscles, and brown fur with a scattering of gray. Rose was sure he had some hare blood in him. As he got closer, she could see the scar along his left cheek and the notch torn out of his ear, souvenirs of a life spent traveling. He saw Rose and nodded as he loped forward. She ran to meet him and they touched noses.

"Tobias! My Lord Harmonizer," said Rose, breathlessly. "So good to see you! Do you have news about the voting irregularities at the Shandy Vale Conclave? What's the final council ruling on the new Presiding Spirit?"

"No news to share yet," chuckled the Harmonizer. "I'm sure everything will be just fine." He nuzzled Rose's shoulder. "You look healthy, Rose."

"Every day a gift," she said. "We've been lucky here at Fallen Oak. The Blessed Ones have been—"

"Living as Yah commands," interrupted Tobias. "We are in His hand."

"Yes, yes of course," murmured Rose. Just then, Freddie showed up with several fronds of fresh dill in his mouth. "Look, my Lord! A small token of our affection for you. Everyone says our dillweed is the best in the Million Acre Wood." She cuffed Freddie lightly behind the ears. "Show your proper respect for our guest!"

Tobias placed his chin on the ground. Freddie put down the dill fronds and licked his forehead. "Greetings, my Lord," he mumbled.

After a few moments, Tobias shook him off and sat up. "Thank you for your kindness," he said. "You're a good lad."

Then, Snowdrop popped out of the warren entrance. "Lord Harmonizer!" she cried. "What an honor it is to meet you! I've prepared your chamber and strewn it with fresh dandelions. And, of course, blueberries."

Tobias touched noses with her and then started munching on the dill fronds. "You haven't lied," he said to Rose. "Fallen Oak Warren still has the finest dill in Yah's creation."

Rose beamed. "Thank you, my Lord."

Tobias sat back as he chewed the fronds. "I wouldn't

mind resting up in my chamber for a bit," he said. "Any burning questions to answer right now?"

Snowdrop led the way toward the special chamber. Rose and Tobias followed, with Freddie tagging along behind.

"There is one," said Rose. "In the Book of Rye 7:13, the passage goes, *And then, Yah smote them with his mighty paw for their iniquities, and he spake in a voice like unto thunder.* Is that last phrase really *like unto thunder* or is it *as though with thunder*? We've had some uncertainty there, and the Rememberer at Blackstone Warren has it differently than I do."

"Not an uncommon question," said the Harmonizer, as he moved along the passage. "These kinds of phrases often get garbled." He paused for a moment, closed his eyes, and put his paws on either side of his head. "The current Conclave memory on that passage is ... *like unto thunder*."

"*Like unto thunder,*" said Rose, savoring it.

"This is so exciting!" squeaked Snowdrop.

"Yes, thank you, Lord Harmonizer," murmured Freddie, dutifully.

Suddenly, a high keening wail pierced the air. It took them a moment to realize what it was. A scream, coming from the main passageway leading to the far side of the warren. A few moments later, a terrified rabbit came bolting down the tunnel, eyes white with fear. As she passed them, she gasped one word: "Weasel!"

Rose stamped, followed by Snowdrop. Freddie felt dizzy. He started to back up. The air was thick with the smell of terror. Tobias disappeared into a side passage. Rose was whispering, "Run, run, run, run, run," and shoving against him, pushing him back up the entry passage toward the outside.

"Save us, my Lord!" shouted Snowdrop, stamping again. There was no answer. More rabbits were rushing down the main passage now, eyes wide and wild. Freddie turned and raced up the entry run toward the light and safety, Rose close on his heels. As he neared the entrance, a terrible, familiar shape rose up and was silhouetted against the light. The small head, the long neck, and the lean body were carved in black against the sun. The sweet, heavy reek of weasel filled the burrow. Freddie felt faint and slowed down.

Rose bit him. "Go!"

The weasels must be attacking as a pair, or maybe there were three or four. Without any sign of hurry, the Blessed One in the entrance of the burrow began to move down the passage, quietly singing her killing song.

"Small little space,
Tight little place,
Great big fear
On your face."

Freddie turned around and shoved past Rose, who was staring into the weasel's eyes.

> *"I've been sent*
> *To collect the rent,*
> *Won't be needing*
> *Your consent."*

As Freddie dashed down the passage, there was a small cry from Rose, and then she was quiet. Snowdrop was gone. The screams from the main passage were louder. Freddie saw a single rabbit, it was Thistledown, dragging himself down the passageway, leaving a muddy trail of dark blood behind him.

The smell of terrified rabbits was overwhelming. Freddie turned, his legs crumbling beneath him. There was no other way out. It was hopeless. He could only wait until the weasels were on him. He felt the Giving begin. He was tired, so sleepy. He could just lie here and soon, he would be with the Loved One in the Lucky Fields, filled with four-leaf clovers and feathery dill fronds and apple twigs as fresh and sweet as the day you were born. His eyelids were heavy. The screams seemed fainter. Everything would be all right.

Then he had an idea: Another way out. A stab of adrenaline burned through him like fire. He bolted upright and ran into the side passage leading to the Reader's room. In a few moments, he was there. And in the roof of the Reader's chamber, as in every Reader's chamber, a small opening let in a shaft of light.

Freddie frantically pushed together all the twigs and leaves and stones and bark that the Reader had gathered, until he had a pile under the small hole in the ceiling. He climbed up, reached up with his front paws, and tore at the earth. It wasn't easy; there were roots around the hole to support it, and that slowed him down. He strained upward and bit through the largest roots, clawing the loose earth down in a shower of debris.

Just down the passage, he could hear a little song.

"Fat little bunny,
Fat little tummy—"

The song stopped, suddenly. Maybe the Blessed One had heard him digging. Freddie paused for a moment, then redoubled his efforts. The warm sun shone down through the ragged gap like a friend. Freddie tore the hole open, and then lunged upward. Raking the sides of the chamber with his rear legs for purchase, he got up into the hole. Then, he seized a root in his mouth while he scrabbled with his forelegs to pull his body up. He was climbing, almost there. One back leg was wedged against the side of the hole, pushing upward, his left leg hanging down.

Suddenly, the weasel reek was thick in the air. A burning pain shot through his hock. The weasel was on him. With the gift of adrenaline and panic, Freddie jerked himself upward, tearing his leg from the Blessed One's jaws. Another moment, and he was through, scrambling past the ferns and trees that grew over Fallen Oak Warren. The weasel leaped upward, missed the lip of the hole, and fell back, thrashing. Bolting as only a terrified rabbit can, Freddie was a hundred yards away in a matter of seconds, his dappled gray body blending with the shadows under the leaves. With his weak eyes, everything was a blur, but as he ran, it seemed as though he saw Tobias standing calmly among the ferns, talking with someone. Talking with a *weasel*.

But that wasn't possible. Freddie shook his head and plunged on, rushing forward into the blue-green smear that was the world.

Chapter 2

Turn your face from me, Hunger Mother. Do not bless me with want this day. Forget me, as one day when the hunting is all done, I will surely forget you.

—Canid prayer

Anastasia

Anastasia crouched as quietly as she could under a laurel bush, eyes huge, hardly daring to breathe. The cicada chorus filled the night air around her. The scent of oak and poplar was strong, and the smell of the little stream she had discovered earlier was bright and moist.

She had never in her life been above ground without the safety of a hole to bolt toward. With her right front paw, she started drawing a circle around herself in the dirt. Little by little, she turned her body as she drew, until the circle was complete.

Quietly, she whispered a soothing, nursery song.

"O, a little tussock of fine fescue,
A sweet little tussock, for me and you."

The night was stifling. She heard her mother's voice saying, "There is only one place for a sick rabbit to go," and fought down a sob. A sob could be fatal. The night was filled with the Blessed Ones, come to take their birthright. A dozen fears clanged in her head. She started to draw another circle. Could she live through this night? *Should* she? She was a sick rabbit, and this was the place for her: Out among the Blessed, waiting to be sent home.

If she could just reach the right state, maybe the Giving would begin and it would all be over, without the terror of the open jaws rushing toward her, the jaws coming to give her what she deserved. She whispered a prayer. "Almighty Yah, creator of the green grass and the apple tree, I beg You for the strength to rejoice in the justice and mercy of Your judgment, so that I may be with You in Paradise."

Then, she felt it: The bump, the small, obstinate *no*. She closed her eyes and prayed fiercely. "Help me, Almighty Yah, Lord of the fox and the rabbit alike ..." But she knew it was no use. Once she felt the *no*, it would never go away. She had learned that over the past year, as she grew from a kitten into a yearling and saw her sisters and brothers taken by the teeth and claws of the Blessed. Weasel. Hawk. Coyote. Fox. She could not give in. She could not.

So, dig. She must dig. Her claws were for something more than drawing circles. All warrens are founded by does, dug by does, enlarged by does. She cast around and saw a massive poplar tree, with a scree of fallen limbs gathered around the base. That would be good. Clutter would help disguise a hole, and the raw earth she would bring up.

Moving as quietly as she could, she crept to the base of the tree and looked for just the right place to start. She found two large roots that grew out close together on one side. A hole in between them would be hard to see. She decided to dig there.

The branches and twigs lay thickly intertwined. She seized one in her mouth and tried to move it, but it was too tangled. She tried another. Same result. Finally, she decided to just chew through the branches in her way. The first few were easy. Then she found one shoot that was especially tough. She could get her jaws around it easily, but it was hard and elastic. It must still be green. She chewed on it for a long time, then stopped and rested, trembling, her ears searching the night for sounds of a Blessed One. The stridulation of the cicadas continued as before. That was good.

She attacked the shoot again, finally wearing it through. One piece of it then fell out of the jumble, its end now worn to a point. Anastasia kicked it out of the way and continued clearing. Soon she was at bare earth, and began to dig.

Her powerful front claws raked the damp earth, tearing it up and piling it under her body. Then she used her large back feet to push it further away, ignoring the pain in her right flank. The wet smell of the heavy loam rose up around her, promising safety.

Every few seconds, she stopped to listen and stare into the surrounding night. Soon her forequarters were well into the hole, with her back legs remaining outside, which made her feel intensely vulnerable. She kept thinking she had heard something, which caused her to back out in a panic. Then she noticed the cicadas were silent, which made her redouble her efforts. She dug fiercely, as fast as she could, panting heavily. If she could just get a hole as big as her body, with a little room to spare, she would be safe, and she could—

Then she heard the sound of a long, drawn-out leaf rattle. *Chik chik chik chik chik.* That was the sound of leaves brushing against a furry coat, each leaf catching on the fur and then releasing. She did not freeze. Rabbits who freeze are dead rabbits. She wriggled out of the hole and raked the darkness with her huge eyes, not making a sound, trying to plot escape routes.

Then she saw it. Fox. The light from the quarter-moon made the teeth shine in the darkness, and the moonlight glinted in the dark eyes. Her heart skipped a beat. She could smell the strong musk. She knew this fox.

The hole wasn't big enough. The two roots hemmed her in, and the scree of branches above kept her from jumping upward and disappearing into the underbrush. She fought down panic.

The fox saw her and stopped moving. Anastasia's heart banged like a kettle drum inside her head. Then he came forward, lips parting to expose his teeth. She inched backward, feet scrabbling in the loose earth, twigs, and shoots. Her mind skittered, even now trying to glean some way out. The stick she had chewed to a point lay beside her, one end buried in the soft earth she had thrown up, and the sharp end pointing away from the hole.

They locked eyes. The moment was brief, then the fox bounded ahead, jaws wide, the killing snarl loud in the small space. Her back against the wall of earth, she scrambled sideways, her powerful legs and feet churning up the loose earth as she fought to put distance between herself and death.

As her back legs flailed, one foot got under the sharpened stick and flicked it into the air, just as the fox lunged. He could not stop in mid-leap, and hurtled forward, mouth open, teeth shining. The sharp end of the stick disappeared into the darkness of his mouth. An instant later, the point reached the back of the fox's throat. The stick, buttressed in the earth, stood fast, and the force of his leap drove the point deep into his soft flesh. The joyful snarl turned into a shriek.

Eyes wild and confused, the fox stumbled backward, the stick stuck in his throat. Thrashing and whipping his head back and forth, he poured forth a storm of yelps and whines. He clutched at the stick protruding from his mouth, his paws slipping down the reddened shaft as he coughed out spatters of blood. He could gain no purchase, and the pointed end of the stick remained buried in the back of his throat. Anastasia wanted to run, but she was terrified to get so close to the enraged and panicking fox, so she stayed still against the dirt.

The fox fell on his left side, dragging his head backward through the damp earth. With his right foreleg, he pushed the stick against the ground as he groaned and heaved. In a few seconds, the stick was covered with earth, and the fox gained enough friction to claw it out of his throat. Then the Blessed One, coughing and leaking red through his lower teeth, bolted into the darkness.

LOVE BUG

Love Bug, a yearling buck with beautiful white fur from head to toe, slipped through the tangle of roots and vines that covered the ground above Moonfall Warren. With any luck, by avoiding the warren passages, he could slip by the First Born who were keeping an eye on the dillweed patch, which was just coming into its prime.

He reached the western edge of the warren, and he could see the dill patch about thirty yards distant, at the edge of a meadow near a wood. Among the feathery fronds were Sweet Pea and Marigold, sisters, both a tawny brown with fluffy white tails. They were pulling down the dill stems and blissfully munching on the delicate tips. The sweet, cool smell of dill wafted toward him in the warm air.

Love Bug quickly washed his face, cleaning his ears one at a time. Then he preened the fur on his chest, and licked his front paws. His spiffing done, he sauntered forward carelessly, singing an ancient bunny dill song in a fine tenor.

"Hey dilly dilly doe
On your dilly dilly hill,
Sweet dilly dally life,
With our dilly dilly dill."

Love Bug reached the dill patch and pulled down a dill stem to reach the sweet, soft tip. Then he turned as though noticing the does for the first time. "Hey, girl," said Love Bug to Sweet Pea. He ran his paw over his fluffy mane.

Sweet Pea looked annoyed.

"Did you thump just now, or was that the earth moving under my feet?" asked Love Bug.

Sweet Pea rolled her eyes and looked away. Marigold smirked and said, "Zat the best you got?"

Love Bug turned to Marigold and batted his long eyelashes at her. "You must be a warm evening in early summer," he said. "Cuz you are *fine*."

Marigold laughed and nibbled a nearby piece of dill. Sweet Pea said, "Do the First Born know you're out here? They said it was only does tonight."

"Oh, yeah, they're cool with it," said Love Bug, nibbling another tip. "We go way back. I'm practically a First Born myself."

Sweet Pea pulled down her left ear and washed it.

"Aren't you, like, thirty-second born?" asked Marigold.

Love Bug lolloped closer and chinned a dill stem in a relaxed way. The sweet aroma of flowers and grass was the perfect complement to the scent of happy, relaxed doe rising from Sweet Pea and Marigold's lush fur. "Ladies," he said, "on a summer evening like this, in Yah's country, birth order ain't nothing but a number."

He saw Marigold's eyes flick upward, focusing on something over his shoulder. "Hey, guys," she said.

Love Bug froze for an instant, then he darted a quick look behind him. There was no one there. He turned back around "Oh, ha, *HA*," he said, amiably. "Okay, okay, you got me—"

Then he was hit from behind and sent sprawling. Sweet Pea and Marigold scattered away, vanishing among the fronds. Love Bug turned to see a squat, ugly rabbit with wide shoulders, who went by the name Stump, one of the First Born of Moonfall Warren. With him was Gaige, another well-fed warren enforcer.

"Love Bug, Love Bug, Love Bug," said Stump, advancing step by step, which caused Love Bug to back up. "This is the third time. What are we going to do with you?"

"It's all good, bro—" began Love Bug. Stump clouted him across the face so hard it made his teeth rattle, and he fell sprawling onto his side. Gaige circled around behind him.

"It's all good, *what*?" demanded Stump.

"It's all good, Third of the First Five," said Love Bug, scrambling to his feet.

"How can it be all good?" asked Stump. "*You're* here." He stepped up to Love Bug, who could not retreat with Gaige pressing against him from behind.

"Who is dill for?" whispered Stump, speaking directly into Love Bug's right ear. Their angry, aggressive scent surrounded him.

"Dill is for does," said Love Bug, his eyes searching the fast-approaching twilight, looking for an escape route.

Gaige leaned forward from behind and fastened his teeth around Love Bug's left ear, applying a light pressure.

"What kind of does?" asked Stump.

"Yearling does," said Love Bug.

"And who else?" asked Stump, as he raised his back foot and placed the claws against Love Bug's soft belly.

Love Bug began to tremble. "First Born," he said.

Gaige tightened his teeth around the base of Love Bug's left ear. Stump's teeth slipped down until they were resting on Love Bug's neck. "Funny thing," he said. "I don't hear anything on that list about late borns from the back runs, do you?"

"No, Third of the First Five," said Love Bug.

"Eating our dill. Talking to our does with your pretty mouth," said Stump. "That's a problem that demands action."

"Wait a sec," said Love Bug quickly. "Warren Mother's not going to like this."

Stump bared his teeth in an ugly smile. "My mother," he rasped, "doesn't even know your name."

Then his long teeth flashed. Love Bug did not even have time to scream.

FREDDIE

Freddie kept plunging ahead, even though now he was far from Fallen Oak Warren. The cries of the rabbits being

Glorified by weasels still rang in his ears, no matter how far he ran. His mother, father, sisters, and brothers were all with Yah. His friends Snap and Tartuffe were gone to the Lucky Fields. All sent to Glory by Blessed, at a moment when they thought they were safe in their own homes.

The grief overwhelmed him. He felt numb, but he could not stop running, even though he knew it was dangerous to blunder through the woods in the full light of day. He murmured verses as he ran. *"Yah is my Prime Buck. I shall not want. He leads me into fields of clover. He shows me the pure waters. He—"*

Suddenly, the smell of rabbit was strong. It jerked Freddie out of his haze and brought him to a stop. He knew there must be a warren nearby. He ran in a circle, nose high, found the strong current of rabbit scent, and followed it. Never had the mingled odors of rabbit fur, raw earth, fresh milk, new kittens, and old urine smelled so good.

Within minutes, he was at one of the holes leading into the warren. He put his head in and hesitated. He wanted to rush in, but that guaranteed a hostile reception. So he stamped instead, not too hard. He didn't want to come across as panicked.

A few moments later, a black and white doe with tiny yellow lantana camara blossoms woven around her ears came out of the darkness and approached the entrance cautiously. She looked Freddie up and down. After a moment, she said, "Holy day."

"Every one a gift," said Freddie, and took a deep breath.

"And you are?" asked the other rabbit.

The words came out in a rush. "I'm Freddie from Fallen Oak. We were just overrun with Blessed. Weasels. Everyone was Glorified. I don't know where to go. So I was just running … and … and … and I smelled your warren."

"Just smelled us, huh?" said the doe.

"Yes," said Freddie. "I'm used to smelling because I'm … I'm farblind, and it helps me—" He trailed off. "May I know your name?"

"Mabel," said the other rabbit.

"May the Loved One smile on you," said Freddie.

"And also on you," she said, but she made no move to invite Freddie in. "We're new here. Came from the other side of the river."

Freddie blinked. It was very unusual for rabbits to travel long distances. "North of the Shandy?"

"Uh-huh."

"What's it like up there?"

Mabel spat on the ground. "Used to be good rabbit country. Now, all of a sudden, Blessed are everywhere."

"Why?"

"Something's changed," said Mabel, her eyes shadowed. "The deer are thinning out. So the Blessed are looking down the chain. When we heard Micah Summerday was hunting rabbits, we knew it was time to leave."

Even in his numbed state, Freddie could hear the new kind of threat in Mabel's words. "Who's Micah Summerday?"

Mabel looked at him with bitter amusement. "You southies don't get out much, do you?"

"What's all that chatter?" called a buck's voice from down the run. A large, brindle buck came into sight and pushed up to next to Mabel. He had fresh bite wounds on his face. "I'm Dogwood," he said.

Freddie hesitated, then just blurted out, "I'm unwarrened. May I ... may I come in?"

Dogwood looked at him without moving. "I'm not sure that's a good idea."

"Please, I have nowhere to go. I'll stay away from the good feeding spots."

Dogwood scratched behind his ear with his hind leg. "We don't need a farblind wandering around and attracting Blessed."

"But I won't do that," said Freddie. "I'll stick close to—"

The large buck leaned toward Freddie. "It's best if you move on, before our First Born come out here to sort you out."

"But why—" began Freddie.

"Sorry," said Mabel, not unkindly. "It's hard times. We

all have to look after ourselves as best we can." She paused. "Go with Yah, friend."

Dumbly, Freddie nodded, and walked away. A few steps carried him over a small rise, and soon, he was looking down toward a creek, choked with brush. He was thirsty after all his running, he went down to drink. Then he began to walk along the stream bank, trying to drum up ideas as to what he should do. The smell of viburnum and coneflower drifted past, then the chalky smell of straightstone. He picked his way forward, stopping to nibble on some watercress and a small patch of radishes. A loon called in the distance.

After a few hundred yards, he came to a large piece of straightstone. It was unusual to see it south of the river, but he had come across straightstone before. The Reader at Fallen Oak—Freddie choked down a sob—used to say straightstone had something to do with the Dead Gods, but most rabbits thought it was just stone that had been flattened by other, larger pieces of stone.

As he walked along it, he came to a crack, which widened into a hole. It was just large enough for him to slip into. He sniffed the entrance. Nothing living in there. It could be a good place to rest and collect his wits. The small entrance would keep out most Blessed. Except weasels. He shuddered.

Freddie squeezed through the hole and found himself in a low, wide space, with a ceiling a few inches above his head that had collapsed in places. It seemed mostly dry.

Some kind of straightstone burrow. He crept along in the half-light until he found a little nook of leaves and clutter near the wall. Then he settled down into the leaves and quietly cried himself to sleep.

ISADORE

Isadore the fox whined as he approached the den where he lived with his mate and three cubs. He paused for a moment in the entrance to their den, letting the comforting smell of fox fill his nostrils. Juliette, nursing the cubs, looked up and saw the dark bloodstains on his teeth.

"And?" she said.

"And what?" said Isadore, his voice raspy. He winced as he spoke.

"Where's the rent?" asked Juliette, her silver ear tips all forward and eager. "I'm starving. You didn't eat it all, did you?"

"Of course not," said Isadore, fighting back a whimper. "I was … I was …"

"Then where is it?"

"I was … attacked," he mumbled.

Juliette's eyes grew wide. "Coyotes? Did one of the *Paresseux*[1] take a bite at you? Was it Edouard?"

---

[1] Lazy.

"No," said Isadore, and lapsed into silence.

Juliette sucked her teeth for a moment. "Then where is my dinner? Where is the rabbit you went to get? Your mouth is bloody. Don't pretend you didn't make a kill."

Isadore slumped down on the cool earth. "I'm bloody because I was bitten," he whined. "In my throat."

"What?" said Juliette. "What was it? A snake?" She crept toward him and nuzzled him. "What was it, honey? Tell me."

Isadore mumbled something and nuzzled under her chin. "What?" said Juliette. "Sorry, I couldn't hear you."

Isadore exhaled a deep breath. "I was bitten," he said, "by a very, *very* ferocious ... rabbit-looking thing."

Juliette blinked several times in silence. "You were attacked by a rabbit," she said, flatly.

"Something rabbit-ish," corrected Isadore. "It was fierce and cunning. It was ... no ordinary rabbit."

Juliette squinted at him. "Have you been eating those mushrooms again?"

"No!" said Isadore. "I said I wasn't going to do that anymore." He looked up for a moment. "Except on solstice." A long growl crept out of Juliette's throat. Isadore took a step backward. "Look, Jul, there's something weird about this rabbit. Yesterday, I started chasing it way out in the boonies, and then, even when I realized it was running toward Bloody Thorn, I just couldn't stop."

"Mmm-hmm," said Juliette.

"I just lost my head. I wanted it. So, I chased it all the way back to the warren."

Juliette cocked her head. "That wasn't too smart."

"I know, I know," said Isadore. "And I don't want the wolves to hear about it, right? So when I was out just now, I smelled her. And I thought, *well, let's just wrap this up.* But instead of a quick kill, now I've got more problems."

Juliette left the cubs, who immediately started whining in protest, and stood up. "Come out into the moonlight. Show me where it bit you," she said, almost tenderly.

Isadore stood up with her and went outside. She examined his neck. He pulled away impatiently. "It bit me *inside* my throat," he said.

"What?" snapped Juliette. "You had its head in your mouth? Why didn't you just kill it?"

"Its head wasn't in my mouth," said Isadore. "It bit me in the back of my throat with a ..." He groped for words to describe something that had never happened before. "It ... bit me with a ... long, sharpy-bitey thing."

Juliette looked at him in silence, eyelids slowly lowering. *Everyone said I should mate with your brother. But no, I had to have you.*

"It just happened so fast," said Isadore. "I saw it. I cornered it. I was going in for the kill like I've done a million times. I thought it was in the Giving. But then it turned its

head at the last second and I felt the back of my throat …
tearing. It hurt me bad, baby."

Juliette licked his nose. "Look at the moon," she said.
"Open your mouth." He did so. She looked down his throat.
"Mmm," she said.

"What?" said Isadore.

"I see it," said Juliette. "That rabbit hurt you all right."

"What do you think we should do?" asked Isadore.

Juliette sat back on her haunches and looked at the
stars. From inside the den, they could hear the cubs whining for milk. She dropped her head to look into his eyes,
and her silver ear tips shone in the moonlight. "We're going
to get that little *criminelle*[2]."

---

[2]   Criminal.

Chapter 3

Be good. And if you can't be good, be Blessed.
—Traditional raccoon toast

ANASTASIA

Overhead, a boreal chickadee was singing. In the warm, early summer morning, Anastasia was finishing digging out her small burrow. The tunnel led downward at an angle for several feet, then turned upward and opened into a larger space, a sleeping chamber that would always be warm and dry. All the while she dug, she was thinking about the fox. The bloody stick had lain just outside her burrow for several hours. She didn't know what to do with it, but finally realized that the smell of blood in the open air was likely to bring other Blessed, so she dragged the stick into the burrow and up into the sleeping chamber, where it lay along one side.

The smell of blood and fox unnerved her, but it was a constant reminder that something had really happened. Something she had never heard of before. *I made a fox go away.*

A fox chasing a rabbit might lose its prey. But a fox that has cornered a rabbit does not miss. *There was a fox. Then there was no fox.* She scratched her ear with her back leg. *What if I could do that every time?* Then she thought, *it's true what they say. I am a crazy rabbit.*

All the digging made her thirsty. She remembered seeing a small stream some fifty yards away the night before. She came to the mouth of her burrow and touched the left side three times, then the right. Then she sang.

"I have seen your summer rose,
She has gone where the warm wind blows."

She patted the earth twice and stepped through. Once outside, she turned and looked the entrance over. The jumble of fallen branches remained, and she had successfully spread the excavated earth out under the scree in such a way that it was hard to see, and was already drying out to match the earth around it. The bright, cleansing smell of white sage drifted from a nearby bush.

Satisfied, she rubbed her chin glands on a stone near the door, leaving a sign that other rabbits could smell, telling them this territory was now taken. Then she set out for the stream. She soon found it, and slaked her thirst under an ancient willow tree.

As she was heading home, she saw a small patch of white under a large agave plant. It didn't look like a flower or a stone, and a rabbit likes to know everything about their territory, so she approached cautiously to investigate. When she got closer, she could smell that it was a rabbit. When she got a few feet nearer, she could smell the blood.

Immediately, her endocrine system began to sing, insistently broadcasting the message: *Injured rabbit! Danger! Flee!*

She fought down the urge to run, and went closer. It was a white rabbit. Patches of drying blood showed several bite wounds scattered over the body, but it was the mouth that seized her attention. It was a mass of crusted blood, swollen and distorted.

As she went closer, she stepped on a twig, which dislodged a small pebble. The white rabbit opened his eyes and saw her.

He made no sound. Wounded prey animals do not whine. That is a luxury that only predators can afford. But she could see he was suffering greatly. Her chemical alarm system was screaming at her: *Blood! Danger! Blessed! Run!* But she forced herself to go forward.

She approached the other rabbit and softly licked his forehead. The other rabbit closed his eyes, and in a few moments, she saw tears welling out from under the eyelids.

"Can you walk?" she whispered. The other rabbit nodded, weakly. "I have a burrow near here. Come with me. You'll be safe." The other rabbit nodded again. Clearly, he could not speak. He struggled to his feet, the movement causing some of the wounds to begin bleeding afresh.

Step by step, Anastasia guided the other rabbit back to her burrow, doing her best to ignore the fact that being near a bleeding rabbit in the open is just begging to be Glorified. Her heart beat a rapid tattoo for the whole journey, and it seemed to take forever before she was back at the door of her burrow.

Quickly, she touched the left side three times, then the right, and hurried through her couplet.

"Summer morning, warm and fair,
Dewdrops scattered everywhere."

Then she touched the earth twice and led the other rabbit into the sleeping chamber. He was so weary and in so much pain that even the bloody stick that smelled like fox musk did not faze him. He could not touch noses in thanks, so he simply rolled onto his side and lay still, his eyes dark with pain.

Anastasia, remembering what she had learned from Nicodemus, ran back down to the stream and chewed off a willow twig and brought it back to the burrow. Once inside, she realized the other rabbit was far too injured to chew the bark for its pain-relieving effect. So she chewed the willow twig herself and let her saliva run into his mouth. He thanked her with his eyes, and then drifted off to sleep.

She settled down near him, pressed against his flank to provide comfort, and began to lick his wounds clean. "If there is a sick rabbit in *my* burrow," she whispered to herself, "there is only one place for them. Here."

FREDDIE

Freddie was dreaming about playing as a kit in the fern groves above Fallen Oak Warren with his childhood friend, Tartuffe. It was cool and green and safe and beautiful. A steady drip of water *plinked* from the tip of a branch into a small pool. Together, they chanted the words they had learned from one of the pages leaning against the wall of Lashonda's chamber, the kind and indulgent Reader of Fallen Oak Warren.

> *"He should not be here.*
> *He should not be about.*

He should not be here
When your mother is out!

Now! Now! Have no fear!
Have no fear! said the cat.
My tricks are not bad,
Said the cat in the hat."

They both laughed and Freddie tickled Tartuffe, who leapt over his head, spinning in mid-air. Full of youth and high spirits, they engaged in the acrobatic frolic that rabbits call *binking*.

Freddie ran up the side of a rock and flipped in the air. Tartuffe bolted toward him, then turned away at the last moment and jumped, executing an aerial somersault. Freddie sat perfectly still for several seconds, then pushed himself upward with an instantaneous kick so powerful he appeared to be levitating in space for several seconds as he soared aloft, and then came to rest on a clump of ferns. Tartuffe giggled. He opened his mouth to speak, and what came out was a peal of thunder.

Freddie woke with a start. It was raining, and he could hear a dying roll of thunder fading away in the distance. When he opened his eyes and the memory of the day before rushed back, he almost wished he had not woken.

But he dragged himself to his feet. Maybe he could stay

here for a few days. He fought back tears and forced himself to overcome the deadly lassitude overtaking him, so he could investigate the area.

Almost immediately, he realized that, although he was standing on dry earth, he was surrounded by walls made of straightstone. The smell of dust and old wood was thick. The low ceiling a few inches above his head was mostly rotted planks, something he had seen only once before. So this place must have been made by the Dead Gods. Their warrens were always filled with straight stuff. They liked things smooth.

The ancient planks had collapsed in some places. There was a spot nearby where a confused heap of rectangles was scattered down a plank lying at an angle. They looked like they had fallen from above. Freddie approached, and could see that some rectangles were falling apart into pages. He was surprised, as he had not seen more than a few pages in his life. And he had never seen a book.

Then he realized that some of the rectangles had writing on them. He strained his eyes to read them.

"The Coming Crash of 2117"

"Anopheles Rex: How Malaria Took The North"

"The End-of-the-World Alphabet"

Freddie caught his breath as he realized what he was looking at. No warren he knew of had more than a few pages, and each warren treasured the pages they had been able to gather. Everyone knew the pages contained the wisdom of the Dead Gods, opaque though it may be. Here were scores of pages, scattered for the taking.

Freddie had always wanted to be a Reader, but his mother had wanted him to be a Rememberer, so he dutifully followed that path. Still, he would often sneak into the passage near Lashonda's reading chamber after morning feed, and listen to her and her apprentices chant their words. Freddie had no idea what the words meant, but they had an incantatory quality that he found soothing.

Then Freddie shook his head. This was no time to get lost in daydreaming about the past and the Dead Gods. Not when the living god, Yah, and all the company of the Blessed Ones awaited him. And a rabbit ignored them at his peril.

DINGUS

"There are too many, too many, too many squirrels!" said Dingus loudly. Then he did his stampy dance on the branch of his oak tree. He waved his fluffy brown tail in an irritable way as he stamped: Left foot, right foot, left foot.

Right foot, left foot, right foot. Then he sang his "Go Away, Squirrels" song.

> "*Ah,*
> *Chek chek chek chek chek chek chek*
> *Chek chek chek chek chek chek chek*
> *Chek chek chek*
> *Chek chek chek*
> *Chek chek chek chek chek chek chek.*"

Just then, he noticed something odd down below, at the foot of his oak tree. It was a lean, brown rabbit. She was standing up on her rear legs and waving her front paws at him. He could hear her voice faintly. "Hey! Hey, squirrel!"

That was strange. He could not remember the last time he talked to a rabbit. Why would a squirrel ever do that? Nonetheless, he ran swiftly down the trunk and sat lightly on the lowest branch, a few feet above the ground.

He twitched his reddish-brown fur. "What?"

"You have hands," said the rabbit.

Dingus just looked at her. Sometimes hot weather made rabbits go simple. "I'm busy," he said.

"I want to ask you something," said the rabbit.

"Okay," said Dingus. He could feel another round of stampy dance coming on.

"If you do something for me, I will do something for

you," said the rabbit. She picked up a thorn that lay at her feet and held it between her teeth. "Can you tie this thorn on my foreleg?"

"Why?"

"To help make a fox go away."

Dingus was incredulous. "You're going to fight off a fox with a thorn?"

The rabbit looked uneasy. "A sharp stick worked once before, but it's too big to carry all the time."

"Why don't you just run down a hole, like usual?" The rabbit did not answer. Dingus noticed a fragment of acorn lodged in the tree bark and picked it up. He popped it into his cheek for later. "So what are you going to do for me?"

"What *can* I do for you?" asked the rabbit.

A ditzy rabbit with a death wish? Nothing. But as she looked at him steadily with her large golden eyes, Dingus heard himself start talking.

"Well, I do have this problem. With squirrels. Suddenly, there's too many of them." Stamp stamp stamp. "Like, anyone can see this is my tree, right? My tree, my my my my nuts. Now there's squirrels with weird accents, probably from *ten* trees away, stealing nuts from all over my crib. And they're not just taking the fresh acorns, they're digging up the ones I've buried. Can you *believe* that? Ah, chek chek chek chek chek chek chek."

"I'm sorry," said the rabbit. "That sounds bad."

"It *is* bad," said Dingus. "I use these fancy hands to gather nuts for the winter. No nuts, no Dingus."

The rabbit pulled an ear down and cleaned it meditatively. "Maybe I could ... dig a deeper hole for you to keep your acorns in. Then the other squirrels couldn't get to them."

"Then how will *I* get to them?" asked Dingus.

"It could be ... a chamber in my burrow, right over there." The rabbit pointed to a nearby poplar tree. "You could get in. Other squirrels, no."

"Why should I trust you with my nuts?" asked Dingus.

The brown rabbit, who had been so serious all this time, looked almost amused. "I'm a rabbit," she said. "Nuts make me sick."

Dingus clasped his hands over his belly and stood like a tiny monk, thinking deeply. The rabbit offered him the courtesy, common among animals, of letting him think his fill. After several long minutes, Dingus suddenly skimmed along the branch, down the trunk, and was standing right in front of her.

He picked up the thorn and turned it over and over with his fine fingers. "If I tie this to your foreleg with grass strips or bark, it's going to slide back the first time you push it against a fox," he said. "You should use the tip of an agave leaf. It's bigger than a thorn, and it has fibers attached to it. I can wrap that around your leg and it will stay in place."

"Thank you so much," said the rabbit. Then she suddenly leaned forward and licked his forehead. Dingus, startled by her large bulk moving so close to him, leaped back. "Sorry," she said. "It's a rabbit thing."

"No reason we can't be friendly, seeing as how we're going to be neighbors," said Dingus, scraping her saliva off his head with his fingers and wiping it on the grass. "Just no more rabbit thing." He came forward and touched noses with her. "I'm Dingus."

"Hi, Dingus," said the rabbit. "I'm Anastasia."

BRICABRAC

Bricabrac found his catamaran right where he had left it, tucked under the broad leaf of an elephant ear growing at the marshy edges of the Shandy River. It was a handsome vessel. The faded green pontoons read "Perrier" faintly along the sides. And like most water rats, Bricabrac preferred a lateen sail.

He clambered aboard, savoring the moist air raising up from the riverbank. The last few days had been a good haul. In his pack, he had seventy-six cents to add to the stash of moneystones he had buried in the soft mud of the riverbank. That put him seventy-six cents closer to having the funds he needed. And he had come back to his ship to pick up more trade goods.

Suddenly, he heard a commotion coming toward him through the woods. Sounded like the short call of a coyote running hard. Shaking off his pack, he quickly climbed one of the sago palms that grew up through the scrub that lined the water's edge. His copper earring shone as he came out into the sun.

At first, he could see nothing, although the short coyote howls were louder. Then he saw a young stag come racing along the opposite side of the river. It stumbled as it ran, and its flanks were covered with foam. Turning, Bricabrac saw a group of five wolves running about a hundred yards behind. The one in the center was a large, golden female, and the two wolves on each side of her were a mixture of gold and gray, and running a pace or two behind. On each side of the wolves were small groups of coyotes, extending the line and curving forward to keep driving the stag straight ahead.

Bricabrac let out a low whistle. He had never seen these wolves before, but he knew immediately who they were. Members of the Summerday Clan, the famous golden wolves of the Million Acre Wood. Even the animals in City of Oom had heard of them.

The stag tripped and almost fell in the soft earth by the riverbank. At the sight, a storm of eager yelps rose from the coyotes. The golden wolves ran in silence, their long legs seeming to barely touch the ground, steadily closing the gap between themselves and their prey.

The stag tried to veer away from the river, but the coyotes had pushed forward and kept him trapped, forcing him to run along the wet ground near the water, which slowed him down. As the wolves drew abreast of Bricabrac, the large female looked out across the river, and Bricabrac could see that her eyes were a startling green.

Just then, the wolf next to her surged forward and pulled even with her. Immediately, she showed her teeth, and Bricabrac could hear her rumbling growl rolling across the water. The other wolf dropped back, and the wolves ran on, silent once again.

The deer was staggering now, eyes white and huge. The wolves and coyotes were arrowing toward him, their curved line drawing tight around him like a noose. The chase would soon be over. Bricabrac made his way down the tree trunk toward his boat. He was already lost in thought about trade goods when the young stag fell for the last time.

ANASTASIA

The agave tip felt awkward tied to Anastasia's right foreleg, but it also felt good. As she busied herself about her burrow, she tried to get used to wearing it. The problem was that the agave tip extended almost an inch beyond her paw, so she was jostling it with every step, and it was hard to hold her paw in such a position that the pointed tip lay flat against the ground. Still, she didn't want to give it up, and she was determined to find some way to make it work. So she paced up to the mouth of the burrow and back to the sleeping chamber over and over.

On one trip, she became aware that Love Bug had opened his eyes and was watching her quietly. He could speak now, but with difficulty. One of his two front teeth had been damaged at the root. It looked like he might lose it.

"Why you help me?" he said.

Anastasia did not answer. She continued her pacing. The next time she entered the sleeping chamber, he asked again, "Why you help me?"

Anastasia stopped and looked at him without speaking. "Crippled rabbit. Fresh blood," said Love Bug. "Blessed coming. Why you stay?"

"I'm sick in the head," said Anastasia, shortly. "I do stupid things. That's why I'm out here, instead of ..." She trailed off and looked down. She patted the floor a few times with her left paw. "Looks like you're out of leafies," she said. "I saw some nice kale down by the stream. I'll go get some."

Love Bug put his paw up to his mouth, but said nothing. It looked like it was bleeding again, from all the talking.

Anastasia paused by the mouth of the burrow and did her exit ritual.

"Fly, fly away my tiny bird,
No one knows what you have heard."

Still, she hesitated. The fox had been here. The fox could come back. A katydid called in the early twilight. The breeze felt cool, laced with the scent of white lilies. No fox smell. She pressed the sharp agave tip against the soft ground and pushed. It sank in deeply. That felt good.

Taking a last look around, she set out for the patch of kale by the stream. She moved cautiously, from cover to cover, bush to boulder to bramble to stump. Not dashing, because fast movement attracts the eye. And the eyes of the Blessed could at any moment be resting on your patch of ground.

She got to the kale patch, and took a moment to devour a fresh kale leaf. The energy of it flowed through her like a waterfall of goodness, the bright aroma enveloping her. She wanted to have five more leaves, but she needed to get a leaf back to Love Bug, and so much time in the open was already dangerous. She dropped her head and quickly cut through the stem of a leaf. Then she picked it up in her mouth and started back to the burrow.

She was halfway home, hunkered down under a crepe myrtle, when she saw the face of a fox with her right eye. He was twenty yards away in the shade of a kudzu bush near the stream. Downwind. That's why she hadn't smelled him.

Instantly, her heart began to hammer. Was it *the* fox? Had he seen her? He was perfectly still, so she could not say. Any movement of her own would cry out for attention, so she stayed motionless while her left eye scanned the route back to the burrow, mapping every leaf and twig.

The whine of a mosquito thrummed through the air. Her muscles tensed. There was nothing else to learn. She broke cover and ran, her back feet digging into the ground and throwing up clods of earth, the kale leaf forgotten. Even her injured right leg pushed strongly, although she felt the skin tear open and begin to bleed.

As soon as she moved, she heard the fox yelp in surprise, and then lash the ground as he hurled himself forward. She had a twenty-yard head start. That was two seconds, a lifetime for a rabbit. But the agave tip slowed her down. Her right forepaw had to fling wide to keep it from burying its point in the ground. The fox was gaining on her.

But she was close to home. She could see the mouth of her burrow. How dark and beautiful it looked. In a few seconds, she would be there.

Then another fox emerged from a creosote bush just to her left. A female with silver-tipped ears. A low, contemptuous bark rolled from her throat.

A terrible jolt of fear burned through Anastasia's veins. But there was no weakening, no Giving. She drove forward. The fox raced to intercept her. Anastasia veered right as the fox pushed her off her direct line to the safety of the hole. She heard the other fox coming up behind her.

The female fox got closer and closer, bending the arc of Anastasia's line even further out. Now she was on course to run past her burrow. Much more of this and she'd actually be running away from it. As the female fox closed to within a few steps, Anastasia suddenly changed course and ran right at her. The fox looked confused for a moment, then opened her mouth wide and lunged forward, the killing joy on her face.

Anastasia leapt high in the air and pushed her right paw forward. The sharp, smooth agave tip buried itself deep in the nose of the fox. A spray of blood spattered out with the fox's next breath. The fox gave out a guttural yelp and stiffened her forelegs to stop her forward momentum and try to pull back from the hurtful thing. But her hindquarters could not stop, and with her forelegs dug in, her hips rose into the air, somersaulting her forward.

The bloody agave tip was forced away from Anastasia's paw, and the fibers wrapping it to her foreleg started to break, unspooling into the warm air. Her momentum carried her forward as the female fox turned in the air over her head. And just as the male fox took his last few steps and arrived, he was greeted by an angry tangle of snarling mate and bleeding nose and agave string.

Anastasia pelted along the last few yards to reach her

burrow. She reached the front door, rushed through her entry ritual, and was in the sleeping chamber a moment later. Love Bug, roused by the commotion, lifted his head. "What, what?"

Anastasia stood over him, her body convulsed with deep, shuddering breaths. He could see a new, very faint spark of fire in her golden eyes. Her scent was warm and spiky.

"What?" he asked again.

"I ... I ..." She sounded confused and amazed. "I stabbed a Blessed. And *lived*."

FREDDIE

It was early morning, and Freddie was out scouting his territory. This is something rabbits usually do in a new area, since a one-second edge is a matter of life and death to a bunny sprinting from a predator. *Big stump here. Large stone makes a tight squeeze there. Go hard left and duck under that log.*

He was down near the stream, and saw a lithe, brown female rabbit come out from under a sweet wintergreen bush and drink water. He made his way toward her.

"Holy day," said Freddie.

The brown rabbit froze for a long moment. Then, she said, "Every one a gift," and drew back under the bush.

"Greetings, sister," said Freddie awkwardly, "I'm un-warrened, and I—"

"Are you sick?" asked the brown rabbit.

"No," said Freddie. He quickly told her what had happened at Fallen Oak Warren.

"I'm sorry," she said.

"So what I'm hoping is," said Freddie, "I might be able to stay at your warren for a few days?"

"I don't have a warren," said the other. "I was ... un-warrened just recently."

"What happened?"

"They said I was sick."

"Are you?" asked Freddie.

She nibbled a piece of fallen apple. "Yes."

Freddie looked down at his toes. "Is it catching?"

"No," said the brown rabbit. She bit into a leaf of watercress, and then said, "Do you know of any painkillers besides willow bark? Something for teeth?"

"No," said Freddie. "Is there something wrong with your teeth?"

"No," said the brown rabbit.

There was an uncomfortable silence. Freddie washed his face. Finally, he spoke. "Are you starting your own warren?"

"A warren?" scoffed the brown rabbit. "I have one burrow. That's a far cry from ...," she trailed off.

"I've been staying in a straightstone burrow, but it's too big and cold," said Freddie. "If you're thinking about founding a warren, maybe I could join up."

She eyed him coolly. "I don't need a buck, if that's what you're thinking."

"No, no," said Freddie, quickly. "I could do something useful." He raked his claws through the moist earth. "I mean, I don't dig, but maybe I could … I could …"

Suddenly, the brown rabbit was very close to his face. "*I don't need a buck,*" she said, spitting the words out. "I'm *not* starting a warren." Then she turned and was gone before Freddie could say another word.

FOXES

The light of the gibbous moon dappled down through the old oak tree and dimly lit a group of very serious foxes sitting in a rough circle. Crickets sawed away in the branches above them.

Juliette spoke first. "This cannot stand." After a moment of silence, there was some harrumphing and possibly even a chuckle from among the circle of foxes. Juliette's hackles rose. "Our blood was spilled. By a rabbit," she said, struggling to keep her voice civil. "What are we going to do about it?"

"Why do we have to do anything?" asked a small, bright-eyed fox named Ariel.

Juliette's shoulders rose, and her ruff as well. "A fox was attacked ... by lunchmeat! This is an abomination. Do you not agree?"

"Must we agree?" asked Ariel. "We're not pack animals."

"It's not like we're *wolves*," said another fox, which caused a snicker to run through the group.

"Hey, sisters, brothers, friends," interrupted Isadore, entering the circle and touching noses with each of the eight foxes in turn. "You've already done us a huge favor just by coming, and I thank you. Again." He stretched out his front legs and bowed for a moment in the manner of a playful cub. "We don't get together enough. Am I right?"

There were some friendly growls of assent. Juliette did her best to seem friendly and not filled with panicky rage. Isadore sat on his haunches and gazed at the other foxes. "Here's the thing. I was out minding my own business, just trying to collect the rent to support my family, and all of a sudden, there's this unprovoked attack from a rabbit. And I have to say, it hurt me pretty bad, inside my throat. With some kind of weird sharpy-bitey magic. Come, look." Isadore opened his mouth and two of the foxes came forward and looked into his throat.

"Mmm, yeah, that's serious," said Ariel.

"Then we tried to deal with this rent problem ourselves,"

said Juliette, "but when we got there, the rabbit-thing attacked me with some new kind of magic stabber."

"I know it's hard to believe, but it's true," said Isadore.

"You can see that my nose is *mal mal*[3]," said Juliette.

Desdemona, an older female with hazel eyes, assumed an ambiguous posture and said, "Young cousin, my love for you is great. And any mate of yours is my friend." Juliette's silver ear tips started to lay back as she heard the slight in this grudging praise, but she recovered and kept her ears high and cheerful. Desdemona continued, "But this idea that rabbits are attacking us is hard to believe. When's the last time a rabbit attacked anything fiercer than a cabbage leaf?"

Juliette's lips curled back, and her teeth shone brightly in the moonlight. Isadore nuzzled her for a moment. Then he turned and looked at the other foxes. "I know you all don't know Juliette well, but you know me. I don't lie."

An older male with a scarred shoulder stepped forward and touched noses with Isadore. "Our mothers were sisters. I was born two summers before you, and I watched you as a cub. I will say this: You are not a liar."

Isadore dropped his head, exposing his neck for a moment. "I thank you, cousin," he murmured.

"Now, we need to go, together, and erase this unnatural creature from the face of the earth."

---

[3]   Hurt bad.

"Then let it be so," Desdemona growled.

"Fear and trembling in rabbitland tonight," snickered Ariel. "Foxes getting their gang on."

FREDDIE

Freddie kept scouting the area for warrens to join, but at Bloody Thorn Warren he was hustled on his way, and at Moonfall Warren, a squat, ugly rabbit actually threatened him. Tense times and rumors had everyone jumpy.

After many days, Freddie was sick of huddling by himself in the cold straightstone cavern, and decided to try his luck with the brown rabbit again. He needed an in. She had asked about painkillers. Maybe he could ... find something?

He nosed around the straightstone burrow and found a partially intact book titled, "Medicinal Plants of Eastern Canada." He spent a couple of days, off and on, poring through it. More than half the pages were rotten, and the dusty smell of crumbling paper made him sneeze, but finally, he turned up a page that looked useful.

Seizing the page in his mouth, he went back to the stream where he'd seen the brown bunny before. She was not there, but of course, no one would dig a warren right on a stream. It would be near enough to be convenient for drinking, but far enough away that it wouldn't flood. The hole would be located where it could blend in with its surroundings, under a bush, or at the base of an old tree with gnarled roots.

Freddie scanned the area along the stream, and started looking in the likely spots, carrying his page with him in his mouth, trying not to let it get soiled. Finally, he found a rabbit hole under an old poplar tree.

As he approached, he could see motion just within the mouth of the hole. It was the brown rabbit. She became still and looked at him without speaking. She was the first rabbit he had smelled in several days. Just the scent of her made him homesick. He willed himself not to cry.

"I would not presume to invite myself into your sleeping chamber," said Freddie humbly. "I bring you this gift as a show of good faith." He leaned the page up against one of the poplar's old roots. There was a picture of a white flower. He read aloud some large words that said, "Feverfew: Headache, stomach ache, toothache."

The brown rabbit scratched her ear and then chewed her paw. "You're a Reader?"

"Not really," said Freddie. "I was a Remembering acolyte. But I liked our Reader and used to hang around her chamber."

"This is helpful," said the brown rabbit. She touched noses with him. "I'm Anastasia."

"I'm Freddie," he said.

She took a step down the passage, then turned and looked at him. "Bring your page."

Chapter 4

Rye in the morning, fescue in the evening,
Millet when the day is hot and still,
Tussock, deer and fountain,
Feather, sedge and mountain,
Every little bunny loves dill.
                    —Traditional rabbit nursery rhyme

Bricabrac

Bricabrac rested under a fallen calla lily leaf and observed the two rabbits. One was chubby, with a face half black and half gray, and a dappled gray and white body. The other was a slender, brown rabbit with quick, nervous movements.

Rabbit warrens could be good prospects, as their Readers often had moneystones. Plus, rabbits were pretty suggestible. But Bricabrac had not heard of any warrens near here. Could be a moony doe, wanting a place of her own, and with her mate tagging along like an old duffer. If that was the case, it was very unlikely there were any moneystones around. Bricabrac pulled on his pack and tightened the straps. Just one way to find out.

He approached the rabbits slowly, stopping to nibble as he went. When he was a few yards away, he showed himself plainly and acted surprised to see them.

"Oh, hey! What up? What up?" said Bricabrac. "How cool is that? Rabbits! I love rabbits!"

Both rabbits looked startled. The black and gray male stamped. The brown female took a few steps toward him.

"Rabbits are so brave. And smart," said Bricabrac. "It's my honor to make your acquaintance, ma'am."

The brown rabbit did not speak, but simply came toward him, looking him in the eye. Bricabrac found it somewhat unnerving. Just when it seemed she was about to bump noses with him, the black and gray harlequin said, "I'm sorry, but you know they carry diseases, right?"

Bricabrac did not even grimace. He had heard this so many times. Anastasia stopped a few inches away. "You have hands," she said. "And a backpack."

"Indeed, I do, ma'am," said Bricabrac. "I've got some items that could be just perfect for a rabbit." He rattled his pack. "Gifts of the Dead Gods. Rare tools. I brought these all the way from Oom."

The harlequin took a few steps forward. "Why don't you just move along, buddy?"

"No, I want to talk to him," said the brown rabbit.

The black and gray bunny looked surprised. "Oh, well, I'll just … keep an eye on things."

The brown rabbit nodded, still focused on Bricabrac. "You have an earring. That's a city thing, right?" Bricabrac nodded. "So you must be clever," she said.

"Born in the deepest sewers of Oom," said Bricabrac earnestly. "My family's still there, bless their hearts. I fought my way out. Learned a trade." He scratched his ear. "Say, is this a start-up warren?"

She ignored his question. "Can you make me something?"

Bricabrac smiled. "That's what I'm here for."

The brown rabbit nodded. They exchanged introductions. Then she stooped down and drew in the dust. "I want something sharp, like a thorn or an agave tip, that can be strapped onto my foreleg, but the pointy part has to somehow go away when I'm not using it, so I'm not walking on it all the time."

Bricabrac chewed his lower lip. "That's a tall order. If you want movable parts, that's high-end crafting. I might have some gear cached near here that would allow me to make that. But it won't be cheap."

"How much?" asked Anastasia.

"Rare materials, skilled fabrication. Mmmm. You're looking at—" Bricabrac hesitated before naming the princely sum he had in mind. "One dollar."

Anastasia looked at him quietly for a moment. She glanced at Freddie. "I can get that," she said. "I have a friend with moneystones."

Bricabrac nodded. "Okay, I'll go look at my materials. What is this for?"

"I just want to make a fox take a step back," Anastasia said simply.

NICODEMUS

The dawn was cool and moist, and the bunnies of Bloody Thorn Warren were out for morning feed. The scent of wild columbine hung sweetly in the air. Tender new shoots beckoned, the midsummer grasses were high, and a sharp-eyed rabbit might see a leaf of wild lettuce and hear its siren call.

Nicodemus came out stiffly. Both his apprentices had errands elsewhere, so he was alone. He was becoming that rarity among his kind – an elderly rabbit. Smarts and luck had gotten him a long way, and he was satisfied with his position as Reader for Bloody Thorn Warren. But he missed his little friend, Anastasia. Surely gone to be with Yah by now.

He found a nice clump of dandelion, and settled down for a feed, savoring the burst of flavor. As the rabbit proverb has it, *dandelion bites you back.* The bitter edge of dandelion was something best appreciated by older bunnies.

An odd movement among a field of crocuses nearby caught his eye. Tentative movement forward, back, side to side. Nicodemus squinted. It was a rabbit. Black and gray face, classic harlequin. Not a local bunny.

Most warrens are jumpy about strangers, and Bloody Thorn was on high alert because of the recent changes. With First and Second Born patrolling the grazing area perimeter, the behavior wasn't surprising. Probably someone unwarrened, nervous, fearful.

Nicodemus took a few steps forward, while continuing to nibble. "Hello, friend," he murmured. "It's all right. I'm not an enforcer." He chuckled. "As I'm sure you can tell. At my age, a tussle with a dandelion leaf is about as much fight as I can muster."

The other rabbit went motionless. "Greetings, brother," he whispered. "Holy day." His scent was sharp with anxiety.

"Every one a gift," said Nicodemus.

"Sorry to bother you, I'm looking for the Reader of this warren. Name's Nicodemus."

Nicodemus started. It had been a long time since someone had sought him out. "Why are you looking for him?"

"It's for a friend," said the other rabbit.

"Who?"

"Are you Nicodemus?"

"Who's the friend?" asked Nicodemus.

The harlequin looked around and then came a few paces nearer. "Do you remember a yearling female who was unwarrened recently?"

Nicodemus felt his heart beat faster. "Is she ... okay?" He did not ask why Anastasia had not come herself. If a rabbit exiled by the Warren Mother attempted to re-enter the warren, that rabbit would likely be killed.

"Are you ...?" began the other rabbit.

"Yes, yes," Nicodemus waved his paw impatiently.

The black and gray rabbit gestured apologetically. "Sorry, one thing I need to check. She said you have a visible scar on the left side of your chest."

Nicodemus sat up and showed the scar. The other rabbit came close to him and peered at his chest. "So? How is she?" asked Nicodemus.

"She's fine," said the other rabbit. "I'm Freddie. I'm staying in a burrow with her and an injured buck."

"Oh, thank Yah," said Nicodemus.

"She's ... more than fine, really," said Freddie. "She's fought with foxes. Twice. *And won*."

"What?" Nicodemus laughed, whether in excitement or disbelief, he was not sure. "What are you talking about?"

"One time, she used a sharp stick, another time, an

agave tip tied to her paw. *She made Blessed go away.* I mean, I'm not sure if it's the right thing to do or not, but I've never heard of anything like it."

Suddenly, Nicodemus realized he was beaming. "She's special," he said. "I always knew she was special."

"Ya," said Freddie. "Looks like any skinny yearling doe, but somehow ..." He trailed off, but then looked Nicodemus squarely in the eye. "It's my honor to meet you, sir. Anastasia has sent me here because she wants to hire a craftrat to make a new thing. A sharpy-stabby thing that works better than an agave tip."

"Okay," said Nicodemus. "I don't know anything about that. Not sure how I can help."

"She needs moneystones," said Freddie bluntly. "She wants to ask you if you will give some of yours."

Nicodemus stepped back. "Those belong to the warren," he said. "I want to help, but they're not really mine to give."

Freddie looked embarrassed. "I know," he said. "I argued with her about this. But she seemed to think it was a good idea."

"How much?" asked Nicodemus.

"She wants a dollar."

Nicodemus sucked in his breath. "That's a fortune." He chewed a front claw. "So what would the plan be?"

"If you could bring them out at the end of morning feed

tomorrow? I realize it might take you several trips. I'll be waiting with a backpack, so I can take them all at once. "

Nicodemus looked at Freddie for a long moment. "So I'm just giving all these moneystones to you?"

"Yes," said Freddie simply.

Nicodemus took a bite of dandelion and chewed thoughtfully. "Everyone who knows me knows I have a scar on my chest," he said. "Anyone could have heard the gossip about a yearling doe getting exiled."

Freddie sat very still. "I can tell you what you said to her as the First Born were pushing her out the door."

Nicodemus felt his eyes go wet. "What?" he said finally.

"*You are strong,*" said Freddie.

A hot tear made its way down Nicodemus' cheek. He looked away and spoke softly. "Be here tomorrow."

BRICABRAC

Bricabrac had set up his workshop in a hollow log not far from the catamaran. He had shoved two green twigs, each with a fork, into the soft and crumbly punk that lined the inside of the log. And he was using them to hold a metal cylinder while he worked on it with his tools. Along the side of the cylinder, wide letters spelled out the word, "X-ACTO."

Near Bricabrac's feet lay a tangle of yucca fibers he had gathered that morning. He kicked it out of the way as he fussed over the cylinder, using a tiny saw that had once been a nail file, and a crow bar that had begun life as a dental tool.

Working with these yucca fibers would be a bear, and he wasn't looking forward to it. They needed to be woven into a snug sleeve to hold the weapon on Anastasia's forepaw. But the tightness of the weave required made even Bricabrac's fine hands seem clunky.

Out of the corner of his eye, he noticed a mouse with a splash of white fur on her back scurry by, and he dropped his tools and ran after her. "Hey, what up? What up, lil doe?"

The mouse darted under a broad thistle leaf. Bricabrac lay on his back and put his hands behind his head. "You know, the craftsmanship of the mice in these parts is straight-up amazing. The fine hand, the skilled eye. Musmuski Grove is everything they say it is. I am gobsmacked."

"What do you want?" said the mouse from under the spiky leaf.

"Oh, nothing, really," said Bricabrac, stretching himself. "It's just that seeing you reminded me of my lil mouse best friend when I was a pup. We lived just down the river. My family's still there, bless their hearts."

"Likely story," said the mouse.

"Okay, I'll cut to the chase," said Bricabrac as he scratched behind his ear. "I've got some yucca fibers I need to have woven into a sleeve. I've got two hardstone loops, so I can set up a circular loom. But it would be awesome to have a tiny person with tiny fingers to do the weaving."

"You got moneystones?" asked the mouse.

"I've got something better," said Bricabrac. He quickly scampered back to his workshop, rummaged through his backpack, and came back with a bottle cap that had "Canada Dry" printed on it. He leaned down and presented it to the mouse with a flourish. "A helmet!"

The mouse partially emerged from under the leaf to sniff the bottle cap. "We can use part of the fabric you make for the chinstrap," said Bricabrac. "So it'll have your own spirit woven right in. So cool!"

"Blah blah blah," said the mouse. "I've got sunflower seeds calling my name."

"Wait!" said Bricabrac. Then he laid down on his belly, so that he looked the mouse in the eye. She was lying on her side, with her head propped up on her tiny hand. "What this helmet *will* do for you is mark you as a mouse to be reckoned with. A mouse who has gone out and done the hard thing and returned to tell the tale. A mouse with character."

The mouse looked back at him, unblinking for several seconds. Then she said, "What does 'Canada Dry' mean?"

"It's a good luck charm. Very powerful."

"Why should I believe that?" asked the mouse.

"Have you ever seen a dead mouse in a Canada Dry helmet?"

"No," said the mouse.

"Well, there you are," said Bricabrac, triumphantly. "Draw your own conclusions." He assumed an earnest tone. "And remember, a mouse with a helmet is a mouse you want to have on your side. A natural leader."

After a pause, the mouse said, "Fine, I'll do it." She came out from under the thistle leaf.

Bricabrac touched noses with her. "I'm Bricabrac," he said.

"I'm Death Rage," said the mouse.

"O, that's nice," said Bricabrac. "Very feminine."

NICODEMUS

It was morning feed. Time to give away the valuables he had been entrusted with. Nicodemus chewed his lip. Who knew where these moneystones even came from? He had inherited them from the Reader before him. *I'm righting a wrong,* he thought. *A young doe was treated poorly by this warren. Now this warren is helping to make up for it.*

Nicodemus rummaged through his pile. He would have to carry these in his mouth, so he selected the highest denomination coins he could find: Three silver 25-cent pieces, each with an image of a moose on one side, and Queen Meghan III on the other side.

He stacked them up against the wall and got a bite on them. They were heavy and awkward to carry, so he had to squeeze strongly. Then he took the lower cross-warren passage, sure to be deserted at this time of day, when everyone was heading outside.

In a few minutes, he was trundling up the slope toward one of the lesser-used entrances. As he stepped into the dawn light, he was just congratulating himself when he ran smack into Briar, who was getting set to do morning perimeter rounds.

"Oof," said Briar. Then, when he had recovered himself, "Holy day."

Nicodemus had to put down the coins to speak. "Every one a gift," he said pleasantly, and started to pick the coins up again.

Briar hummed tunelessly for a few seconds, then said, "Where are you taking our moneystones, Honored Reader?"

Nicodemus cursed himself for not having prepared a cover story. Where *was* he taking them? What *was* he buying with the warren's money so early in the morning, with no peddler in sight?

"I'm ... I'm ...," he began, but could not get any traction. Buying *what*? From *whom*? A brief, nasty vision of himself getting unwarrened, with this very clod shoving him out through the night gate flickered in his mind. He shivered, and strove to keep his scent neutral.

"You're gonna do something really smart with them, eh?" said Briar. "Something all boring and Readerish?"

This broke the logjam in Nicodemus' head. "Absolutely," he said brightly. "I'm taking them out to … set them all in a circle, a henge, really, and, uh …" He trailed off.

"And what?" asked Briar, chewing a fescue seed head like a wad of chewing gum.

"And … and … and use them to focus the sun's rays toward a central point," Nicodemus said, authoritatively. "It's called a…solar oven. I read about it in a couple of pages from *Labrador Life* over at Fallen Oak Warren. Yah rest their souls." He dropped into his singsong Reader's lecturing voice. "You see, these disks are shiny, so, in addition to having value as moneystones, they also have *reflective* value, which can be diagrammed as—"

"Thank you, Honored Reader," said Briar hastily. "Well, I've got a patrol to run."

"Oh, well, perhaps another time, then," chirped Nicodemus.

Briar took off on his morning round. Nicodemus said a little prayer of thanks, hastily picked up the coins, and lolloped toward the crocuses. In a minute, he could see Freddie, unsuccessfully hiding his black and gray form among the green and purple flowers.

FREDDIE

Freddie crouched among the flowers, wearing a hastily made grape-leaf backpack that Bricabrac had assembled for him. He had just watched Nicodemus having a long conversation with a rabbit, who he assumed by his manner to be a First Born, and he had begun to feel hot and nervous.

Now he saw Nicodemus coming toward him, carrying three silver disks in his mouth.

"Holy morn," said Freddie.

Nicodemus dropped the moneystones at Freddie's feet, more than a little out of breath. "You tell Anastasia that I'm considering this a loan. When she's all grown up and has her own warren, all plush with Readers and moneystones, I want her to pay me back."

"I'll do that, sir," said Freddie, with a small smile. He didn't bother to say, *If you ask her if she's starting a warren, she bites your head off.*

Nicodemus picked up the quarters one by one and put them in Freddie's backpack. Then he went back into the warren to get the rest. After a couple of minutes, Freddie started to get anxious, but then he saw Nicodemus coming out with three more moneystones in his mouth.

A moment later, he deposited two dimes and a nickel in Freddie's backpack, and pulled the fastener shut with his teeth. "Good to go."

"Thank you, Nicodemus," said Freddie. "I won't forget this."

Nicodemus double-nose-bumped his flank. "Tell Anastasia not to forget *me*," he said, and turned and hopped stiffly homeward.

Freddie immediately took off toward the burrow, following the series of low-lying landmarks he could see, even with his farblindness. Anastasia had talked him through them earlier this morning.

In a few minutes, he was back at the burrow. Bricabrac was there with a bulging backpack, standing with Anastasia between the two large roots that hid the doorway. Love Bug was lying just inside the entry passage. His wounds were mostly healed, and helped by the feverfew, the swelling in his mouth had gone way down. He was almost his old beautiful self again.

"I've got the moneystones," Freddie said. Anastasia came to him and nose-bumped his flank.

"Thank you," she said.

Freddie shimmied out of the backpack, and it fell to the ground with a clank. Bricabrac opened it and quickly counted the moneystones. "What? No tip?" he said.

Anastasia looked at him blankly. "What?"

"Just joking," said Bricabrac, as he opened his own backpack and stowed the coins inside. "But seriously, once you see what I have for you, you're going to be thinking this is a tipping situation." He started to pull out an object, and then stopped and looked at them. "I'm about to show you something no rabbit in the Million Acre Wood has ever seen before. A fossilized dragon claw, crafted into a bespoke weapon for a discerning client."

He pulled out a metal cylinder loosely wrapped in a fabric sleeve. On the side, the rabbits could read "X-ACTO" through the fabric.

"Looks like regular hardstone, right? But watch this." Bricabrac picked up the cylinder and made a flicking gesture with it. There was a scraping, *zhing!* sound, and a triangular blade slid out of the end of the cylinder and locked into place. "The claw of X-ACTO, the mighty one, at your service," he proclaimed proudly.

"Oh, my Yah," said Freddie. Anastasia said nothing, but she stared at the blade. Love Bug came forward and sniffed at the edge. Bricabrac snatched it away.

"No!" he shouted. Love Bug jumped back. "That's very dangerous," said Bricabrac. "If you sniff this claw carelessly, it could cut your nose open." Love Bug took another step back.

"Who's X-ACTO?" asked Anastasia.

Bricabrac stood on his back feet and reached up as high as he could with his front paws. "In life, X-ACTO was a dragon of enormous size. She was taller than ten rabbits. Or even eleven rabbits."

All the rabbits looked skyward, boggling at this monstrosity. "Sounds horrible," said Freddie.

"Her claws were retractable, like mountain lions', who have not been seen in these parts for many a generation, thanks be to Yah," said Bricabrac. "The claws lived inside her bones. With a flick of her paw, she could extend them, and then pull them back in as needed. When she died, her bones, as all dragon bones do, fossilized. They turned to hardstone."

"Awesome," murmured Love Bug.

"Put it on me," said Anastasia, her breath coming a little faster.

Bricabrac sprang into action, tugging the sleeve up over her right paw and tightening the metal tube against her foreleg with a set of straps. "I've made this so you can do all this with your teeth," said Bricabrac. "Now shake your foreleg, like this." He showed her the special flick. She imitated him, and the blade came forth. "Now do this," said Bricabrac, showing her a lateral jerk with the paw held aloft, which caused the blade to disengage and slide back into the tube.

"Got it," said Anastasia, after a few tries.

"Now," said Bricabrac, holding up a green twig, smiling, "show this bunny-killer who's boss."

Anastasia looked at him for a moment, then flicked out the claw, *zhing!* and swept her paw forward, slicing the twig cleanly in two. The blade was back in its metal holster before the twig hit the ground.

Love Bug whooped. "Fear the Claw!" he shouted, triple-stamping in affirmation.

Anastasia felt a hot flush flow through her. Her eyelids fluttered. She stood upright and held her paw over her head. The diamond-cut letters spelling out "X-ACTO" caught the early morning sun and gleamed like fire.

Freddie sat perfectly still. His old life had ended when Fallen Oak Warren was overrun, and he had shed many bitter tears over that. But now, he had a sense that something new was beginning. Perhaps something never before seen.

"Book of Thorns, 7:19," he murmured. *"Now I am become Death, the destroyer of worlds."*

ISADORE & JULIETTE

Isadore and Juliette lay on their bellies under the big rhododendron bush, squinting through the thick curtain of leaves in the dawn light. Juliette squirmed around, trying to get comfortable. Thirty yards away, upwind, they could see a lean brown rabbit leaping and turning in the air at the foot of a poplar tree. The smell of rabbit was making the foxes salivate.

"What is she doing?" asked Juliette.

"It's that stupid *binky* thing rabbits do," said Isadore.

"That seems strange," said Juliette.

Isadore licked his nose. "Why?"

"Frolicking?" said Juliette. "That seems very playful for an attacker of innocent foxes."

Now a black and gray rabbit was visible. It jumped toward the brown rabbit, and she turned in the air to meet him, batting at him with her front paws. He landed lightly and bounced toward her again, his mouth open. She flicked him away with her front paws, and then curled into a ball when she landed, rolling away from him. The black and gray rabbit jumped on top of her, and she squirmed out from under him.

"They're flirting," said Isadore.

Juliette said nothing for a moment. Finally she spoke, "Nah ... I don't think so."

Now a third rabbit had joined them. A white rabbit. He also sprang at the brown rabbit, mouth open, like a Blessed going in for a kill. The brown rabbit scrubbed her paw across his face as she somersaulted in the air over him.

"She's ... practicing," said Juliette, slowly. "They're play-fighting. Look at how she uses her front paws. She's hitting their faces. Just like with me. That wasn't an accident."

"It's all about her magic stabby thing," said Isadore. "So, we should ... turn our faces away from her front paws? Our faces are the most vulnerable."

"Yeah," said Juliette. "Getting stabbed in the nose is like, blinding. But a puncture wound anywhere else is just trivial. You shake it off."

"This was such a good idea to do this," said Isadore. "Thank you, Jul."

Juliette touched noses with him. "So when we bring your family back here to kill this thing, we need to warn everyone: Look away from her paws. Come at her from the side or behind."

Isadore nodded. Then he said, "Look!" Juliette followed his gaze. "They're going to the blueberry patch again, just like yesterday."

"That patch is a ways off," said Juliette. "Maybe we can wait til they go there, then get in between them and their burrow and—" She licked her lips. "Turn the problem into a meal, you know? Get our foxy going."

Isadore nuzzled her. "We get hurt and we get back up," he said. "That's what I love about us."

Anastasia

In the cool before the dawn, Anastasia found Love Bug and Freddie dozing in the run outside her sleeping chamber, and double-bumped them in the ribs.

"Hey," she said. "I need help digging the nut chamber for Dingus. We owe him, so we have to do it. Come help me."

Love Bug yawned and stretched, then sat up at attention. "It's an honor, *Belle Dame,*[4]" His injured tooth had fallen out, so now he just had one incisor, but his wounds were almost entirely healed.

Freddie looked confused. "Um," he said, "I'm a buck. I don't really dig."

Anastasia almost looked as though she might smile. "If you live here, you dig," she said. "C'mon, I'll show you."

They took it in turns, one digging the nut chamber itself, one pushing the dirt down the main passage, and one kicking the dirt out the door. They got into a rhythm and worked in silence for awhile. Then Anastasia spoke. "Freddie, I have a question for a Rememberer."

"Okay," said Freddie.

"I don't really want to hurt the Blessed Ones," said Anastasia. "I just got this Claw because I don't want the Blessed Ones to hurt me. That's okay, isn't it?"

"Well …" Freddie mumbled. "We're not really supposed to fight back against the Blessed. The Glorified are supposed to find joy in their Glory."

"But everyone runs," said Anastasia.

"Ya, but that's our weakness," said Freddie. "Book of Kale, 22:12-13. *I am weak even as you are weak, saith The*

---

[4]   Beautiful Lady.

Loved One. I say, I will not run, and yet I run. Even though Yah's love awaits me on the other side of Glory."

"I know I'm weak," said Anastasia as she shoved along another load of dirt. "And everyone says I'm sick in the head. Maybe Yah will forgive me for pushing back against the Blessed Ones because I'm crazy."

"Maybe," said Freddie doubtfully.

"If I run into some Blessed, I'll just stick them in the nose with the Claw, and they'll go away. It's not perfect, but it seems like a compromise everyone could live with."

"Doesn't seem like Yah compromises a lot," murmured Freddie.

"What happens if you hurt a Blessed One real bad?" asked Anastasia.

Freddie chewed one of his foreclaws. "Um, I think Yah hurts you for a million summers, and each summer is itself as long as a million summers."

Anastasia was silent for a moment. "That makes my head hurt."

"Remembering is tough," said Freddie. "I wanted to be a Reader."

Love Bug came back from pushing earth outside the burrow. "*Magnifique*[5] sunrise out there. Who wants blueberries?"

---

[5]   Magnificent.

Anastasia pulled on her Claw. In just a few days, she had gotten rather good at getting it strapped into place, and the sparring drills with Freddie and Love Bug had helped her learn how to hit with her paws while in the air. Of course, using the Claw with Blessed would be another story.

Love Bug went out first, followed by Freddie. Anastasia stood in the entryway, leisurely touching the left side three times, then the right side. She sang her couplet cheerfully.

"Blueberry shine in the sun and rain,
Have it one time, you'll be back again."

Then she patted the earth twice and they were off.

"Why do you do that?" asked Freddie.

"Do what?" asked Anastasia.

"That thing. Touch the walls, sing a song when we go in and out."

Anastasia looked at him coolly. "I don't know what you're talking about."

"But—"

"If we see any Blessed, run for the burrow," said Anastasia. "My Claw will help me slow them down a bit, then I'll follow."

"Okay," said Freddie. "Will do."

Love Bug threw a withering glance at him. "Seriously?

This lady saved my life. I'm not leaving her outside with Blessed."

Freddie just barely stopped himself from rolling his eyes. "That's what she just *asked* us to do."

Love Bug muttered something about "low-rent mama's boys."

"It probably won't come up," said Anastasia. "Just keep your bunny watch up. More rabbits attract more Blessed."

They set out for the blueberry patch, with Love Bug shouldering roughly past Freddie. Moving from cover to cover, leapfrogging each other, and proceeding slowly so as not to attract attention, they covered the ninety yards and were soon gorging on ripe berries by the stream. Nearby, a red-breasted robin sang in the cool gray light.

"Blueberries on a warm summer morning," murmured Love Bug. "This is one of the times when it's good to be a rabbit."

"This is the day that Yah hath made," said Freddie, mouth full of blueberries. "It is holy."

"Every one a gift," said Anastasia. Then her eye fell on a shiny quartzite boulder at the edge of the stream. Immediately, there was the insistent *thrum* pulling her toward it. She knew from long experience there was no point in resisting. It was like her doorway ritual: she could not *not* do it. "I need to go touch that rock," she muttered. "Be right back."

Freddie and Love Bug hardly noticed as she drifted carefully several yards down the stream bank. She reached the shiny boulder and touched it with her forepaw. Then a small movement caught her eye. It was a fox tail flicking under a bougainvillea bush forty yards downwind. She was very still for a moment. Then, she began to move back toward the other rabbits. "Don't dash. Don't stamp," she said quietly. "Blessed under that bush. Fox. Just start moving toward the burrow."

"Got it," said Love Bug, who instantly left the ripe blueberry he had been biting into and started to drift toward the burrow. Freddie froze. Anastasia lolloped past him.

"Easy now," said Anastasia. "Just take a few steps, Freddie." Then she saw another fox, not far from the first. Her heart raced. "Go now," she hissed. "*Walk*. As soon as you bolt, they will break cover."

Terrible things were happening in Freddie's mind. Sounds and images from the day Fallen Oak Warren had been destroyed, only three weeks before, were rushing together in a cacophony of fear. A mocking little song played over and over.

"Fat little bunny,
Fat little tummy."

Freddie broke and sprinted at full speed for the burrow. The instant after he moved, the meadow was alive with foxes.

Anastasia saw four, *five?* come bursting out of different bushes and start racing toward her. Her back claws raked the ground as she accelerated instantly into full flight. Freddie was ten yards ahead of her, and Love Bug was off to her right. His lithe young body gliding over the ground like a ghost.

Her heart hammered in her ears, but she could see that they were okay. They were fast. They would make it. The foxes were arrowing toward them, but they had too good of a head start. Soon they would be back home and then they could make plans to leave this wretched area with its fox infestation that never seemed to end. Even a bunny with a Dragon Claw could not survive here. They would be smart and leave, as rabbits have done for millennia, and—

Then three more foxes broke cover between her and the burrow. One was almost under Freddie's feet, but he let Freddie dash past. His eyes were locked on Anastasia. With a sick feeling, she realized she knew this fox, knew his mate with her silver ear tips. They were back. Back to kill her. Only her. The crazy one. Hated by Yah. Hated by Blessed.

Love Bug was running alongside her. He was saying something to her. Yelling. But she could not hear. The blood roared in her ears. The foxes in front were converging on her. The two she had hurt, and a third, older female with hazel eyes.

There were eight, nine foxes racing toward her. But she had the gift. The gift from herself. She had the Claw. She would die today, as rabbits always did. But today, for the first time in the history of the world, a fox would die, too. A Blessed One would be Glorified.

The silver-eared fox reached her first, jaws wide, tongue lolling. And then a miracle happened. Just as she reached Anastasia, she turned her head away. Suddenly, she wasn't a set of spikes reaching out to crush Anastasia's small body. She was a smooth expanse of fur covering a taut, curved neck.

Anastasia launched herself into the air. She flicked her right front paw. The blade came out singing its killing song. *Zhing*! As their momentum hurled their bodies together, she drove the fine steel point of the X-ACTO blade into the flesh of the neck, then pulled down with all her strength. The blade fell through the flesh like a heavy rain.

A spray of red hit Anastasia in the face and drenched one side of her body. Her momentum carried her past the fox, who was still hurtling forward and trying to turn as her legs buckled in shock. Terrible sounds came out of her throat. Anastasia landed and fell onto her side, rolling toward the second fox, who also turned her face away from Anastasia as she approached.

Anastasia was tumbling, too low to reach the fox's neck. But as she slid under the fox's belly, she reached out with the Claw and flailed at the legs, the blade flickering in dramatic chiaroscuro. A moment later, Anastasia was sliding into the open air, unsure where she was.

Blinded by the blood, she could not see the third fox, the original attacker, who she knew best of all. But she could smell him, and she was terrified. She scrubbed her eyes with her front paws, and finally got the blood clear in time to see the fox's head, thrusting toward her, jaws wide open, aiming to seize and tear apart her soft belly. She could not reposition herself in time, and she knew these were her last seconds.

Just as the jaws were about to close on her, a white shape flashed in from her right. It was Love Bug, and he closed his teeth on the fox's nose, driving his single upper incisor deep into the mass of nerves that lie just under the exposed black skin. The fox, suddenly weighted down and feeling a blinding jolt of pain, staggered forward, snarling, falling toward the ground.

Anastasia rose on her hind legs and dragged the X-ACTO blade across his face, just missing his right eye. The fox groaned and jerked his head away from her Claw, rolling toward the foxes coming up the hill. Anastasia saw the five foxes converging on her abruptly slow down, looking at each other as they trotted, and then finally walked forward, heads low, tails dragging. The three injured foxes filled the early morning air with shocking, unearthly noises.

Anastasia stood on her back legs and raised her right paw high over her head. The dawn sun made the bloody blade gleam, red and shiny. The five foxes bellied down on the grass, whining. Then one turned and ran for the stream. An instant later, the rest followed him. Then one of the injured foxes rose and tottered after them, whining.

The other two foxes lay still as their blood drained into the thirsty earth.

Anastasia and Love Bug touched noses, then turned and walked toward the burrow. It was done. Rabbit beats foxes. A set piece played out for the ages.

LOVE BUG

But then Anastasia stopped. Love Bug stopped also, gazing at her through his left eye, breathing hard. She was still for what seemed like a long time. Then she said, suddenly, "Run get some spider web."

No one had ever said these words to Love Bug before, but there's a funny thing about fox killers with magic Dragon Claws: You don't argue with them.

Love Bug remembered seeing an orb weaver down by the stream with a web between several stalks of cattails. He turned and ran down there and found a couple of large webs. He stared at them for a second, unsure how to proceed, then just started raking his paws through the web, doing his best to ball the sticky mass up into a wad between his paws. The spiders weren't pleased, but he growled at them and they took off, sitting on the underside of an elephant ear and glowering at him with all sixteen of their eyes.

When he finally had a good-sized ball of spider web, he stuck it to his chest and ran back to Anastasia. She was standing near Juliette, applying a large wad of spider web to the freely bleeding wound in Juliette's throat. The sticky mass stuck to the wound.

"Spider web for healing," said Anastasia. Then she pulled loose fur from her own chest and spread it over the spider web. "Fur to stop the bleeding."

Nearby, Isadore growled feebly, but was in too much pain to do anything.

Anastasia took Love Bug's wad of spider web from him and began spreading it across Juliette's wound. They would need more.

"Go get Freddie and get him to help," said Anastasia.

Love Bug nodded and ran toward the burrow, his mind a confused jumble. *Why is she doing this? Why? Why? Why?* Love Bug reached the mouth of the burrow and rushed inside. He found Freddie just inside the entryway, pressed against the wall, staring at the earth.

"Is it over?" asked Freddie.

"No," Love Bug said brusquely. "We have to gather spider web. Right now."

"What? Why?" asked Freddie.

"Anastasia's helping the foxes."

Freddie sat bolt upright. "Are you serious? Why?"

"Don't know," said Love Bug. "I'm … I'm …" An image of himself, bloody and waiting for death under the agave plant came to his mind. And then a vision of Anastasia appearing as the angel that saved his life. "I'm … doing it. Are you going to help?"

"That's crazy," said Freddie.

"*You* ran," said Love Bug, coldly. "*We* fought. If you want to make up for that, help me now, you yellow belly."

Freddie groaned and heaved himself to his feet and followed Love Bug out of the burrow. They scurried down to the stream where the biggest spider webs were and collected big, sticky wads. Then, they dutifully trekked back to where Anastasia stood over Juliette.

Anastasia took the spider web and pressed it into the laceration, then told Love Bug and Freddie to pull loose fur from their own bodies and pack in on top of the spider web. Gradually, the long slash down Juliette's body was matted over, with the blood drying.

Isadore groaned and dragged himself toward Juliette. The rabbits moved toward him. He lay beside Juliette, pressing against her flank, and offered no resistance as they pressed spider web to his face, working quickly under the mid-morning sun.

Chapter 5

The mouse has short teeth but a long sword.
—Shandy Vale proverb

ANASTASIA

The day warmed up and became hot and bright. After Juliette and Isadore lay for many hours, slowly recovering their strength, Ariel and some of the other foxes crept back and helped them drag themselves away. They were silent.

Love Bug sat by the entrance to the burrow, slowly cleaning himself, which meant licking a heavy spray of blood out of his fur. So all morning long, his mouth was filled with blood and hair. Freddie worked on finishing digging the nut chamber, excavating the earth and pushing it down the hallway by himself. A few hours later, Dingus showed up with cheeks full of acorns and began to stow nuts in his chamber, packing them in tightly. They were silent.

The sky was empty. The songbirds sat in the branches, in small groups of twos and threes. They did not sing. They had seen what had happened in the meadow. They were silent.

No one knew what to make of what had happened. Kill a predator. Yes. That was the dream. The fantasy. Not even spoken of, it was so absurd. A flicker of a thought between eyes closing and sleep coming. A hot flash in the mind after seeing a loved one crushed to death in the jaws of the Blessed Ones.

But it could never happen. That's what it meant to be named a prey animal. An animal awaiting Glorification. Yah touched you when you were not yet born and said, "This one will die to be someone's meal." Or more clearly, "This is a dying animal. This animal lives only until it is needed." Needed by someone more important than you.

And everyone knew there was no getting out of this. This was your assignment, because Yah said so. And there was no fighting back.

So kill a Blessed One. Huzzah. Love it. It's the second coming. The twelfth imam. The final avatar of Vishnu. Do this and we will welcome you, Lord. You're a killer, but you're *our* killer. We will lay ourselves and our babies at your feet.

But kill a Blessed and then save that Blessed's life? What was that? Is that you, Lord? In the big space where the amazing victory lap should have been there was an enormous nothing. And no one wanted to enter that nothing.

So Anastasia paced. From the mouth of the burrow to the sleeping chamber. From the sleeping chamber to the nut room. From the nut room to the mouth of the burrow. Then to the oak tree, and back. Then out to the meadow where the blood lay smeared on the grass, and back. Then down to the blueberry patch where she had first seen the fox. And back.

She could not rest. The Dragon Claw was heavy with sticky blood, the blade stuck in its chamber. She plodded along with it. Once she had marveled at it. Now she felt the weight of it. Is this what it's like to be a Blessed? *You* will die. *You* will live. It was a heavy burden. More than she wanted to carry. The next time her steps took her to the sleeping chamber, she shook off the Claw and left it lying in the dirt.

When she returned to the mouth of the burrow, there was a heavily pregnant amber and white rabbit crouched between the roots. She looked at Anastasia with huge eyes.

"Are you the one who Glorifies Blessed and then brings them back to life?" asked the pregnant rabbit.

Anastasia stared at her. Finally, she said, "What do you want?"

"Are you the Warren Mother?" asked the other rabbit.

"No," said Anastasia stonily.

"May I stay with you?" asked the rabbit.

"Why?" said Anastasia.

"I think my babies would be safe here," said the rabbit in a whisper, her scent bright with desperation. She shifted her weight and Anastasia noticed that she was missing her left front leg. It had been bitten off just below her shoulder, and it had healed as a ragged stump. Having all her weight resting on her right leg made her sit awkwardly, her heavy body twisting. "I've been cast out, because my warren— my old warren—thought I would attract Blessed because now I'm crippled and ... and pregnant." She hung her head. "So please, great lady, if I might ..."

Anastasia suddenly found she had tears burning in her eyes. She leaped forward and pressed her wet cheek against the cheek of the pregnant rabbit. She whispered, *"You are strong."* Then she turned to Love Bug, still covered with dried blood, and said, "Can you ...?"

"What?" asked Love Bug.

"Dig her a chamber ... near mine? See if Freddie will help you."

"Oui, Dangereuse,[6]*"* said Love Bug.

The pregnant rabbit tried to kiss Anastasia's forehead. "Thank you, Honored One," she said, with tears in her voice.

---

[6] Yes, Dangerous One.

Anastasia pulled back. "No," she said. "I'm no one. Love Bug will help you." Then she turned and darted away from the mouth of the burrow, heading upstream, into the ferny woodlands where it was dark and cool. And peaceful.

NICODEMUS

Nicodemus was in his Reader's chamber, trying to calm himself by sorting his collections of lungwort and oakmoss, when Briar appeared in the doorway. "Honored Reader, Warren Mother requests your presence in her chamber."

"Oh, of course," said Nicodemus. He rose and followed Briar through the maze of passages to the Warren Mother's chamber. When he arrived, he saw that Aiden, Rememberer of Bloody Thorn Warren, was already there, although Olympia was not.

Aiden looked at him coolly, his creamy fur dense and luxurious. "Friend of yours, wasn't she?"

"Oh, not really," said Nicodemus, trying to sound casual, even though his heart rate kicked up a notch. "I mean, we've chatted over a clump of fescue, but she wasn't one of my apprentices."

"Ah," said Aiden.

Olympia came in. Her sleek form filled the entryway for a moment. Nicodemus glanced up and forced a casual smile. She skipped the usual formal greetings. "You've heard about it?"

Nicodemus nodded. "Ya, I just came in from morning feed. The songbirds were all over it." He tried to keep his nose wiggle slow and calm.

Olympia laid down beside him, her flank against his. Aiden looked surprised.

"Help me, dear Reader," Olympia murmured. "Rabbit goes crazy, attacks foxes, dies quickly. That, I understand." She laid her paw on his. "Rabbit goes crazy, attacks foxes, hurts them bad. That, I don't understand." She chewed a front claw. "But rabbit goes crazy, attacks foxes, hurts them bad, and then *heals* them? What world are we living in?"

Nicodemus could feel Aiden's eyes drilling into him. "These are strange times," said Nicodemus. "The Rememberer would probably know better than me …"

Olympia turned her gaze to Aiden. "What wisdom does the Word of Yah have to offer?"

Aiden cleared his throat. "*He that turn from Glory and seek life shall find neither.* Letter to the Cruciferous, 11:23-24."

"And yet she lives," said Olympia.

Aiden looked upward and spread his forepaws slightly. "*The rabbit shall lie down with the wolf, and the thistle grow as soft as asparagus. When you hear these things, ye shall know the end is nigh.* Book of Ruminations, 16:35-37."

Olympia gazed at him for a moment, then turned her eyes back to Nicodemus. Her breath was warm on his cheek. "Old friend," she said, "Anastasia loved you."

"She loved *you*," said Nicodemus quickly. He felt himself getting hot, and he fought to keep his scent from broadcasting his alarm. *Happy thoughts. Carrot tops. Peppermint and rue.*

"She loved you as a friend," said Olympia. She sat up and closed her eyes. "She loved me as a mother." Her eyelids flicked open. "Did she say anything to you about this? How did she do it? *Why* did she do it?"

Nicodemus looked down. "It's a mystery to me, Warren Mother," he said. "I had affection for the child, but never saw any indication she could ..." He hesitated.

"Murder a Blessed One?" said Aiden.

"Why would she bring such dishonor on our warren?" asked Olympia. "And now of all times?" She stamped. "Why?"

Briar put his head in from his post in the passageway. "All good, Honored Mother?"

"Yes, yes," said Olympia, irritably.

"I don't think she wanted to do that," said Nicodemus. "She was sick ... in her mind."

Olympia looked at him without speaking.

Nicodemus started again, "That's why you —"

"I?" Olympia's tone was dangerous.

Nicodemus realized there was no way that sentence would end well. "Sorry, what I meant was … that's why the decision had to be made … by everyone … to unwarren her. It was the best thing, at that moment … for every ... all the bunnies." Nicodemus felt he was babbling. He glanced at Aiden, who gazed at him, unblinking. "But we need information. The songbirds are saying that rabbits are going there, to join her. Maybe we could send someone?"

"She's not going to let anyone from Bloody Thorn in," snapped Olympia.

"Someone she doesn't know?" said Nicodemus.

"She knows most of the Readers and their apprentices from the other warrens in this area," said Olympia. She turned to look at Aiden. "What about the Rememberers? Does one of them have an acolyte we could recruit? Someone strong in the ways of Yah."

Aiden nodded. "Almost certainly, Warren Mother," he said. "I will investigate."

"Holy day," said Olympia as she swept out of the chamber.

"Every one a gift," Aiden called after her.

ANASTASIA

After she had gone a few yards into the coolness of the wood, Anastasia began to move faster. Soon she was running. Then sprinting. The bright scent of the pines and eucalyptus trees was sweet and cleansing. It felt good to dash just for the pure feel of it, her powerful rear legs driving her forward. No fear. No death. No Claw. Soon she could smell the salt mist coming in off the ocean, and hear the faint crashing of waves. Through the trees came occasional glimpses of dark blue water.

She was running up an old streambed, dodging around a thick litter of boulders, roots, dead branches, and overhanging ferns. About a hundred yards up, she rounded a stump and ran right into a small creature the same size as herself. The impact bowled them both over and they fell down into a small space between two boulders. A sweet, heavy reek told Anastasia the space was being used as a den by a family of weasels.

The creature sank its teeth into Anastasia's shoulder, and she responded by biting the other's big droopy ear. Her teeth met through the cartilage, and she tasted the salty blood. Then she felt an enormous, clawed foot land on her abdomen, and the kick sent her sprawling.

She yelped in surprise and rolled backwards. Then she flung herself upright, teeth bared, twigs crackling under her back feet, her front paws slashing. *Why had she gone out without the Claw?* The other creature thrashed for a moment, growling. Then it stood still, glaring at Anastasia.

She had never seen anything like it. The forehead was

broad and heavy, with deep-set, dark eyes. The pelt was loose and baggy on its sturdy frame, the hips were wide, long ears hung down to the ground, and the paws were huge. It looked like a tiny grizzly with long ears. But it smelled strangely familiar. It was hard to sort that out with the reek of weasel and dead animal flesh overlaying everything.

The creature growled again, and Anastasia took a step back. She felt damp earth behind her. Her shoulder was wet with blood. There was only one way out of the space.

The animal came forward, shambling like a bear, a trickle of blood running down its left ear. Anastasia suddenly noticed it was wearing a necklace which appeared to be strung with several claws. Anastasia took up her fighting stance, head low and moving side to side like a snake, shoulders high and jutting. This was going to be a nasty fight. Suddenly, she realized why the smell was familiar.

"You're a rabbit," she said, stunned.

The animal looked at her suspiciously.

"You're a *rabbit*," she said again.

The other creature growled. "You rabbit?"

Anastasia laughed nervously. "Of course I'm a rabbit. But what … happened to you? Did you … break your ears?"

"Bah," said the other animal.

As Anastasia stared, she felt a faint tickle in the back of

her mind. Something Nicodemus had once told her. "Are you ... a br ... a breed? Like from the Dominion?"

The strange rabbit waved her question away. "Where is world?" it asked suddenly.

"What?" said Anastasia.

"World!" The creature barked. "Where is? I want find."

Anastasia could see a little bit of the teeth of the other creature flash when it talked. They didn't look like canines. Clippers, not rippers. Definitely a rabbit. Finally, she said, "Don't know."

"You stupid," said the other animal.

You crazy, thought Anastasia. Aloud, she said, "Weasels live here. We shouldn't stay." She started edging forward.

"What is 'weasels?'" asked the other rabbit.

Anastasia blinked. "Blessed Ones. They kill ... us," she stuttered. "You've never heard of weasels?"

"I know killers," said the strange rabbit. "They fly. Hawk. Owl."

Anastasia pushed her way past the other rabbit and out through the front doorway, then turned and said, "Okay, listen. Weasels are walking hawks. We have to leave now, or we'll be dead." She hesitated. "You want to come with me to my burrow? There's a few people there."

The other rabbit shook its head. "I want find world."

You more crazy than me, thought Anastasia, a little sadly. Aloud, she said, "Holy day." The other rabbit said nothing. Anastasia looked up and down the streambed. Were those some snaky shapes coming out from behind that dying fern? "May Yah watch over you," she said. Then she turned and ran.

ARIEL

Ariel the fox crouched in the entrance to her den under the chokeberry bush. Her eyes were still bright, but now they were glassy. She stared straight ahead. Some of the other foxes had gone back to help Isadore and Juliette. Ariel had not gone back.

After awhile, she saw a dirty-gray coyote come limping through the brush. It was Gaetan. He stopped to eat a windfall apple lying on the ground under the gnarled branches of an ancient apple tree. Ariel moved, crushing some dried leaves. The coyote looked up.

"O, hey, cousin," he said. "Did you hear … about the rent riot today?"

"I was there," said Ariel.

Gaetan looked surprised. "I'm so sorry, *ma chère,*[7]" he said. He limped toward her, favoring the right front leg he had broken as a pup, which had never healed right. He nuzzled her neck and shoulder. "What I heard sounds crazy. I'm sorry so many foxes were hurt." Ariel did not move or

---

[7]   My dear.

respond. After a few moments, he stopped. "Can you tell me what happened?"

"Problem tenants." Ariel was quiet for a few moments. "Went crazy and attacked us." Then she said, "I'm leaving."

"Where are you going?" asked Gaetan.

"I don't know," said Ariel. "Far away."

Gaetan lay down near her and again nuzzled her coat. "But your whole family is here. Ariel, *what happened?*" he persisted. "It can't be what they're saying."

Ariel pulled away. "When you see a rabbit tear open a fox's body with a touch, you don't wait to see more," she said. "Blood Father is looking at us."

"No, he's not," said Gaetan. "Blood Father loves us. He's looking far away. This is just … a freak accident."

For the first time, Ariel gazed directly into Gaetan's eyes. "You weren't there." She stood and shook off the dried leaves, her gaze shifting. "I'll tell you this, cousin. If you come across a rabbit …"

The sentence hung in the air. Ariel took a few steps up the trail. "What?" said Gaetan, finally.

She glanced back. "Think twice."

LOVE BUG

It was the morning after the fight with the foxes. The Blessed were still giving the area around the incident a wide berth. And the skies were still clear. In the distance, a blackbird sang.

Love Bug came out the main entryway and inhaled the lush scent of grass rising up from the meadow that stretched from the burrow to the stream. Not even a hint of Blessed. He saw an elderly buck huddled next to one of the roots. "Holy day," said the buck, faintly.

"Every one a gift," said Love Bug. He chinned the big stone near the door. "How can I help you, friend?"

The old buck looked sad, and his fur was a thinning brown going gray. "I've been unwarrened," he said, and Love Bug could hear the fear in his words. "I'm almost blind now, and they say I'll be attracting Blessed. I heard about the killing and I thought maybe this is a place that's not so afraid."

"It wasn't exactly a killing—" began Love Bug. The pain on the old rabbit's face stopped him. "But I think the lady who lives here would be glad to welcome you."

Tears came to the elder rabbit's eyes. "Thank you very much, Honored First Born and Door Warden—"

"I'm not a First Born," said Love Bug quickly. "But I'll show you where you can rest." He touched noses with the other rabbit. "Name's Love Bug."

"I'm Grégoire," said the other rabbit.

Love Bug turned and led the way down the main passageway into the warren. "Do you mind nuts? We have a room we dug for nuts, but it has quite a bit of space at the moment."

"Why do you have nuts?" asked Grégoire.

Love Bug started to answer, but realized it would take a long time. "Squirrel outreach," he said, finally.

He got Grégoire installed in the nut room, then headed back outside, passing the newly dug chamber where the pregnant Holly was resting. Much of the floor and walls were already covered in soft down she had pulled from her body to prepare for her young ones.

When Love Bug got back to the main entrance, he found two kits about four months old, both black and splashed with gray. They told him their names were Chervil and Juniper. Their mother had dug a burrow a few hundred yards away by the light of the last-quarter moon, but she had been killed by an owl a few days ago.

When Love Bug asked them why they had come here instead of going back to their mother's home warren, they said they had heard that the Warren Mother here had killed many Blessed. So maybe this place was safer?

"Well, that's not quite what happened," said Love Bug. "Plus, the lady that was doing the fighting isn't really a Warren Mother, although ..." He trailed off as he looked into their big eyes staring up at him. "But, of course, you can stay, little friends," he said, touching noses with them. He led them into the burrow, roused a somewhat grumpy late-sleeping Freddie, and asked him to help the young ones dig a sleeping chamber.

When Love Bug returned to the main entryway, he found a group of rabbits, some injured, some very old, some kits, waiting for him, along with a family of field mice.

Up above, he could hear Dingus giving a tour to a group of squirrels. "And just there, you can see the actual hole of the Rabbit Who Killed Seven Foxes With One Blow. Ah, chek chek chek chek chek chek chek."

Love Bug was starting to feel a little overwhelmed by the parade of needs. He noticed the group contained a young buck, who seemed capable and energetic, and approached him. "Hi, I'm Love Bug," he said.

"I'm Coriander," said the buck, who had copper agouti fur and teal blue eyes.

"And you're here because—"

"I'm here to join the warren," said Coriander cheerfully.

"Why?" asked Love Bug.

"Doe kills a fox, then *brings it back to life?*" said Coriander. "You got my attention. I wanna see this up close."

Love Bug was intrigued that this rabbit seemed to have a somewhat better grasp of what had actually happened, but he felt driven to argue details. "Well, it's not really a warren—"

"Looks like a warren to me, dude," said Coriander.

"For where two or three or a dozen are gathered in my name, it shall be a warren, and it shall be holy, saith the Loved One." He smiled. "Book of Fluffy, 2:16-18."

Love Bug looked around at all the rabbits. "Well, hard to argue with that," he said. "Coriander, can you take this group into the warren and organize them into teams to rough out sleeping chambers?"

"This is a warren where bucks dig?" asked Coriander. "Wow, now *that's* disruptive. I guess this is one of those new-fangled warrens—"

"You could say that—" began Love Bug.

Then Anastasia showed up, returning from a long recon through the surrounding territory. The voice of Dingus was suddenly loud, just above them in the old poplar tree. "Open your eyes, my squirrellies! That is Anastasia Bloody Thorn, Champion of the Field, Killer of Foxes, Protector of Nuts. Ah, chek chek chek chek chek chek chek." The squirrels in the tour all clapped.

The rabbits and mice, hearing this, swarmed around her. Grégoire, Chervil, Juniper, and Freddie came out. Even Holly woke up and joined them. They all cheered her. "To the killer of Blessed!"

Anastasia immediately began shushing the crowd. "No, no, no," she said. "This is the world that Yah has made, and we share this world with the Blessed Ones. All I want is some breathing room."

"Three cheers for breathing room!" shouted Holly, huge with her litter of unborn kits, followed by more cheers and hubbub.

"A warren without Glorification!" shouted Freddie.

Grégoire took a few steps up onto a rise and called to the crowd, "*Bienvenue dans le Garenne Sans Gloire!*[8]"

There was a loud round of cheers.

"Warren *Sans Gloire*," said Love Bug to Anastasia, with a smile. "*Dirigé par une belle dame.*[9] Sounds fancy."

Anastasia looked at him for a long moment. "Are we fancy?"

"We're alive," said Love Bug. "That sounds pretty fancy to me."

Coriander came over to Anastasia and kissed her forehead. "It is my honor to meet you," he said, smiling warmly. "I'm Coriander."

Anastasia looked at him, her gaze taking in the way the sparkly pigmentation in his agouti fur gave his muscular, copper body an almost iridescent sheen. She also noticed that he had kind eyes. "Welcome, Coriander," she said.

Holly came alongside Anastasia and snuggled against her flank. Juniper and Chervil climbed up, so they could lie

---

[8] Welcome to the Warren Without Glory!

[9] Run by a beautiful lady.

in the warm space between them. "Yay, Warren Mother!" they shouted.

"No, no," said Anastasia. "I'm not the Warren Mother."

"Yay, Loving Auntie!" they shouted.

Anastasia looked at them for a long moment, and then kissed them. "You may call me whatever you like," she said.

Dingus ran forward and presented Anastasia with a fresh dandelion. "Behold, the Loving Auntie!" he proclaimed. Anastasia took a bite out of it, then he whisked it away. They both laughed. A young bunny did a backflip *bink* right over them. Anastasia looked happy. A family of chaffinches began to sing.

The rabbits and mice and squirrels in the crowd chattered away. The smell of happy, relaxed little animals flowed over the greensward like a river of joy. Love Bug felt a warm glow building inside of him. This could be a new kind of warren, without First Born and other bullies. Maybe it could be a place where no one would be unwarrened because they were sick, or old, or injured. A place where even the Blessed would have to show them some respect. A place that Love Bug would be proud to call home.

As he sat, smiling, in the early-morning sun, he looked up and realized that dark shapes were gathering in the skies overhead. A chill overtook him. The raptors were back.

BRICABRAC

Bricabrac was back at his workshop in the hollow log, working on cleaning Anastasia's Dragon Claw. The fox blood had filled the inner chamber and dried, locking the blade inside like a hard, sticky resin. He had set up three split green twigs so they were holding the Claw in place against the soft punk that lined the inside of the log. Now he was alternately pouring in water from a stainless steel thimble and digging out the dried blood with a brush he had made by chewing the end of a hard maple twig.

Bleh. I need to rethink this design. Bricabrac stopped for a moment to cogitate, and carelessly sucked on his twig brush. *Mmm. Aged fox blood. You don't get that every day.*

With his sharp ears, he heard tiny footsteps outside his log. He flicked a glance in that direction and saw a familiar dark shape with a splash of white fur on the back enter a small grove of poinsettias gathered around a puddle of clear water. Soon, he heard a small voice singing a morning liturgy he recognized.

"I see you,
You see I,
I and thou,
In my eye.

What shall we do,
I and you,
This day to
Make the world?"

Bricabrac chuckled. *These crazy cults are everywhere now*. Then he busied himself with his cleaning. Soon, with the side of his eye, he saw the dark shape creep into his log, and he smelled the wispy, warm smell of mouse. "Death Rage! What up, cousin?" he said, then sat down and offered her the twig in a companionable way. "Fox blood?"

Death Rage made a face. "How can you eat that crap? Blood is for spilling from the veins of my enemies."

Bricabrac shrugged. "Grab the blessing of the day and stuff it down your throat, that's what I always say."

"Feh," said the mouse, and started to turn away.

"Well now," said Bricabrac, "how did I not mention how awesome your helmet looks? Have you been getting compliments on it?"

"Some," allowed the mouse. "I got invited to a duel."

"Fantastic!" said Bricabrac.

"But I didn't go, because my weapon was in the shop."

"Oh, that's a shame."

"Not that it makes much difference," said Death Rage. "Most of our weapons are wood. We don't have any sharpstone, so things are pretty sleepy around here. After awhile, dueling other mice for honor points gets boring."

"Well hey, I'm tweaking this Claw that you helped me with. I need a cuff to cover the hole where the blade comes out. It has to be flexible, and sewn onto the sleeve. I was thinking that's the kind of thing a Musmuski Grove artisan could make with pineapple skin?"

Death Rage thought seriously. "That would be possible," she said, finally. "What's on offer?"

Bricabrac frowned judiciously and reached into his pack. "This will be harder than weaving the agave fiber, so I have something extra-special for you." He pulled out a stainless-steel needle. "The finest sharpstone. Never goes crusty."

Death Rage's eyes grew large. She reached for the needle. He pulled it back. "So will you do it?"

"Let me feel it," she said.

He handed her the needle. "This could be a rapier for you. You can use some of the pineapple skin to make yourself a grip."

Death Rage hefted the needle. It suited her tiny hand perfectly. "This is good. Very good." She tried a few lunges. "Okay, I'll do it." She did some squats and settled into a deep stance. "What is that Claw thing for, anyway?"

"It's for a rabbit to kill enemies, as needed," said Bricabrac.

Suddenly, Death Rage put together the stories she had been hearing with her freelance work for Bricabrac. "A rabbit ... Glorified a fox with that?"

"Cut its throat," said Bricabrac, nonchalantly.

"And lived?" asked Death Rage.

"So did the fox," said Bricabrac. "It was quite a day."

A moment later, the mouse was standing very close to him. "Cousin," she said, "when you go back, take me with you."

"Why?" asked Bricabrac.

Death Rage twirled her repurposed needle before turning her eyes on him. "Destiny calls."

GAETAN

Gaetan limped toward the clump of tamarind trees where Clan *Paresseux*, the casual coyote pack south of the Shandy River liked to gather. He noticed a fresh new tomato on the vine growing next to the oak stump. He picked it up in his mouth and made the mistake of entering the clearing without eating it first.

"Hey, it's the vegetarian," called Edouard, his yellow eyes lazy and smiling. "Did that tomato run you ragged, brother?"

A general chuckle ran through the pack of several dozen coyotes as Gaetan walked awkwardly into the space under the tamerinds, his right front leg dragging. "I take care of the slows and the stupids," he said, affecting an amiable tone. "That's my job."

"I'll bring you back an ear next time I make a kill," said Edouard. "Put some meat on your bones, *chien bâton.*[10] "

"Oh, hush," said Lilou, stretching her tawny back legs. "You haven't killed anything bigger than a rabbit in weeks."

Gaetan was embarrassed that his older sister was always sticking up for him. "Very kind of you to offer an ear to a fat *saucisse*[11] like me," he said. "When I lose a few pounds, maybe I'll take you up on it." He eased his lean gray frame down onto a soft, grassy spot near Lilou.

Benoit, a rangy, gray elder lying on a flat rock in the warm sun, growled. "Let's get back to the issue at hand. Micah Summerday is saying no more deer hunting unless we're doing it *en banc*[12] with the wolves. What are we going to do about it?"

"Micah Summerday can eat my scat," said Edouard, his yellow eyes rolling.

"*Sooo* brave," said Lilou. She licked up a bug crawling

---

[10] Stick dog.

[11] Sausage.

[12] Literally, "in bench." Figuratively, "as a group."

between her ecru forelegs. "When the wolf's away, the coyboys play, eh?" There was a light riffle of snickers.

"Ain't scared of that yellow dog," said Edouard.

Benoit stood and shook the dust out of his coat. "As I see it, we have two choices," he said. "We can just ignore it, or we can tell him *casse-toi*.[13]"

"I may not be a Landlord, but I know how to collect the rent as well as the next *voyou*,[14]" said Edouard. "I don't need any team-building tips from the golden yakkers."

"Why pick a fight with the wolves?" asked Lilou. "Just ignore him. He can't watch us every second."

"No, but the crows can," said Benoit. "They're always happy to carry tales."

"We're free, gray, and Blessed," said Edouard. "I say we do what we want. If Summerboy has a problem with that, let him tell us."

There was some lazy cheering, and then the group gradually fell silent in the warm afternoon.

"Have you heard about that rabbit thing south of Musmuski Grove?" asked Gaetan, casually.

"The what?" asked Benoit.

"Oh, that thing with the foxes?" said Lilou.

---

[13] Literally, "break yourself." Figuratively, "shove off."

[14] Thug.

"A rabbit refused the rent. Attacked some foxes," said Gaetan. "Hurt them pretty bad."

"Oh, you're scaring me," scoffed Edouard.

"I talked to a survivor," said Gaetan.

"A *survivor*?" laughed Edouard. "A fox has to *survive* an attack by a bunny now? What's the Million Acre Wood coming to?"

"Foxes are nitwits," said Benoit. "Next thing, you'll be taking up a collection for foxes that got mugged by a mouse."

"This is real," said Gaetan. "Everyone's talking about it. Something weird is happening." He paused, and the hot whine of a mosquito vibrated in the dusty air. "We're the alpha hunters south of the Shandy. We should have a plan."

"Oh, now you're the boss of me, *blaireau*?[15]" asked Edouard.

"We should at least send someone to check it out," said Gaetan.

There was a chorus of general chaffing, mixed with cries of *"Garçon!*[16] More rabbit!"

Gaetan put his chin down on his paws and growled. "This is what I hate about these *andouille*[17] coyotes."

---

[15] Literally, "badger." Figuratively, "jerk."

[16] Boy.

[17] Literally, "blood sausage." Figuratively, "stupid."

Chapter 6

Live in my belly and pay no rent.

—Coyote proverb

WARREN SANS GLOIRE

It was late afternoon, and Anastasia's single burrow was busily turning itself into a bustling warren. Coriander turned out to be a capable digger, even though, like all the bucks, he was new to it. And he was always ready with a friendly smile or a kindly quote from the Word of Yah.

Grégoire was nearly blind, as he had said, but he had a keen understanding of plants, and could tell the roots of plants underground just by their scent. This enabled the digging teams to avoid wasting time on runs that would be blocked by huge tree roots, while helping them find areas with a filigree of fine roots that would help support walls and ceilings.

Juniper and Chervil were diligent in pushing the loose earth out. They made a game of it, even getting the other young bunnies to join them. And when they cried for their dead mother at night, many a doe would offer kindly kisses and a warm, furry flank to snuggle into.

Holly would have her kits any day now. And many rabbits came in from the two daily feeds with extra leaves in their mouths to leave in her chamber. When the warren was quiet, everyone could hear her singing quietly to her children who were about to be born.

"Sweet, tiny babes,
Stay close and warm,
Inside is safe,
Outside, the storm."

Anastasia had deputized Dingus to organize the local squirrels and offer safe, centralized nut storage in exchange for keeping an eye out for Blessed and sounding a warning when they saw them approach. Most of the squirrels were enthusiastic. They forgot where they buried half their nuts, and although this is how forests are planted, it did end up being a lot of wasted work for the squirrels. Plus, they thought of Anastasia as some kind of wizard who killed foxes and brought them back to life, so they were happy to be on her good side.

The Blessed were still keeping their distance. Sure, the dark flecks of raptors were circling above, but there had been no attacks. And the ground-based Blessed Ones where nowhere to be seen.

Anastasia herself was often away from the warren, which she still habitually referred to as "my burrow." She had her Dragon Claw back, in good working order, and she roamed the area around the warren memorizing every tree, bush, and stone, hypothesizing about coming dangers and trying to work out solutions.

This left Freddie and Love Bug to manage the minute-by-minute needs of the warren. They weren't always the best of comrades. Love Bug thought of Freddie as an out-family weakling from the lower runs, and made no secret of it. Freddie saw Love Bug as a rich boy slumming. He was part of Moonfall Warren's founding family bloodline, with all the privilege that entailed. And even though Love Bug had been attacked and run out of Moonfall by bullying older brothers, he hadn't lost his aristocratic confidence with the does. Freddie couldn't help being envious.

Still, they had worked it out that they took turns overseeing the digging and standing as Door Warden of the main entrance. Because every day, more little creatures came.

On this afternoon, Love Bug was at the front door. It

was too early for evening feed, so the landscape was deserted. Bored, he chinned a nearby twig. Then a pebble he hadn't noticed earlier. Suddenly, he caught sight of a mother rabbit trying to shepherd four young kits along from cover to cover. Now under a bougainvillea, now under an ocotillo cactus, they moved slowly and erratically.

The mother was copper-colored with streaks of white, and she must have Hotot blood, since she had the rim of dark fur around her eyes. Her four kits were the color of ash, tamarind, storm cloud, and honey. They looked to be just two months old: frolicsome, easily startled, and snuggly all at the same time.

Love Bug watched their slow progression with unease. A hundred yards away. Eighty yards away. Fifty. "Come on, come on," he murmured. Thirty yards. Love Bug felt a sick sensation in his gut before he knew why. Then he realized what it was. One of the dark specks in the sky had begun to drop. A raptor was coming to collect his birthright.

Love Bug froze for a moment. Then he darted forward. "Hey!" he shouted as he ran. "Hey! Mother! *Raptor falling!* Run!"

The mother tried to herd her kits forward. The storm-cloud gray kit ran toward Love Bug and the entrance of the warren. The tamarind and ash kits hid in a clump of petunias. The honey-colored baby doe ran the wrong way, into the bare meadowlands. Mother bunny looked desperate.

"I'll get her," said Love Bug, as he ran past the mother rabbit. She pushed the other two toward the entryway. Love Bug glanced up as he ran, and saw the alternating rows of dark and light feathers on the body of the Blessed, now falling like a stone from the clear blue sky. Northern goshawk. His heart skipped a beat.

Where was that baby? Love Bug leaped, catching quick reconnaissance glimpses over the fescue clumps. There she was, huddling under a thistle. The goshawk was a descending hammer. Love Bug shouted, "Come to me, baby girl! Come to me!" The baby did not move. Without looking, Love Bug knew the yellow talons above him were opening, steel-sharp points aimed downward, wind rushing past them.

He forced himself forward. In a few more steps, he was there, near the child. He could smell a bright bloom of fear. She was petrified, long gone into the Giving. Love Bug seized the scruff of fur at the back of her neck in his mouth, and turned back toward the warren entrance. There was a jolt of pain from his single upper tooth. She was heavier than he expected, and he couldn't lift her cleanly. He stumbled. The baby squealed, shocked awake.

Love Bug stole a glance upward and saw the goshawk just seconds away, great wings beating the air now to slow its descent. Love Bug hurled himself ahead, dragging the baby with him. She shrieked and fought, limbs pinwheeling. His back claws dug in and found purchase against an ancient clump of purslane. Then his body was lunging forward. The weight of the kitten was dragging his neck to the side, but still they were moving. The pain in his tooth was hot as fire.

He could see the mother running toward him now. Something was interfering with his vision. *Flick. Flick. Flick.* Suddenly, he realized it was the wings of the goshawk beating above him. He knew what was coming next. The beak slicing down like a lancet, shredding fur, rending flesh.

He heard a scream. His back claws raked the ground and he staggered ahead, teeth clenched in the kitten's fur. A moment later, he was rocketing forward, light and free, and the baby was gone. He looked up just in time to see the tiny creature being lifted away. The huge wings beat the air fiercely as the goshawk climbed.

With his very next step, he crashed into the mother, and they rolled together on the ground, the terrible cry of her heart breaking burned into his ears.

NICODEMUS

Nicodemus the Reader and Aiden the Rememberer sat in the warm sunshine near the main entrance to Bloody Thorn Warren, playing the ancient game of the northern rabbits,

Terre Soleil.[18] In between them was a patch of bare earth, and in the earth, there were twenty-five small holes, arranged in five rows. Some of the holes were empty. Some had pebbles in them. In the center hole was a small sunflower. Its sweet, light scent rose gently in the summer air.

Nicodemus picked up a flake of flint from the small pile in front of him and held it carefully between both paws. "Second of the Third Four has been born," he said, and placed the pebble in the row in front of him. "Why do rabbits have so many children?"

Aiden scratched his ear with his hind leg. "Because Yah loves us," he said. Then he put his paw into a hole in front of him and scooped up a bright piece of iron pyrite, pushing it into the next hole forward. "Trickster sees a blueberry." He chewed his front left paw. "Why do rabbits want what cannot be had?"

Nicodemus wiggled his nose slowly. "To be alive is to desire," he said. Then he moved a green pebble to the side. "Dill seed blows on the wind." His eyes flicked up, and for a moment he looked into Aiden's eyes. "Why do the Blessed Ones Glorify so many rabbits?"

Aiden held Nicodemus' gaze. "Because Yah loves us," he said coolly. Then he looked down and nudged a fragment of chert toward the center. "Fool lies in the sun." A

---

[18] Earth Sun.

butterfly landed on the sunflower for a moment, and then flittered away. "Why does a rabbit steal moneystones?" asked Aiden.

Nicodemus froze for a moment, then he remembered to start wiggling his nose again, slowly. It was the seventh round, traditionally the time for a personal question. *Does he know something? Has that lout Briar been talking?* Nicodemus pulled his ear down and washed it. This was not the time to smell anxious. *Happy thoughts. Radish tops.* "So that the moneystones do not steal the rabbit," he said, with a small smile. Aiden inclined his head slightly. Nicodemus picked up a fragment of black anthracite and laid it in the same hole as Aiden's chert. "Dark days for Fool." He inhaled deeply. "Why does a rabbit fight another rabbit?"

Aiden looked down at his pebbles. "Yah is a jealous god," he said. Then he pushed his fragment of chert forward. "Fool advances." He glanced up into the bright blue heavens. "Why should a rabbit who aids an outlaw not be cast out as well?"

There was no sidestepping this threat. Nicodemus was old and very satisfied with his position as Reader at Bloody Thorn. He had hoped to die here, serenely, in his sleep. The ultimate rabbit victory. As he gazed at Aiden, he felt a taste of the old rage that Readers have felt for Rememberers for aeons. He was silent.

"Well?" asked Aiden.

This was a breach of protocol, very unusual among the learned strata of rabbit society. It was tantamount to a declaration of war. Nicodemus used both paws to pick up his amethyst and held it over the earthboard. He looked Aiden steadily in the eyes. "Loved One takes Fool."

FREDDIE

Anastasia, Love Bug, Freddie and Coriander were sitting in a side chamber at *Sans Gloire*. Anastasia was drawing a complex pattern of triangles on one wall, then taking three steps and drawing the same pattern backward on the other wall. Back and forth.

"The breathing room from the raptors is over," said Freddie. "They've figured out they don't have anything to fear from us."

Love Bug looked lost in thought. At last he spoke, "You know, if I had just gone the other way coming off that clump of purslane, that little kitten would still be alive right now."

"Don't go down that hole," said Freddie. "You'll never come out."

Love Bug slowly came back from his thousand-yard stare and focused on Freddie. "Fine, wise words," he said, "from a rabbit who doesn't fight."

Stung, Freddie turned to the other two and said, "We

see the problem. The question is, what should we do about it?"

Neither of them answered him. Anastasia continued her pacing. Coriander looked as though he might be praying. "A new tactic," said Freddie. "Something that would scare off the other raptors. Something that will show them that we will exact a cost—."

"Hawks have been Glorifying baby bunnies for a million years," said Coriander. "It's sad for us in the moment, but it's part of Yah's grand plan for every living creature."

"But we need to *do* something—" began Freddie.

Coriander began to sing very quietly.

"All my days of pain, O Yah, I give unto You,
My darkness and my rain, O Yah, I give unto You."

Anastasia stopped pacing, suddenly. "Yes," she said. "Yah created this problem. We should pray to Him for guidance."

"But how shall we do that?" asked Freddie. He resisted adding, *if Yah wanted us to have any answers, we'd have them now.*

"We will ask every rabbit to pray," said Anastasia.

"That sounds like a wise plan," said Coriander.

"Let's start now," said Anastasia. "And let's not just ask every rabbit here. Let's ask the rabbits here to ask all the rabbits they know."

Freddie ground his teeth. "Very good, Loving Auntie," he said.

Coriander looked at her with his kind, beautiful eyes. "Yah is with you, Anastasia," he said.

DINGUS

It was late in the day, close on to twilight. A whippoorwill was calling. Dingus balanced with insouciant ease on an oak twig as he addressed the squirrels gathered before him. One family had traveled for seventy-nine trees to see the famous *Glorification & Resurrection of Foxes By the Rabbit Without Antecedents*. Business was good. Very good. Seventy-nine trees was a long way to travel. Dingus was thinking of opening—he had just learned this word from Freddie this morning—a "hotel."

"You can just leave your nuts in the hollow of the tree there," said Dingus. "One per visitor, or three nuts for four. Ooo, a pistachio. *Exotique!*[19] Now," he folded his hands over his tummy, "let me take you back in time to the moment, many days ago, when a plethora of foxes came to this place, this very assemblage of poplar and stream and meadow and blueberry patch." Dingus paced back and forth on his branch, his fine hands shaping the air as he

---

[19]   Exotic.

spoke, "Thinking they would Glorify a bunny of no particular stature, a brown bunny who had just dug a hasty burrow here and was beginning to think of a longer stay, when, without warning—"

Dingus had a habit of resting his eyes on the underbrush in the middle distance as he spoke, and he suddenly realized he was looking at a familiar gray shape moving slowly through the brush. Very familiar. Very gray.

"Coyote!" he squeaked. The squirrels in the tour perked up. *This* was new.

Dingus stared. The coyote was moving strangely. It did not have the lazy slinkiness of movement that one usually saw when these quiet gray killers were about. It took a moment for him to realize that the coyote was limping. One of its legs dragged as it walked.

"What happened with the coyote?" piped up one of the younger squirrels on the tour.

The question kicked Dingus into action. "*Oyez, oyez, oyez,*[20]" he shouted, racing around the perimeter of his oak tree. "Blessed spotted! In the brush by the saguaro! Warn everyone! Take action!"

The squirrels in the other trees came alive. They had all been promised extra nuts for a vigorous response. The poplar tree's primary squirrel-in-residence dashed down the

---

[20] Literally, "see, see, see." Figuratively, "hey, listen up, everyone."

trunk and into the main entrance of the warren. An instant later, Coriander came racing out of the entrance and started rounding up stragglers from evening feed. The squirrels on the tour looked excited and pleased.

"Pine tree squad," yelled Dingus. The squirrels who lived in the pine tree were already out on their branch ends, each holding a pine cone. "There!" called Dingus, indicating the coyote. Immediately, the squirrels began to bombard the coyote with pine cones. The coyote froze at first, then looked up to see the ranks of squirrels above him. The pine cones didn't hurt, but all the commotion made sure that every creature within a quarter of a mile knew he was there.

There was no more element of surprise. The coyote turned and limped away into the gathering twilight.

One of the squirrels in the tour elbowed the squirrel next to her and said, "*So* immersive. Definitely worth a pistachio."

FREDDIE

Freddie was taking a shift as Door Warden at evening feed. The scent of woodland irises drifted on the cooling air. As the rabbits filed out into the twilight, excited to hunt for fresh herbs, he said, over and over, "Hawk danger is high. Stay close and under cover. Keep your eyes up."

As he spoke, he could hear Love Bug under a nearby

rhododendron bush, chatting up a fluffy-tailed doe who had just arrived two days earlier. "Ya, when you take on a fox and you come out alive, every day after that is just, like, more vivid, you know? It's like you're pulsing with the life force. Say, what are you doing after evening feed?"

Freddie rolled his eyes and glared out across the meadowlands. Suddenly, he caught a whiff of something gamy. Something dead. There was a rustling in the brush on the far side of the poplar tree. Freddie stamped. Immediately a dozen rabbits near him stamped. And an instant later, every rabbit in or near the warren was on high alert.

A small, bearlike creature with long ears that hung down came around the side of the tree. Freddie took a few steps backward, and then forced himself to stop and drop into fighting stance. He was gratified to see Coriander, Love Bug, and half a dozen other bucks and does line up beside him.

The strange animal laughed, "You some scared *coineanaich*.[21]" The gamy smell was a lot stronger now. From the voice, it was clear the creature was female. She appeared to be wearing a necklace, which no rabbit in the Million Acre Wood had ever done.

As Door Warden, Freddie felt like he had to marshal the situation, even though he hated this sort of thing. "Umm, we live in peace, and respect all who want peace.

---

[21] Bunnies.

But we can defend ourselves," he said, sternly. Beside him, Coriander growled.

The other animal laughed again, "You pray for help with raptors. God send me to you."

Freddie sat up, "Yes, rabbits prayed for help. What are you?"

The strange animal grinned and showed her long yellow incisors. "I rabbit," she said.

A murmur ran through the crowd. "What happened to your ears, sister?" asked Coriander.

She waved away his question with a large paw. "Bah."

"What do you know about raptors?" asked Freddie.

The rabbit moved her paw toward her necklace, and Freddie realized with a start that it appeared to be strung with several claws. She touched each claw in turn. "Hawk. Owl. Osprey. Hawk. Falcon."

Is she saying she killed these raptors? Freddie had never heard of such a thing. He walked forward to take a better look. By the time he got close enough to see the necklace well, it was clear the dead animal reek came from the claws.

"Oof," he said, stepping back. "How did you get these?"

The strange rabbit licked her paw. "I bite off."

Freddie felt his head buzzing. "If you can kill hawks, you were indeed sent by Yah."

"Yah moves in mysterious ways," said Coriander, who looked pale under his fur.

The rabbit laughed. "What is Yah? I said God sent me." She lollopped forward and touched noses with Freddie. "Now, you want kill hawks, or you want stamp and jabber all night?"

"No, not kill hawks," came a voice from the back of the crowd. It was Anastasia, just coming out of the main entrance. "We are rabbits. We are beloved of Yah. We do not kill Blessed." She came forward and double-bumped the shaggy rabbit's flank. "But we do ask them nicely to take a step back." Anastasia flicked her front right paw, and the Claw came singing out of its holster. *Zhing!*

The strange rabbit grinned. "You nice lady," she said, her long teeth flashing in the setting sun. "I could tell first time we met." She nose-bumped Anastasia's shoulder. "I want something."

"What?" said Anastasia.

"All these walking hawks here make me tired. I want place live until I find way back world."

Anastasia looked at her for a moment. "Done."

The shaggy rabbit licked her paw and touched Anastasia's forehead. "Done."

"We weren't introduced before. I'm Anastasia."

The strange rabbit belched loudly. The stench was horrific. The nearby rabbits scuttled backward. Anastasia's golden eyes narrowed, but she did not move.

"I Wendy," said Wendy.

AIDEN

There was a space among the thorn bushes that grew over Bloody Thorn Warren where the earth was packed firm, overlaid with a carpet of dead leaves. The thorns grew thickly about, creating an airy meeting chamber also difficult to see into. There was only one way in, a short run that ramped up from Olympia's chambers.

Olympia and Darius were reclining on the leaves, chewing some fresh apple twigs that Aiden had ordered brought in. Fufu, a little gray and red orphaned robin who Olympia had adopted and raised from a hatchling, fluttered about, pecking at seeds that fell from the trees above.

Nicodemus was gone from the warren, and so unable to join them. Aiden had contrived his absence by telling him about some fascinating new reindeer lichens growing down by the stream. Aiden surveyed the scene with satisfaction. *I think we can get on just fine without that old fool.*

The spy Aiden had placed in Anastasia's warren should be here soon. He would have preferred to interview him first, alone, but Olympia had been quite insistent. There was a light scrabbling on the entry ramp, and a handsome rabbit with copper agouti fur appeared.

"Ah, Coriander!" said Aiden, touching noses with him. "Welcome, dear boy."

"Holy day," said Coriander.

"Every one a gift," said Aiden.

Olympia and Darius laid their chins on the earth, and Coriander dutifully licked their foreheads. "Warren Mother," he murmured. "Prime Buck."

"What can you tell us?" said Olympia.

Coriander sat up very straight. "First, let me thank you for offering me this commission. For a rabbit from the lower runs in a poor warren, this is a high honor."

Olympia nodded, "It's my pleasure to offer advancement to a handsome lad like yourself."

Aiden looked annoyed and coughed into his paw. "Yes, well, let's not keep the Warren Mother waiting. Out with it."

Coriander clasped his forepaws together. "I beg your indulgence," he said, "Your estranged daughter—"

"Beloved daughter," interrupted Olympia.

Coriander looked confused. Aiden waved him a private "get on with it," sign. Coriander straightened up. "Your beloved daughter is not living according to the Word of Yah. She has created her own interpretation, which some might call …" Coriander trailed off, suddenly afraid to say the next word.

"Speak, child," said Darius, kindly. "There's nothing to fear."

"Apostasy," said Coriander.

There was a moment of silence. Olympia's ocean blue eyes bored into him. In a far corner of the thorn chamber, everyone could hear Fufu murmuring, "Apostasy, apostasy," in her tiny voice as she pecked at the fallen seeds.

Coriander took a deep breath. "As the new Presiding Spirit of the Shandy Vale Conclave, I know this must be bad news for you."

"What is the nature of the apostasy?" asked Olympia.

"She is resisting Glorification," said Coriander.

Darius sucked in his breath. "A rabbit's finest hour."

"Quite right," murmured Aiden.

"Every kitten who has been properly catechized knows that it is only through Glorification that a rabbit may cross over to the Lucky Fields and be welcomed into the bosom of the Loved One," said Coriander.

"We are in His hand," said Darius.

Coriander nodded at the Prime Buck and continued. "Of course, many rabbits run from what is vulgarly called 'death'— apologies for this language — but Yah in His mercy forgives us this weakness."

Olympia rose and strode forward several feet, and then lay down so that her face was just a few inches from Coriander's.

"So what is my daughter doing, exactly?" asked Olympia.

"She has obtained a magic weapon of great antiquity that enables her to kill Blessed at will." Coriander lowered his voice. "It's not just the foxes. She is about to apply some killing magic to the raptors as well."

Aiden found the *tête-à-tête*[22] between Olympia and Coriander altogether too cozy, so he took several steps forward himself, and assumed the Sphinx pose at a right angle to the Warren Mother with his face close to hers. "Anathema," he said. "She is taking the power that Yah has reserved for Himself. Deciding who lives and who dies."

"Anathema," chirped Fufu, coming close to Olympia's shoulder.

Olympia groaned. "Is there no end to the mischief of this girl child?"

Coriander gathered himself to speak again, "Withal, she loves Yah," he said. "He is ever on her mind. Her understanding may be imperfect, but she yearns for righteousness."

"But if she brings down dishonor on this family ..." said Olympia.

"Don't even think it," murmured Darius.

"I could lose my position," said Olympia. "I just got elected." She sat up and covered her eyes with her paws. Her scent was hot and dark. At last, she said, "Give me wisdom, counselor."

---

[22] Head to head.

Aiden sat up straight. "Yah's justice is always leavened with mercy," he said, placing his front paws together wisely. "With the austere doctrine of Glorification comes the beneficent gesture of the Giving." He lifted his face to the sky and Fufu fluttered across his line of vision. He felt like he was floundering. "Let her find her feet. She might yet find her way back into fellowship with the Conclave. There may be no need for harsher measures. And in the meantime," he turned to Coriander, "stay in her good graces, but do your best to temper and guide her."

"I will, Honored Rememberer," said Coriander.

Aiden stretched out on the leaves near Olympia. "Does this counsel please the Warren Mother?"

Olympia looked at him for a long moment without speaking. Then she rose to her feet. "Ish," she said.

Aiden looked alarmed. "How may I address your concerns—"

"Wait," said Coriander.

Aiden glared at him. "Speak freely, please."

Coriander spread his paws. "I believe she will ... attempt to Glorify a raptor soon." His eyes darted back and forth between Olympia and Aiden. "Should I ... seek to dissuade? Fight back? Obey?"

There was a long pause. Aiden racked his brains for something smart to say. He tried to fluff up his scent to project confidence. "Erm—" he said, at last.

"Do not call attention to yourself," said Olympia. "We at least need to know what's going on, for Yah's sake."

"Yes, Warren Mother," said Coriander. "It is my honor to be guided by you."

"Obey the Lord in all things," said Olympia. "And your reward shall be great in heaven." She swept down the ramp.

"Holy day!" called Aiden after her. There was no reply.

A few moments later, Darius rose and lollopped toward Aiden. "Next time, maybe you could bring some asparagus tips?"

FREDDIE

All the rabbits in *Sans Gloire* were gathered in the under-hall, a newly dug large chamber with its extensive earthen ceiling supported by the roots of the poplar tree. Like the Reader's chamber, there was a small hole to let in light. Wendy was speaking about her plan to fight the raptors. The pungent reek of her claw necklace filled the room.

"Feh," murmured Freddie to Grégoire, who sat next to him. "Next time, we should meet outside, eh?" Grégoire nodded absently, his eyes locked on Wendy.

The plan was complicated. Most of the other full-grown bucks and does already had roles. One by one, they had volunteered. Yasmin, the Hotot mother who had lost her baby a few days ago wanted to be part of it, but Anastasia had softly led her from the room. "Too soon, mother angel," she had whispered.

"Next job most dangerous," said Wendy. "I did twice." She turned to the side and with her forepaw riffled the dark brown fur along her flank and abdomen. All the rabbits could see the scars of deep puncture wounds. "Who will do now?"

There was a long silence in the room. Freddie found himself avoiding the eyes of nearby rabbits. Faintly, from outside, came the sound of a night bird calling. The silence dragged on. At last, Anastasia said, "I will do it."

There was an immediate chorus of protestations. "We can't risk you, *Tante Aimante*,[23]" said Love Bug. "Without you, there would be no Warren *Sans Gloire*."

Anastasia nodded, and lay down. There was another pause. Finally, Wendy said, "Bah. I do it."

"No," said Anastasia. "This is your plan. You're the only one who knows how this whole thing is supposed to work."

"'Kay," said Wendy. Her eyes swept across the crowd. "Come on." She patted the center claw in her necklace. "Get one of these."

"I'll do it!" rang out a voice that managed to be tiny and huge at the same time. It was Death Rage. She was standing by the doorway where she had just entered, her bottlecap

---

[23] Loving Auntie.

helmet gleaming. "You say what is needed, and the mouse will do the dangerous deed." She drew her needle and held it aloft. "*Timent muram!*[24]"

Wendy grinned. "Big heart. Body too small," she chuckled, and reached out with her forepaw to pat the mouse's head. Death Rage's needle flashed, and Wendy jerked her paw back, splashing a heavy crimson drop on the packed-earth floor. For a moment, it looked as though she might smack Death Rage and send her reeling across the room. Death Rage held her needle *en garde,*[25] point quivering.

"*No,*" said Anastasia.

Wendy dropped her paw and licked it sullenly. Anastasia turned and faced the wall. "I'm looking at no one," said Anastasia. "But if you are the one, you will know."

Freddie scratched the earth under him. Now the only ones left were the kits and the elders. His gaze fell on Death Rage. *Even the mice are raising their paws.* He gazed stonily at the ground. *My whole warren was destroyed. Weasels killed my mother, my father, my sisters, my brothers. Haven't I been through enough?* He chewed a foreclaw. *I was one of the first ones here! Isn't that worth something?*

---

[24]   Fear the mouse!

[25]   On guard, a fencing position.

There was a sick, growly feeling in his belly. He shifted position to try to get more comfortable, and was surprised to find himself raising his paw and saying, "Me."

Chapter 7

At the end of the Dominion, the woods were filled with animals. But the same Winnowing that took the Dead Gods took many of the animals, too. In the end, only six kinds of creatures were left in the Million Acre Wood for the canids to hunt: Deer, raccoon, rabbit, squirrel, rat, mouse.
—Thimble Thimbalian, History of the Known World

ISADORE & JULIETTE

Sixteen days after she had almost bled to death, Juliette nursed her cubs again for the first time. Isadore had scrambled to find wet nurses to stand in for Juliette as she lay in their den on the brink of death, the cubs frantic with fear and hunger. He had begged his female relatives who had cubs of their own, and finally found two who would visit on alternating days.

He had hunted her favorite delicacies, wood mice and rats, though it was harder to hunt with the tight scar across his muzzle, now stiff with proudflesh. And rats were so rare now. Once, he had found a clutch of eggs in a hermit thrush nest. And he had carried water to her in the only container he had, his own mouth.

Foxes have no Readers, so Isadore had no word for "infection," but he knew there was bad magic that sometimes happened that made serious injuries even worse. He could see that the spider web was keeping the wounds healthy and healing, so every day he gathered more and applied it.

Now he lay alongside her back, licking her neck and ears as she nursed. "Sweetheart," he murmured, "I'm so glad you're coming back to me. I was so scared."

She turned her head and licked his muzzle. "You're my angel," she said.

"In a couple more weeks, when you're healthy and ready to travel, we can get out of here," he said quietly. "Take the cubs and find a new place where there are no ..." he trailed off for a moment, then resumed. "Ariel got out. Maybe we could go way down the coast, to the southern marshes. Find a new place that's good for foxes. Put our lives back together."

The cubs changed positions, yelping as they did so.

Juliette shifted her weight. Finally, she said, "My babies are not going to tell the story about how mama ran."

Isadore was startled. "What?"

"My children are not going to grow up and hear about the whole family running like … mice, just because new, nasty animals moved into the neighborhood."

Isadore got up and stepped over her, so he could see her face. "Nasty animals? Babe, we almost—*you* almost—got killed."

"Nasty animals, nasty little rabbits," said Juliette. "Not paying rent."

"What are you talking about?" asked Isadore. "Let's just get out. We're alive. We still have a chance."

Juliette stood, and immediately all three cubs whined in protest. "Foxes are too nice," said Juliette, her eyes dark and unreadable. "Foxes are good people. What we need are some mean little killers."

Isadore pressed his muzzle against hers. "Honey, please. You're not well. Just rest."

The cubs crawled toward her. Juliette took a few steps away, then stopped and turned in the mouth of the den. "Don't worry," she said. "I know just where to find them."

WARREN SANS GLOIRE

Anastasia crouched under a sage bush, anxiously patting the ground and then touching five branches around her in a particular order. Lowest, second-lowest, highest, third-lowest, second-highest. Repeat. A mosquito whined past her ear. The scent of sage was bright in the still air.

Thirty yards away, in the meadow, Freddie was lying in the open, casting a long shadow in the late afternoon sun. A thick layer of leaf litter and twigs was strewn around him, but there was no shelter from the radiant blue sky. He was moving awkwardly, jerkily. Changing his position, but not really advancing. His long shadow amplified his motions. Everything about him screamed "injured rabbit."

High above, the dark specks swirled lazily, riding the thermals that billowed upward in the summer heat. Anastasia rushed through her rituals. Pat pat pat. Touch touch touch touch touch. Sing quietly.

"Three little bunnies sang a little song,
Two were right and the other was wrong."

One of the specks started to drop, spiraling down in a huge circle. Soon, it was clear the trajectory would take it over the spot where Freddie lay, still struggling feebly. Anastasia squinted and could just make out the gray and white plumage. Gyrfalcon. Male. The biggest of the falcons, his wings spanning six feet. He could easily pick up a full-grown rabbit.

The spiral was steepening now, feathers held close against the body. Anastasia was biting her lip so hard that she could taste blood. The gyrfalcon augered downward in a fast glide, wings wide and flat, pointed beak cutting the air. Faster, then faster, coming down at an aggressive angle, moving like the ancient machines that the Dead Gods once called *fighter-bombers*.

Suddenly the body flipped. Now the feet were leading, claws opening, black talons shining in the golden sun. Now the wings were beating hard, slowing the descent.

Freddie jerked, then seemed to hug the ground. The talons reached for him hungrily. Anastasia's wide eyes captured the motion as though it were crawling. Now the claws were spreading. Now they were closing around Freddie's body. Now he screamed as the points pushed through his fur and skin.

The gyrfalcon's momentum carried him forward, but he could not lift Freddie from the ground. As the feet pulled up, Anastasia could see the loops of agave fiber wrapped around Freddie's body, anchoring him to roots deep in the earth. And she could see the dark spots of blood appearing around the talons.

The gyrfalcon refused to let go of his prey, so a moment later, his body outpaced his legs and he was pulled into the earth in an ugly crash-landing. His breastbone took the shock of the crash, and a wheezy groan escaped his mouth as his lungs were compressed and a rush of air was forced up his windpipe.

Anastasia leaped forward, her back feet throwing up earth and leaves as she ran. And other rabbits were bursting out of hiding places in dense foliage all over the meadow.

The huge wings lifted high, and then beat downward. As they touched the earth for the first time, the leaf litter around Freddie erupted and two rabbits appeared, one on each side of him, shaking the dirt from their eyes. It was Love Bug and Coriander, rising from trenches where they had been lying, covered with leaves and earth. They lunged toward the leading edges of the wings, jaws open wide. Coriander closed his teeth around the radius, the delicate bone forming the leading edge of the wing. Through the feathers and skin, he could feel the muscles working. He focused on hanging on, his body now a dead weight holding the wing on the ground.

Love Bug missed his first grab and the wing rose above him, blotting out the sun. Then he was rolling on his back in the dirt, scrabbling to get his paws under him. He noticed a strange, guttural sound near him and it took him a moment to realize it was Freddie groaning as the black talons penetrated the sheath of muscle around his body.

The wing descended and Love Bug threw himself upward, mouth open. When the leading edge of the wing struck him, it felt like being smacked in the face by a log. He closed his jaws and felt his upper tooth enter a wad of cartilage and tendon. The wing jerked as the gyrfalcon tried to lift it, but Love Bug's weight held it down.

Rabbits were now streaking toward the crippled raptor from all directions, with Anastasia in the lead. Wendy was second-closest, having come out from under a hydrangea forty yards away. The gyrfalcon fought back with his one remaining weapon. He darted his head toward Coriander, trying to get the tip of his curved beak under the rabbit's skin, so it could rip down his body and skin him alive. The beak hit Coriander's skull just behind his ears and dug out a gobbet of flesh, but he was able to jerk away before the rip began.

Again the beak drove downward. This time, it hooked behind his shoulder, and Coriander felt a burn of adrenaline light up his nerves. But before the gyrfalcon could jerk his head and sentence Coriander to death, Anastasia arrived and launched herself at the bird's head, shouldering it out of the way.

A second later, Wendy and a dozen other rabbits arrived, all sinking their teeth into the wings and legs. The gyrfalcon let go of Freddie and tore the ground with his claws as he struggled to move forward, take off, and escape. The beak came down again and hit Anastasia in the forehead, tearing her skin as the gyrfalcon stabbed at her eyes.

She let go of her grip on the wing and flicked the Claw out, its quiet song lost in the noise. She drove the point up into the wing. Out of the corner of her eye, she saw a small, dark shape clinging to the end of the wing, getting walloped against the ground. It was Death Rage, and as she hung on with her teeth, she drove her needle into the tendons around the metacarpus. Her bottlecap helmet had come loose and was hanging by the strap, flapping.

A moment later, Anastasia saw Wendy's dark brown shape appear suddenly on the gyrfalcon's back, her claws flashing and teeth biting everywhere. With the strange weight pinning it down, the gyrfalcon's eyes widened with terror, and for the first time in her life, Anastasia heard a raptor shriek in fear.

It felt good.

Then, the blood from her head wound started running into her eyes. She stopped fighting for a moment to try and wipe it out. She mostly succeeded in just smearing the blood, so she was still looking through a fog when she realized Coriander was shouting in her ear. "Wendy! Wendy! Look!"

Anastasia looked up to see Wendy sitting astride the gyrfalcon's neck. With her two front paws, she was holding the head under the chin and pulling it up and back. And her head was darting down, her mouth yawning open, trying to sink her teeth into the exposed throat.

In a few seconds, the gyrfalcon would be mortally wounded. Not the plan. Not the deal with Almighty Yah.

Anastasia's back legs sent her soaring upward. Her forehead hit the underside of Wendy's jaw, splashing blood across it, and both tumbled to the ground.

Wendy was up immediately, shouting a string of unintelligible curses. Anastasia, foggy with pain and half-blinded by her own blood, managed to bark out a single command. *"No kill!"*

As Wendy raged for a few more seconds, the gyrfalcon, without the weight on his back, began to rise. Love Bug lost his hold on the joint and slipped off. Then the rabbit next to him fell. The raptor was able to raise one wing. Suddenly, the outcome was in doubt.

Wendy lunged at the gyrfalcon's feet and fastened her jaws around the central claw, biting hard, her head twisting and pulling. The pain caused a loud cry from the raptor, which startled the rabbits holding down the wings. Several lost their holds, and the gyrfalcon took another step toward freedom. A few seconds later, it was rising, huge wings beating the air, an astonishing series of shrieks pouring from its beak.

Wendy stood below, with a bloody raptor claw in her teeth.

A few feet behind her, Freddie lay on his back, very still, blood oozing from the puncture wounds in his sides. The hot, coppery smell of blood hung in the air. Anastasia ran to him. His eyes were closed. "Freddie, Freddie, Freddie," she whispered, fiercely. "Freddie, you did it. We won." He lay without moving.

Wendy galloped up, with the bleeding gyrfalcon claw in her mouth. "You fighter!" she shouted. "You *saighdear!*[26] I blood you now!" She picked up the claw with both her front paws and smeared the wet, gory end across Freddie's face.

"Get that thing out of here," snapped Anastasia, slapping the claw out of Wendy's paws. Then she turned back to Freddie, nosing along his flank, examining his wounds.

"No," said Freddie at last, very quietly.

"What?" asked Anastasia.

"I want it," said Freddie.

"Want what?"

He opened his eyes and looked at her. "I want my claw."

Death Rage whooped, followed by several rabbits. Wendy came close to Freddie and this time Anastasia did not object. She lay down beside Freddie and licked his wounds.

"You killer," said Wendy. "You dangerous bunny."

She laid the bloody claw on Freddie's chest, and he closed his front paws around it, hugging it tightly. Just before he passed into unconsciousness, he whispered, "I'm dangerous."

---

[26] Soldier.

Gaetan

Gaetan could hear a raucous mixture of yelps, howls, laughs, and snarls when he was still two hundred yards away from the tamarind trees. Tonight was solstice, and Clan *Paresseux* was getting lit.

As he got closer, he could hear Edouard yelling, "Welly! Welly! More Micamac Golds!"

Gaetan entered the tamarind grove and saw Wellbutrin the raccoon standing near his travois of fermented apples. Probably brought it down the trail from Stranglethorn just that morning. Looking around the grove, Gaetan could see that lots of the coyotes were wearing their moneybags around their necks, which they only did when they were in the mood to spend.

"Sup, bruh?" said Wellbutrin as he sidled over, walking on three legs and carrying a reed basket of fermented apples in his left front paw. His eyes were bright and lazy at the same time.

"Hey, Welly," said Gaetan.

Wellbutrin dug around in his basket with his long-fingered hands, and came up with a mushy brown apple with wrinkled skin and one side smashed in. A strong reek of alcohol came out of the basket with it. "Ooo, here's a long happy night," he said, passing the apple under his nose. "From our last surviving tree of Mangrove Jacks. This apple is *dirty*," he grinned. "And we age them with Russets, so the tannin is there, but it doesn't take your head off." He proffered the apple to Gaetan. "As long as you're having a good time, why remember it? Amirite?"

Gaetan sniffed the apple.

"Seven cents and it's yours," said Wellbutrin. "Or no, six cents for a friend."

Gaetan laughed. "You're singing my song, *mon pote*,[27]" he said, then shook his head. "Maybe later. Have you seen Lilou?"

"Over by the hydrangeas earlier," said Wellbutrin. He dropped the apple back into his basket and pointed at Gaetan with both his index fingers. "Catch you later, gator."

"Thanks, Welly," said Gaetan.

As he limped toward the hydrangeas, Edouard appeared suddenly and fell into step beside him, stumbling a little, his scent brash and overloud. One of his sidekicks trailed after him. "Hey, Gaetan," he said, companionably.

"*Salut*,[28]" said Gaetan, feeling suddenly guarded.

"So, you went to visit the rabbit assassins, eh?"

"Yes."

"And you made it back safely?" Edouard looked at him, earnestly. "Blood Father loves you."

---

[27] My friend.

[28] Hi.

Gaetan stopped. "Look, they didn't attack me," he said, simply. "But I did notice something else." A couple of other coyotes who were passing by stopped to listen.

"What?" said Edouard.

"The lunchmeat were cooperating," said Gaetan. Out of the corner of his eye, he saw Lilou come sauntering up.

Edouard frowned. "Lunchmeat don't cooperate. They're too stupid to do that."

"That's *why* they're lunchmeat," added Edouard's buddy, Lucien, who had a dark gray smudge of fur running down his back. Edouard chuckled and did a quick nose touch with him. Some other coyotes came and sat down.

Gaetan shrugged. "Saw it myself. I just slipped over, very casual. Not hunting. When the squirrels saw me, they alerted other squirrels, and then the rabbits."

Lilou nuzzled Gaetan's shoulder briefly. "What happened then?"

Gaetan licked his paw. "Rabbits went underground, like always. The squirrels threw pine cones at me."

Edouard guffawed. "O, those meanies!" Several of the other coyotes started laughing, too. "You scared the crap out of me, *casse couilles!*[29] I thought you were going to tell me the lunchmeat were getting some kind of lemming

---

[29] Literally, "shell breaker." Figuratively, "pain in the butt."

freakout together, so they could come nibble us to death."
There was much hilarity and hiccupping.

"This is weird and different," said Lilou. "Squirrels don't attack coyotes. And why would they care about rabbits?"

Edouard ignored her and lurched toward Gaetan. He threw an overly companionable front leg over his shoulders. "*Mon ami,*[30]" he said, and belched. "Do yourself a favor and make more kills. All that vegetation you're eating—and I say this as a friend—it's rotting your brain."

Gaetan shrugged off the dominance gesture. "Edouard—and I say this as a friend—your nards look dry. Go lick them."

Edouard and Lucien shrieked with laughter and rolled on the ground. In the distance, Benoit's hoarse voice floated on the warm air, "*Garçon*! Three more Yellow Bellies over here!"

Love Bug

Love Bug bit through the stem of another asparagus shoot. Now he had five. He gathered them all up in his jaws and trekked back toward the side entrance to Warren *Sans Gloire*. As he drew near, he saw Freddie lying off on the side

---

[30] My friend.

under the large leaves of a dyphylleia. He still had patches of spider webbing and fur from Anastasia and Yasmin stuck to his wounds, and he lay, breathing shallowly, with his eyes half-closed. A cool green smell surrounded him.

Love Bug headed toward him and dropped off the asparagus shoots. Freddie opened his eyes a little and smiled. "Asparagus! Aww, you shouldn't have."

"This one here looks pretty tender," said Love Bug, nudging a fresh tip toward Freddie's mouth.

"I'm going to have to check your work on that," said Freddie. He took a bite and chewed it with relish. "Mmmmm! Excellent choice."

Love Bug sat down near Freddie and washed his face. He looked out over the meadowlands for a few moments. "I know I haven't always been the nicest bunny," he said, finally. "I'm sorry I said you were a rabbit that doesn't fight. What you did out there with the hawk was like ..." He shook his head and exhaled sharply. His eyes flicked towards Freddie. "Respect."

Freddie finished eating his piece of asparagus. "You were right," he said. "I didn't fight. I was scared to death." He picked up another piece of asparagus and munched it. "I grew up in a warren that never got attacked. Lucky Fallen Oak, everyone called it. Then, when it happened one day and everyone was killed, I thought bad luck had attached itself to me. I thought I was about to die every second."

"I'm sorry, Freddie," said Love Bug. "Did it help being a Rememberer?"

Freddie sat up, gingerly. "I didn't want to be a Remembering acolyte, but my mother made me do it. She said, 'Look, you're farblind, you're a slow runner, and you're not part of the warren's founding bloodline. The other bucks are already cuffing you around. Do you want to be a lowbie buck down in the mud runs your whole life? You need a role that's going to earn you some respect. Do this.' So I did," he sighed. "I wanted to be a Reader. I did manage to learn a few things on the side."

Love Bug pulled down one ear and cleaned it. Then the other. "I'm a lateborn," he said. "Being part of the bloodline doesn't help much when you're in the thirties. My mother hardly knows me. Prolly hasn't even noticed the First Born ran me out."

Freddie stretched and groaned a little. "Oh, Yah. One of those talons got me right under my third rib," he said. "Ow, that hurts when I move."

"You want some willow bark?" asked Love Bug.

"Nah, I'm already so full of it I feel sick to my stomach and my ears are ringing," said Freddie.

They sat in silence for a few moments. Some visiting does lolloped past. Love Bug engaged in his usual banter and they giggled and flashed their tails.

After they moved on, Freddie rolled over so he could look Love Bug in the eye. "Hey," he said. "You're so good with the does, you know? All that cool talking? Maybe you could give me some tips."

"Well," said Love Bug, as he licked his paw, and then fluffed his facial fur, "I'm not sure I can teach you how. It's all about being in the *maybe of love*, you know?"

"Not really," said Freddie.

"Being in the maybe of love means being aware of the possibility that you might connect with another person."

"Oookay," said Freddie.

"It's like, when you meet a doe, say something nice. About her. Don't just say, 'Hey, you down for some humpty-hump?' That's not very maybe."

"What kinds of things are nice?" asked Freddie.

"Well, it could be something you've learned. Something hip and suave, like 'Hey, are you a warm summer evening in May? Cuz you are *fine*.'"

"Oh, that's good," said Freddie. "I'm going to remember that."

"But the best ones are things you just make up on the spot, because you're looking at her. Like, 'Wow, these forget-me-nots are so beautiful. They're the exact same color as your eyes. I could *never* forget them.'" He scratched his ear. "The thing is, everyone wants to be seen."

"Okay, okay," said Freddie. "I think I'm getting it. Like …" He held out a paw. "'Whenever I eat a blueberry, I think about your eyes.'"

Love Bug looked up into the clouds and thought deeply for a few seconds. "Dude, you gotta relax," he said. "Remember, hooking up with a doe is just a good time. It doesn't mean anything."

"What if it does mean something?" asked Freddie.

Love Bug looked at him. "If it means something, you're doing it wrong."

ISADORE & JULIETTE

"Are you sure this is a good idea?" asked Isadore, again.

"Yes," said Juliette, impatient in the moonlight. "Sassy and I grew up on the same streambank." She reached down and licked the pink scar that crossed her throat at an angle, then trailed away down her side. "We learned to kill together. She would go in the holes and I would catch whatever came out."

"I mean bothering the weasels on solstice?"

"If not now, when?" snapped Juliette. "This is one of the few times of year when they're all together." She turned and nuzzled Isadore. "Darling, I know I'm being cranky. Go home and be with the cubs if you want. I'll be fine."

Isadore shook his head. "I don't want to leave you out here."

"Then hush for a minute." They were both silent. A nightjar called. Faintly in the distance came the sound of four eerie notes in a descending sequence. They tinkled in the night with a strong metallic flavor. "That's them," said Juliette. "I used to hear that coming through the doorway of my mother's den when I was a pup."

She led the way through the thick brush toward the music, with Isadore trailing after. In a few minutes, they had crested a hill, so they could look down into a grassy dell with a fairy circle in the center. The ring of mushrooms was more than thirty feet in diameter, and it was filled with a boogle of weasels, swaying to the music. The deep, earthy smell of the mushrooms mixed with the sweet reek of weasel and filled their nostrils.

In the center of the circle, an older female with a dark back and fawn underbelly stood next to two small logs. Across them were laid four metal bars that had once belonged to an ancient Xylophone. They shone brightly in the cool moonlight, and their names were cut into the metal: B♭, A, A♭, D. In one of her hands, the weasel clasped a length of wood with a knob at the end, and she swayed as she struck the metal bars, playing the creepy riff over and over.

The weasels in the circle were holding seed pods with dried seeds in them, and they played them to good percussive effect as they high-stepped around the circle, their slender bodies rolling as they moved, and their long necks undulating like snakes. Clearly, they had an affection for backbeat.

Juliette spotted a gleaming white weasel with shiny dark eyes, and ran forward. "Saskatoon!" she called. "Saskatoon!"

Several weasels turned around and showed mouthfuls of spiky white teeth. Juliette stopped moving. A weasel is smaller than a fox, but any one of them could easily kill her. And a group of weasels could strip her to the bones in minutes.

"Sassy!" said Juliette, quietly urgent. "It's me, Juliette! From the old streambank."

The white weasel paused, head tilting at the sound of her voice. A moment later, she leaped lightly over the mushroom wall and shimmied toward Juliette. "Julie-Wulie," she cried, laughing. "Look at you, all grown up!" She touched noses with her. "What brings you out on the birthday of the Goddesss?"

"Well," Juliette looked back at Isadore, who was just coming up, "something bad is happening. And I thought you should know."

"What?"

"Rabbits are ... attacking Blessed."

Saskatoon stared at her for a moment. Then, she giggled. "I think I had one too many mushrooms tonight," she said, finally. "What?"

"A rabbit has a magic weapon, and it almost killed several foxes," said Juliette.

Saskatoon did her best to look concerned. "Ohhh, sweet

foxiesss. Hurt by a bunny? That's so sad." She fought down a smirk. "But foxies aren't known for being the best fighters. No offenssse." The weasel smiled, her white teeth shining.

Juliette tried to keep the rage out of her voice as she said, "Have you ever seen anything like this?" And she raised her head, so that her newly-healing pink scar, seamed with proudflesh, gleamed in the moonlight. Saskatoon leaned forward and scanned the scar carefully as it crossed Juliette's neck at an angle, then cut down across her shoulder.

Her dark eyes got huge. "A *rabbit* did this?" Juliette nodded. Isadore turned his head, so Saskatoon could see the scar across his face. "And this?" asked Saskatoon. He nodded.

Juliette nuzzled against Saskatoon's shoulder. "A new thing is happening. A bad thing. If we're going to fight it, we have to do it now. But foxes can't do it." She shared a brief glance with Isadore. "It needs to be serious fighters. People who can go *in*."

Saskatoon looked at Juliette seriously, then walked a few paces away from the fairy ring. She settled down on the warm summer turf. "Tell me everything."

Warren Sans Gloire

Holly gave birth to her kittens the next morning. And everyone in the warren took it in turns to admire the babies—hairless, blind, and beautiful. Love Bug brought blueberries from the patch by the stream. Grégoire sang quietly to the kits about the old rabbit legends, like the story of the peach tree with the sweetest fruit in the world.

> *"C'est beau the peach, ma fille*[31]
> *C'est beau the peach, my lad,*
> *'Twas just one peach, but a very fine peach,*
> *One taste would drive a rabbit mad."*

Anastasia spent the afternoon nursing Freddie, cleaning his wounds, and packing in more fresh spider web brought in by Coriander, helped by the agile fingers of Dingus.

Wendy spent much of the day working on Freddie's gyrfalcon claw. She gnawed the flesh away until it was just the talon and the bone up to the first knuckle. Then she asked Death Rage to braid an agave cord to use as a necklace. Death Rage was willing, and went out to gather fiber.

Juniper and Chervil took it on themselves to look after Yasmin's young kittens, so she could have some time to herself to grieve the child she had lost to the hawk. She spent the afternoon in the bramble maze on the far side of the poplar tree. When Anastasia was

---

[31]   It's beautiful, the peach, my girl.

done with nursing duty, she came and lay down with the kits, nuzzling their tiny ears and covering them with kisses.

The dark specks in the sky had shown no signs of dropping all day. For the moment, the rabbits' attack on the gyrfalcon was buying them time. The successful attack bought them something else, too. For the first time, for most of them, they felt a little bit less like somebody else's meal waiting to be served, and a little bit more like something they had as yet no name for.

The attack boosted the warren's reputation, so more and more rabbits were coming every day. Not just loners and outcasts now, but some from other warrens. Introducing themselves, making inquiries. Wanting to meet the rabbits who fought Blessed and won.

Love Bug was on top of his game: A boyish, cute, warrior with a story to tell and a steady string of wide-eyed does to tell it to. Even Freddie, the chubby, wounded hero of the battle of the gyrfalcon, was making some new friends and enjoying some gingerly snuggling.

Wendy's droopy ears, shambling gait and necklace of raptor talons fascinated the visiting rabbits. They were also afraid of her, and her brusque manner didn't help. She tended to be followed by a group of curious onlookers wherever she went, carefully keeping their distance and openly speculating about her parentage.

"Half rabbit, half hound," said one black and white pie-bald visitor.

"Hounds are a myth," said another rabbit, authoritatively.

"Two scoops of rabbit, and a skosh of brown bear," said a third.

"Bah!" said Wendy, with a wave of her huge paw, which caused the group to scatter momentarily, only to re-form a minute later.

Coriander was given to stating that Yah moved in very, *very* mysterious ways, and often peppered his conversations with quotes from the Word about "leviathan."

But it was Anastasia they wanted to see the most. The founder. The warrior. The killer. The saint. She mostly avoided visitors, playing with kittens in the private parts of the warren, or else roaming the area, obsessively scouting.

Bricabrac came by the warren around dusk, ever smiling, ever looking for work. Some of the rabbits shunned him, as they would any rat. "Run along, little rat," said Grégoire. "We don't need any *épidémiques*,[32] eh?"

Bricabrac smiled blandly, saying, "Never fear, sir. I've had all my shots," as he continued into Anastasia's chambers.

Anastasia came out of the entrance to her meeting room, and patted Grégoire kindly. "Bricabrac is a skilled

---

[32] Epidemics.

and valued craftrat," she said. "And a friend of this warren." The older rabbit went on his way, muttering about dirty animals.

"So sorry," said Anastasia. She took him for a private chat in a comfy spot in the back of her area. It was stocked with blueberries, strawberries, and parsley. They each settled down and munched in companionable silence for a minute or so. The bittersweet smell of parsley filled the chamber.

"How are you, friend?" she asked.

"I'm good," said Bricabrac. "How does it feel to be the hero of every rabbit in South Shandy?"

"That's a bit of an overstatement," said Anastasia.

"Depends on who you ask," said Bricabrac.

"We have made a little space," said Anastasia, "but our enemies are close at hand."

"True dat," said Bricabrac.

As usual, it was hard for Anastasia to avoid coming immediately to the point. "We need more weapons," she said. "The Claw is awesome, but one person can't do everything. Many rabbits are coming. Squirrels. Mice. All want to fight."

"I see that," said Bricabrac. "It's amazing." He picked up a strawberry and toasted Anastasia with it. "Of course, I'm not a fighter myself." He bowed ironically. "I'm a businessrat."

"Can there be more weapons?"

"Of course," Bricabrac smiled.

"Can there be more Claws?" pressed Anastasia.

Bricabrac sucked in a breath between his teeth. "X-ACTO's retractable Claws are very rare. She only had twelve toes. That's why they're so hard to find—and expensive."

"What else is there?"

"Sharpstone. Pointystone. Of all kinds. The Dead Gods made a lot of it." He smiled. "They can be made into a variety of weapons. I'd be glad to provide you with a price list." He stood up and spread his arms wide. "Then you can go shopping!"

Anastasia remained seated. "We don't have a lot of moneystones," she said. "I had to borrow the moneystones I used to buy the Claw."

Bricabrac sat down and steepled his fingers. "Yes, this can be a challenge. Artisanal expertise is a significant investment. But the total cost of ownership—"

Anastasia laid her paw on his arm. "Bricabrac," she said, "would you consider joining us?"

Bricabrac looked at her blankly. "I'm certainly always available—"

Anastasia lay down and looked him in the eye. "Not as a businessrat. We're trying to build something here. You could be part of it."

Bricabrac gazed steadily at her. "Are we talking about me fabricating weapons for free?"

"No, of course not," said Anastasia. "I'm talking about you being part of a *community*—"

Bricabrac put his finger on her lips to silence her. "I guess you didn't know this," he said, "so, I won't be offended."

"Know what?" asked Anastasia.

Bricabrac looked at her for a long time. Finally, he spoke. "*Rats is for rats.*"

SASKATOON

A day later, Juliette, Isadore, and Saskatoon were lying on their bellies about a hundred yards from Warren *Sans Gloire*, covered by a scramble of kudzu vine climbing a dead tree. "The one with the magic Claw went out earlier this morning," said Juliette. "She's usually gone all day. So you can just slip in, scout around, take down a couple, scare a few out for us. You know, a rent collection, with late fees."

"If you're comfortable with that," added Isadore.

Saskatoon smiled and looked at him. "Why wouldn't I be?"

"No reason," murmured Isadore. "Just don't want anyone to do anything they're not … comfortable with."

"You are a sweetheart." Saskatoon touched noses with him. "Julie, you have to tell me where I can get one like him."

"Probably best to get going," said Juliette to Saskatoon. "We'll split up and keep an eye on the two most common routes back to the warren. If we see anything, we'll let you know."

"Fine," said Saskatoon. As she moved out from under the kudzu, she surprised a young squirrel on an overhanging tree branch. Startled, it chattered angrily at her for a moment, then bolted up the tree trunk.

Saskatoon moved toward the warren in a relaxed saunter. With her small size, it was easy for her to slip through the plentiful vegetation. The wonderful smell of rabbit drifted towards her on the breeze. She was aiming for a side entrance to the warren, lightly concealed under a camelia bush. When she saw the hole, no one was guarding it. At this time of day, late morning, most of the rabbits would be inside, sinking into a doze after a hearty morning feed. A small yawn escaped her. Just another day at work for a weasel, excitable foxes telling tall tales or no.

She slipped into the entrance, quietly humming her killing song. Just a few steps in, she saw a very old bunny with thinning fur. He looked almost blind from cataracts. It would be a mercy killing, really. Saskatoon sang quietly in a soothing voice.

"Hey, old timer,
With the cloudy eye,
Put your troubles behind you,
It's a good day to die."

The elderly rabbit froze. Saskatoon just looked at him, half-smiling. The old ones generally slipped right into the Giving without making a sound. Then she would just bite through the large blood vessels in his neck as he lay paralyzed with fear, and he would quietly bleed out as she finished her business with the rest of the warren.

Instead, the old rabbit stamped and then bolted down the passage. *That's weird,* Saskatoon thought. Then she shrugged. *Guess there's life in the old boy yet.* She continued along the tunnel in her strolling shimmy. A few seconds later, she lifted her nose as she caught a bewitching fragrance.

"I smell young bunnies,
So soft and sweet,
They go down like honey,
My favorite treat."

She would be on them any second now. Mother bunny would fight, of course. They always did, the poor dears. Saskatoon licked her lips. She came around a bend and saw a brown and white rabbit with one of her front legs missing. Behind her, four new kits, still blind with just their first light fur grown in, mewed and struggled feebly as the heavy reek of weasel reached their noses.

"Hey, mama, hey, mama, hey," murmured Saskatoon. "Today is a good day. Your suffering is over."

The mother rabbit stamped, then stamped again, pushing her kittens behind her as she backed down the tunnel past a side passage. "Run while you still can," she said, glaring fiercely at the weasel.

Saskatoon smiled. *So* brave. "You're a good mother," she whispered. "You and your children will be together in Paradise."

A rabbit with a black and gray harlequin face came around the mother rabbit. He moved stiffly, probably injured. He came to a dead stop when he saw Saskatoon, and his legs buckled for a moment.

This one seems to be entering the Giving, at least. "Hey, buddy," smiled Saskatoon. The harlequin bunny appeared to have a vine around his neck with a leaf attached to it. *This is a strange bunch.*

"No weasels," said the injured buck. "Fair warning. I'm dangerous." He crawled forward, passing the three-legged mother, putting his body in front of hers. *Beautiful,* thought Saskatoon. *Welp, time to wrap this up.* She opened her jaws and lunged at the harlequin, spiky teeth flashing like a handful of nails. Instead of fleeing, the rabbit seized the thing that was hanging around his neck with his jaws and slashed at her face.

What the—? Saskatoon closed her teeth on the thing and discovered that it was not a leaf, but something very hard, and very sharp, with a hooked point that was now tearing at the inside of her cheek. She backed up in a hurry, opening her mouth to release the pointed thing, and was startled to find the crippled mother rabbit biting her left ear. Frightened and angry, she turned to tear the rabbit's throat open.

But before she could make contact, a copper-colored doe came flying out of the side passage, followed by an agouti buck, both of whom fastened their teeth in her long neck. Their weight dragged her neck and head down and kept them pressed into the damp earth. And without her long flexible neck, she could not execute the rapid series of lightning-fast strikes, each one from a new angle, that usually terrorized, blinded and killed prey within a matter of seconds. She was almost defenseless.

Then came a rabbit-sized bear-thing that leaped onto her back and started chewing through her fur toward her spinal cord. An instant later, a horde of rabbits pushed into the space. Suddenly the passage was filled with bunnies driving their half-inch-long incisors into her flesh, and using their heavy back feet to pound against her abdomen, forcing the breath out of her in a frightened, wheezy gasp.

And while all this was happening, the injured rabbit in front of her with the curved pointy thing in its jaws was hitting her in the face with it again and again, clearly with the aim of driving the point into her eyes.

Saskatoon's nerve broke. The cool killer from thirty seconds ago vanished. By flailing her four clawed feet in every direction, she managed to make some space around herself. Then she tore at the faces of the two rabbits holding her neck down, and got them to loosen their grip as she shredded their fur and skin. And once her neck was free, she could turn and rain down spiky teeth on the thing on her back, and get those bulldog-like jaws away from her spinal cord.

An instant later, she was racing up the passageway at full speed, eyes wide and straining to see the light of the entryway, and freedom. In her mind, over and over, the voice of the crippled mother played: *"Run while you still can."*

SLUMBER PARTY

It was Juniper's idea.

Having the weasel get into *Sans Gloire* was a near thing. And even though the bunnies had rallied valiantly and pulled off an almost unheard of victory, it was a solemn reminder to everyone just how relentless a siege they lived under.

Juniper, just two months away from her mother's death, was determined that they should seize some good times amongst the endless battles. And what better way than a slumber party? So she found a wonderful spot in a wooded glade not far from the warren. There was a small pool with a lovely sprinkle of watercress, mint, and endive growing around the edge. And an old apple tree with branches hanging down near the ground offered some sweet twigs for nibbling.

Then Juniper started following Anastasia around and cajoling her into taking the time off to do it. At six months old, Juniper was the equivalent of a bossy sixth-grader, and she was well-suited to this task, as Anastasia would not have taken this much guff from anyone else.

After Juniper had trailed her for two days, alternately wheedling and badgering her, Anastasia finally said, "Fine, I'll do it! Not too many people."

"Yay!" shouted Juniper, and did her happiest little dance. "I'll take care of everything."

So the next warm night, Anastasia found herself in the glade by the pool, sitting in a circle with Holly, Yasmin, Juniper, and Death Rage. Juniper greeted them with a heap of fresh flowers she had collected in a reed basket woven for her by the mice.

After an opening snack of apple twigs and mint, Juniper sat up tall and put her paws together. "Welcome, sisters," she said gravely. "We are a new breed at *Sans Gloire*. We're coming to know well the arts of war. Let us also know well our own hearts. And the hearts of our friends. Here's our chance to share all the feels." She poured out the basket of flowers into the middle of their circle. A bright array of scents rose up, some sweet, some spiky, some musky. "Choose a flower. The first one that calls to you."

They reached into the heap of flowers and began to turn them over, looking for just the right blossom. There was a dazzling array of colors. To the rabbits' eyes, attuned to the yellow-blue spectrum, the blossoms were azure and lapis, canary and gold, onyx and silver, all shining under the bright moon. They chatted a bit as they looked. These were comrades who worked together daily on a task that was so large it was as yet unnamed, but in some ways, they hardly knew each other. The laboring, the inventing, the surviving, took up all the time.

After a couple of minutes, they had each chosen a flower. Juniper got out her set of bobstones, a kind of ancient dice that rabbits use to play games during the winter months. She cast the bobstones and stared at them intently. Then she looked up at Death Rage, who was holding a silver blossom as large as herself. "Smoke iris," said Juniper, naming the flower. "Why did you choose that?"

Death Rage looked at the others for a moment. "Mice fight all the time," she said. "We have almost no sharpstone, so we are dueling with wooden weapons. We don't die, but you feel the kiss of a Musmuski blade, even if it's made from a twig." She sat up and drew her dark hands up her body, ruffling her fur and revealing a filigree of white scars on her dusky skin. "We fight for honor points. Good fighter. Good family."

There was a moment of silence. "That's nice," offered Holly.

"Actually, it's stupid," said Death Rage. "What difference does it make if my family has ten thousand lifestrikes if the next day a fox can devour me on his way out to move his bowels?" She drew her needle. "I want my sword to make the world different than it was before." Death Rage took hold of the flower petal and wrapped it around her rapier, cradling it lovingly. The delicate powdery scent rose up around her. "I chose the smoke iris because, like my weapon, it is the color that Bricabrac calls *steel*. It is the color of death. And change."

Juniper leaned forward and very lightly kissed Death Rage's forehead. "Mad respect. I am proud to call you 'sister.' And I think ... many will be touched by your steel."

Death Rage looked amused. "And how do you know this?"

"My mother told me," said Juniper simply.

Death Rage shot a glance at Anastasia, and then looked back to Juniper. A concerned glance riffled around the group. "I'm sorry," said Death Rage. "I thought ..."

"Yes," said Juniper, her black and gray face serene. "She was Glorified two moons ago. But she loves me. And she comes to me at night to tell me about love, and flowers, and things that are yet to be." She reached up and touched her cheeks softly. "When she kisses me, it's like tiny petals falling on my face."

Holly, who was sitting next to Juniper, felt her eyes go wet. Thoughts of her own young kittens, snug in their burrow, washed over her. She put her remaining foreleg around Juniper and embraced her. Her mouth was next to the little black and gray bunny's ear. "Your mother loves you very much," she whispered.

"Thank you," said Juniper. She held the embrace for a moment, then let go and washed her face. "Sorry, didn't mean to cause a scene."

"Nothing to be sorry about," said Yasmin.

Juniper took a deep breath and threw the bobstones again. She peered at them and looked up at Yasmin, who was holding a large flowerhead comprised of small blue blossoms twinkling in the moonlight. "Delphinium," she said. "Why did you choose your flower?"

Yasmin ran her paw through the pool of water. The moonlight made the dark circles around her eyes stand out in sharp relief against her copper-colored fur. "I was born in Warren Azure, in the dunes by the sea. I loved to look at the water when I was a kitten." She nuzzled into the delphinium cluster and inhaled the cool, clean scent deeply. "My mother was a wanderer that the warren had taken in. I didn't realize that the dark circles around her eyes marked her as a Hotot, a foreigner."

Death Rage crept across the circle and sat next to her. Yasmin rubbed her back and continued. "One day, not long ago, after the Blessed had made several savage attacks on the warren, the First Born decided that the foreigners were bringing bad luck. They turned us out." She looked out at the ripples in the water. "Some of us survived to reach *Sans Gloire*."

Holly kissed her forehead. "I'm so sorry that happened, Yasmin," she murmured. "But I'm so glad you're here."

Anastasia nuzzled her from the other side. "*Sans Gloire* is the home warren for no one. And everyone," she said. "There are no foreigners here."

Juniper touched some of the blue flower petals. "Delphinium speaks of grace and coolness. One day, I think … your cool head … will save many." Yasmin nodded seriously.

"These tiny blossoms will make perfect circlets for your ears," said Death Rage. She plucked several and wove them together quickly. Yasmin lowered her head and Death Rage stood on her tiptoes to place the circlets over her ears.

"Beautiful flowers, beautiful spirit," said Holly. She touched noses with Yasmin.

Juniper cast the bobstones again. "Holly," she said. "Why did you choose your flower?"

Holly held a Tuscan yellow lily close to her chest, and the creamy, aromatic smell rose up around her. "I love the sunset," she said. "I love the warm light that, just for a moment, says the world is good and safe." She looked deep into the lily and took a breath. "A fox took my front leg when I was a kitten. My brother saved my life and lost his own. He was brave, like you, Death Rage."

Death Rage rubbed the side of Holly's paw. Holly kissed her head.

"I thought I would never find a mate," continued Holly. "But when I did, he was so perfect." She hugged the lily tightly. "Amaranth was his name. And he loved me like a sweet summer afternoon." She took a deep breath. "My warren had often been uncomfortable with me, because of..." she indicated her injured leg with a grimace. "So we were talking about moving out and trying to start a warren of our own. We were still thinking about where to do it when an owl took him one night. After it became clear I was pregnant, the Warren Mother decided to be done with me for good. Because everyone knows there's only one place for an injured rabbit." She looked down.

"Here," said Anastasia.

Yasmin hugged her. "We are so glad you are part of this warren," she said fiercely.

"Your warm heart carries so much love," said Juniper. "I think … there *will* be a world that is warm … and safe," she rubbed Holly's side. "Somewhere."

"Maybe at *Sans Gloire*," said Yasmin.

"I don't know," said Holly. She looked at Juniper steadily. "But I'll fight for my babies any day. Every day."

Juniper cast her bobstones again. "Loving Auntie," she said, "Why did you choose the golden rose?"

"Because it's beautiful," said Anastasia.

"Not because it's prickly?" asked Juniper innocently.

"Watch yourself, young lady," said Anastasia. "I'll have Death Rage show you a thing or two about respecting your elders."

Death Rage laughed. "Look, you can braid the petals and fibers from the stem together to make a golden circlet," she said, her fingers working quickly. "And then, just slip it over your ears and — *voila!* — you're beautiful." She stood back with her hands on her tiny hips. "Look in the pool and see."

Anastasia glanced in the pool briefly. "I'm not beautiful," she said. "I'm a plain brown bunny."

"Don't talk about my Loving Auntie that way," said Juniper. "You're a boss babe."

"You're strong," said Death Rage. "That's the best kind of beautiful."

"Anyway, it doesn't matter," said Anastasia. "I don't need a lot of bucks hounding me. I've got you all."

"And we love you," said Holly, and the others murmured assent.

The golden circlet did look lovely against Anastasia's brown fur. Juniper came near and traced it with her forepaw. "Golden is precious, golden is queen," said Juniper. "There is one thing, though. My mother says ... one day... you will pay a great price for your crown, Loving Auntie."

"I don't *want* a crown," said Anastasia, flipping it off her head irritably. "This game is stupid. Are we finished here?"

"I'm sorry," whispered Juniper, pressing her face into Anastasia's fur. "That's just what my mother told me. I don't know what it means."

Anastasia took a deep breath and kissed her forehead. "You are a sweet girl. I'm just being a poopyhead."

Chapter 8

Crow is the all-seer. Wolf is the all-doer. Open your eyes and be a crow.

—Corvid proverb

GAETAN

She was the most beautiful wolf in the world, scion of a family of golden wolves that began thirty generations before, when a genetic mutation bred true and launched a clan of wolves with fur as radiant as the sun.

The rich ambers of the golden fleece on her back hugged her muscular form, while the lighter cornsilk gold of her underfur clothed her belly and the insides of her legs like a soft down. Her eyes flashed as green as a maple leaf when she lifted her head to look out over the Shandy River, its bright blue arc separating the northern and southern parts of the Million Acre Wood.

Gaetan had seen her stop for a moment on the high bluff overlooking the river, while her hunting companions had gone on down to the river plain. In the yellow-blue spectrum that coyotes can see, she shone like fire against the pale blue sky.

He had been following her for the better part of two days. He hoped she would remember meeting him at the Shaman's Conclave the year before.

Canids have no Readers, but most wolf packs have a Shaman who passes on the lore of the night sky and seasons of the hunt. Some coyote packs have Shamans, but most are too casual and disorganized to sustain the role, and the training required. Gaetan had a love of knowledge, so even though he had no Shaman to mentor him, he had gone to the Conclave in hopes of learning something. He had come away with a new theory developed by Shhhh, one of the owl Shamans, that the sun hunted and ate stars.

Gaetan entered the clearing and made a deep bow, almost scraping the ground with his belly. Her scent was glorious, and it made him light-headed. He blanked on her title for a second, and then remembered it and got started. "Fair Greetings to Lady Aliyah Summerday, Third She of the Summerday Clan, and Golden Spirit of the Million Acre Wood."

Aliyah yawned as she looked at him. "What?"

"Fair Greetings to Lady Aliyah—" Gaetan began again.

She squinted at him. "Were you at that Shaman thing last year?"

That's one thing this limp is good for, thought Gaetan. Aloud, he said, "Yes, Third She."

"I don't care about being Third She," said Aliyah, as the wind ruffled her gold tresses. "I'm the Lead Striker."

"That's very … bold," said Gaetan.

"It would be if there were any big stags left around here," said Aliyah. "Mummy says we'll all be eating mice soon if we keep getting new wolf packs coming down from the uplands."

"Wow, that's awful …," said Gaetan, as he noticed the little tufts of golden fur on the tips of her ears.

"It's worse north of the river, but I'm sure you've seen it down there in trot-over country."

"Ya, we've seen some wolves down there, mostly lones, not packs, really. But … we figure wolves are your business, not ours."

"It's not easy being the Landlords of the Million Acre Wood," said Aliyah. "Anything goes wrong, who has to deal with it? The Summerdays." Even the whine in her voice was cute.

"That's tough," agreed Gaetan. "Why are new wolves moving in?"

"Daddy says it's the bears," said Aliyah firmly. "Now they're not satisfied with City of Oom. They're pushing out into the surrounding lands." She scratched her ear. "The freelance wolves can't hunt in the uplands anymore, so they come down here."

"Bad news," said Gaetan.

Aliyah nodded. "That's why Mummy and Daddy instituted the ban on coyotes hunting deer alone. There's so little hunting now, there's not even enough for the Landlords. That's like, a crime against nature."

Gaetan scratched his ear and tried to sound casual. "Do you think it will be strictly enforced?"

Aliyah turned and rested the full weight of her gaze on him. Gaetan found it unnerving. "Are you asking if Daddy would kill a coyote found violating the ban?" she asked, slowly.

"Well, I don't know if … I guess, you know, I was just … asking for a friend," Gaetan mumbled.

Aliyah rested her chin on her paws. "Tell your friend it would be a terrible thing to put Micah Summerday in that position," she said mildly. "He would have no choice."

"Understood," said Gaetan.

"This is the hour to stand firm," said Aliyah. "These are strange and difficult times."

"There's some weird stuff happening in the south, too," said Gaetan. He moved a little closer and inhaled more of her scent. "I don't know if you've heard. It has to do with rabbits—"

"A rabbit doing something interesting? That's new," said Aliyah.

"Well, it is interesting, if you want to call it that," said Gaetan. "These rabbits are attacking Blessed."

Aliyah looked surprised, and then laughed. "Are they hopping on you?"

"They almost killed some foxes," said Gaetan patiently.

Aliyah scrunched up her wolfy face. "How?"

"One of them has a magic paw or claw or something. It can hurt you by touching you," said Gaetan. Aliyah snapped at a passing butterfly. "And the other weird thing is that the lunchmeat have started cooperating."

"Lunchmeat?" said Aliyah, wrinkling her nose. "That's not very respectful. Mummy says we should call them *luncheon meat*." She turned and glanced down toward the river.

"Of course, of course," said Gaetan. "Sorry, I'm just a coyote. You know how we are." He forced out an awkward chuckle. "But this is like, nonpayment of rent. So I just thought somebody should know …"

Aliyah's maple-green eyes flicked back to Gaetan's face suddenly. "Clan *Paresseux* should be able to manage rent withholding on the rabbit level. That's why we made you our agents in the South Shandy."

A hot prickle ran down Gaetan's back. He shifted uneasily. "Of course, I mean … yes, we're handling it."

"If there's a problem managing small tenants, maybe we should look into other agents. Get you some help."

Gaetan bowed deeply and tried to add some heft to his scent so he would seem confident. "There is no problem. So sorry to take your valuable time, Lead Striker of the Summerday Clan, wise and kind stewards of the—"

"Fine," she cut him off. "Okay, gotta lope. See you later, Daetan."

"It's Gaetan," he said quickly. "Not that you'd have any reason to know that or anything."

"Great," she said carelessly, and moved down the steep slope toward the river plains at a rapid trot.

"Hey," murmured Gaetan, as he looked after her. "You should come down to the South Shandy sometime. We could have a pair of Mangrove Jacks by moonlight. My treat."

FREDDIE

Freddie came across Anastasia on the same warm afternoon, practicing with her Claw under a maple tree. A large branch had fallen across some boulders, creating an environment with multiple levels and angles, perfect for some bunny parkour. Freddie stood quietly, watching her launch off the fallen log, executing spiral thrusts and zig-zag slashes in mid-air. A leaf drifted down from the maple. Anastasia speared it with her Claw, and then sliced out through one side.

This was the perfect moment. Freddie took a deep breath. "Hey, are you a warm evening in May—"

"What?" interrupted Anastasia.

Freddie went for it, then lost his nerve. "Cuz you are fine ... nally getting the hang of that Claw."

She dropped onto the turf and squinted at him quizzically. "You're in a funny mood."

"Yeah, I'm funny...." mumbled Freddie. *Good going, you fat stupid doofus.*

She slipped the Claw smoothly back into its metal sheath and inspected it for a moment. "Anyway, I wish I had fifty of these," said Anastasia. "Enough for an army of rabbit dragons."

"Yeah," said Freddie, and winced a little from his injuries as he turned.

Anastasia came over to Freddie and sat down next to him. "How are you doing, Freddie?" she said. "I heard what you did with Holly and that weasel. That was ... very brave." She patted his paw. "Twice in a row now. You gotta slow down, buddy. We can't be wearing our heroes out."

Freddie snuggled next to her, his soft gray and white fur enfolding her taut ropy muscles. "Thank you for helping me," he said. "When those gyrfalcon claws were stabbing into me ... I wasn't sure I was going to make it."

"I'm so sorry, Freddie," said Anastasia. She laid her cheek next to his. "If I had my way, no one would ever feel like that."

"Thank you," he whispered.

"And, now you have your claw necklace to prove who won that fight," said Anastasia. She rolled over on her side, still pressing against him as she looked up through the green maple canopy. "And the way you used the gyrfalcon claw on that weasel ... I've been thinking," she mused. "If we can't get a whole bunch of Dragon Claws, maybe a weapon you wear around your neck and grab with your teeth in a fight could be good." She licked her front paw. "Blessed wouldn't see *that* coming."

"How could we get them?" asked Freddie. "Right now, all we have is Bricabrac, and—"

"He's expensive," said Anastasia. "He's got skills and he knows it."

"Yep."

"Can't blame him for that, but ..." She sucked her teeth. "*Sans Gloire* is made up of refugees. They come with nothing. We have nothing."

"It's a wonderful nothing," said Freddie.

"Ya," said Anastasia. She sat up. "We have a lot of love, and that's great. But you don't love a Blessed One's teeth off your neck."

They lay quietly for some minutes, watching dragon-flies zoom through the nearby hollyhocks. "I don't know anything about moneystones," said Freddie. "But I was talking with Bricabrac last time he was here, and he was saying what a hassle it was that all his materials have to be brought from Oom."

"Yeah, he's always talking about that," said Anastasia.

"It's because there's no sharpstone or hardstone out here in the woods. He said transport is all by water or air, and air's expensive. Whatever that means."

"Rat talk," said Anastasia. "I don't know if *he* always knows what he means."

Freddie rolled over and looked at Anastasia. "Well, the place I stayed for a few nights before I met you … it was all straightstone and pages and other Dead Gods stuff. There could be more things there. Things Bricabrac would want."

Anastasia sat up. "Really?"

Freddie sat up and spread his paws. "Not sure how much. But it could be a lot."

"What kind of stuff?"

"Don't know. I didn't look." Freddie shuddered at the memory of the crushing grief that had consumed him during that time.

Anastasia looked thoughtful. "We can't tell Bricabrac about it, cuz he'd go clean it out."

"Ya," said Freddie.

"In a few days, when you feel better, could you go and see? Take a couple of good fighters with you for safety."

Freddie sat up, a little gingerly. "I think I could do that," he said. "Although I'd miss everyone here."

"We'll miss you, too," said Anastasia, and kissed his forehead. "Bring Dingus along to talk to the local squirrels and set up an early warning system."

"Okay," said Freddie, a little glumly.

Anastasia touched noses with him. "Thanks, buddy," she said.

GAETAN

"Rabbits are all we have left," said Gaetan, as he stumble-walked through Clan *Paresseux*.

"No hooves. No horns. Fine with me," said Benoit, and burped. There was a riffle of snickers.

"Rabbits are soft and easy *now*," said Gaetan. "But look at those killer rabbits near the Shandy. They've fought off fox, falcon, weasel. *They* are not soft. And everyone's talking about it. More rabbits are joining them all the time. What if this spreads to other warrens? No more rabbits? That will mean death for us. You know the upland wolves will never allow us in their territory."

Edouard growled, yellow eyes half-closed. "Raccoon is tasty."

Gaetan laughed bitterly. "You want to turn all those clever *crapauds*[33] against us? They live in fortified camps, *stupide*.[34] You'll kill one raccoon and never get another one. Plus, you can kiss your dirty apples goodbye."

Benoit laughed. "I might have to kill you myself, Edouard."

Lilou scratched her side. "So, what are you saying we should do, Gaetan?"

Gaetan stopped pacing and looked at them. "Hit them hard. Today. Tomorrow. Until they are gone. Stop this before it spreads."

All the coyotes were silent for a moment. Then Lilou stood up. "Your leg is weak," she said. "But your mind is strong." She turned and faced the other coyotes. "We should do it, *copains*.[35]"

"There are squirrels as lookouts," said Benoit.

"We can do a surround from a hundred yards out," said Gaetan. "Then a rush, cut a bunch of them off from their holes. We won't get them all, but we can hurt them bad."

"There was a long, quiet moment, then Benoit said, "I could use a bite." Some of the other coyotes growled in assent.

---

[33] Toads.

[34] Stupid.

[35] Friends.

"Okay, let's go snag that rent," said Edouard.

"This isn't rent collection," said Gaetan. "These are scofflaws. And it's time they were put down." He looked from face to face. "For the good of the realm."

"Lead on, lil bro," said Lilou. "I got your back."

So an hour later, Gaetan was hunkered down under a swath of chaparral, keeping an eye on Lilou, who was parked behind some gorse bushes seventy-five yards away.

She turned and looked at him, giving him the head toss that signaled, *everyone's in position.* He signaled back with a toss of his own head, then raised up on his back legs for a moment. She mirrored his gesture, and he knew the coyote on the other side of her was doing the same, and so on around the string of coyotes spread out in a circle around the warren. He turned and looked the other way and saw Lucien up on his hind legs.

Gaetan took a deep breath and launched into his best approximation of a sprint, headed straight at the warren. He knew Lilou and Lucien were following him inward, and in a few seconds, all the coyotes would be. It was now late twilight. By the time the squirrel lookouts saw them and raised a cry, they would be on the rabbits, a killing whirlwind.

Gaetan's injured leg caused his body to drop down every fourth step, slowing him down and making his gait a clumsy shamble. He knew the other coyotes were already taking the lead. He would be the last one there.

He prayed under his breath as he ran. *"Turn your face from me, Hunger Mother. Do not bless me with want this day. Forget me, as one day when the hunting is all done, I will surely forget you."*

A few seconds later, he broke out of the brush near a stream. On the far side of the stream, about fifty yards up the slope, he saw the poplar tree where the warren was. Other coyotes were already hurtling into the grassy area. Overhead, the squirrels were yelling, and underfoot, dozens of rabbits were pinballing around the space, eyes wide and frantic. The warm smell of many rabbits was intoxicating.

Gaetan knew he had just a few seconds of opportunity. Near him, he saw two young rabbits, black and spotted with gray, only about six months old. He raced toward them. They launched into a sprint. He kept up, and then gained on them. Even with his damaged leg, he was faster than a young rabbit when running in a straight line.

He managed to ride on their left flank, keeping them pinned against the stream. Their back feet threw up tiny clods as they ran. He closed ground on them rapidly, one stride of his matching ten of theirs. In a few more steps, he would be on them. One of them looked back at him, then suddenly changed direction, and veered back, running almost between his legs.

Gaetan did not even lower his head. Long experience had taught him that was useless. Instead, he accelerated at the remaining rabbit, who was just now looking back to see what happened to his companion. The young rabbit saw him coming and tried to put on a burst of speed, but it was too late. Gaetan's hungry jaws swept him up.

In a moment, it was done. Gaetan felt the killing pleasure as he made his meal. Then, feeling the hunter's joyful pride, he turned to see what else was happening. The grassy area was empty. Several coyotes were eating. Benoit and Lilou were standing at the foot of the poplar tree, digging at the ground.

Gaetan loped toward them. As he got closer, he could see that Benoit was digging in the main entrance of the warren, between two large roots. His excited whines filled the warm air, and Lilou was crouched next to him, her front paws pulling freshly dug earth away from the hole. Benoit was laughing and cursing as he dug.

This made Gaetan giggle as he ran forward. "What you doing, *ami?*[36] Getting your weasel on? Aren't you a little big for that, you *gros*[37] slug?"

Suddenly, he heard Benoit scream and leap backward awkwardly. His body twisted at a strange angle, his front left paw appeared to be stuck to the loose earth. Then he dragged his paw away from the hole, and Gaetan could see there was a rabbit attached to Benoit's paw. It looked like

---

[36] Friend.

[37] Fat.

their paws were touching. He shook his head, trying to see better in the rapidly dimming light.

Benoit was crying and flailing at his left paw with his right, which appeared to accomplish nothing. The rabbit looked like it was pulling back on its paw, but it seemed to be stuck. Lilou had the presence of mind to strike downward with her open jaws. But just as she was about to seize the rabbit, a mouse with a bottlecap on its head came racing out of the hole, ran up the rabbit's back, and touched Lilou's eye with its hand.

Lilou shrieked and jerked her head away, then bolted for the cover of the brush. Her actions spooked the other coyotes, who had been converging on the spot. They suddenly slowed to a walk. Gaetan continued to press forward, now with a sick feeling in his stomach. He had a better idea than the others what he was looking at.

When he came up next to Benoit, he saw a lean brown rabbit, half dragged out of the entrance hole of the warren, pull her blade out of Benoit's foot. Benoit roared as the moving blade cut his foot open further, then he staggered away into the darkness as fast as he could.

Gaetan stood frozen with shock. The rabbit withdrew into the hole. The mouse stood on a clod of earth near the hole and shouted threats at him in a tiny voice. Then it dashed towards him suddenly, and he turned and bolted for the safety of the tamarind grove.

CORIANDER

It was late morning at Bloody Thorn Warren. Though the sun was hot, Olympia's meeting chamber amidst the thorns was cool and shady. A hummingbird zipped through the twisted branches. Fufu sat on a twig near Olympia and sang quietly about a beautiful worm she had seen yesterday.

"The weasel escaped," said Coriander, the lacerations on the side of his face from the weasel's claw still visible. "The coyotes got away. But Anastasia could have let the gyrfalcon be killed. She fought another rabbit to save its life."

"So whatever she's doing, she's not becoming a Blessed-killer," said Aiden. Coriander could see Darius recoil from the phrase, and he mouthed, "sorry."

"She wants to live by the Word of Yah," said Coriander. "She's just—" He looked at Aiden.

"Changing what she thinks the Word of Yah means," finished Aiden.

"So not apostasy, but heresy?" said Olympia. "You said this was good news?" She lay stretched across the center of the meeting area, one of her back legs slowly scraping a hole in the dry earth. Fufu started a new song about heretics and worms, and Olympia shushed her.

"It's a dreadful stain on the family name," murmured Darius.

"She's still a believer," said Coriander. "There's a chance for reconciliation."

Olympia bounded upright. "Heresy is worse," she hissed. "That means the sickness is still alive and eating at the body of Yah." She smacked at the pile of asparagus tips that Aiden had ordered brought in for the meeting, and the pointed green shapes scattered across the leaves. "I was just elected the Presiding Spirit of the Shandy Vale Conclave," she growled. "They can't let this stand. They could vote me out. Or force an honor killing. Or worse."

Coriander made placating gestures. "Surely not, Warren Mother," he said, earnestly. "I know for a fact the Rememberers at the Conclave hold you in the highest regard."

Olympia looked at him with heavily-lidded eyes. "It's not about *regard,"* she said. "Every warren in our Conclave would like to have what we have, and they would quite happily use this against me." She stamped. "Why do you think Bloody Thorn Warren has been so fat and happy recently? It's because I'm Presiding Spirit that the Blessed—" She cut herself off suddenly. Then she dropped her body down between her legs and slowly walked, lizard-like, toward Coriander. When her face was very close to his, she said, "You've made me angry and loosened my tongue."

Coriander crouched down and made himself as small as he could. "I am so very sorry, Honored One," he said quietly, looking down at the dead leaves.

Her ocean blue eyes rested on him for a long time. "It's my fault," she said, finally. "I've forgotten how little acolytes know."

"Your kind heart is legend," murmured Coriander.

Olympia turned to Aiden. "Send for the Lord Harmonizer, Tobias," she said. "It's just past solstice, so he'll be at the Known World Symposium right now."

"Yes, Honored One," said Aiden.

Olympia looked back at Coriander. He forced himself to hold her gaze. "Coriander," she said, "you know what an honor killing is, don't you?"

Coriander shifted his forepaws uneasily. "Yes, Presiding Spirit."

"Are you prepared to do what is necessary, so help you Yah?" Her eyes were very close to his.

Memorizing thousands of verses had not prepared him for this moment. He thought of himself as a scholar, a counselor, a healer, a poet, not— An image flashed in his mind of himself in deep shadows, jaws creaking open. He banished the thought. There was only one answer. He did not blink. "Yes, Warren Mother. So help me Yah."

WARREN *SANS GLOIRE*

A day later, the working council at Warren *Sans Gloire* was in its chamber near the underhall.

"You are a mighty hunter before the Lord," said Anastasia, and licked Death Rage's forehead. The mouse stood proudly with Anastasia's saliva flattening the fur on her head. She had even taken off her Canada Dry bottlecap helmet for the occasion. "If I'm ever in trouble," said Anastasia, "I want you by my side, stabbing coyotes in the eye as needed."

"I will be there, Loving Auntie," said Death Rage.

"I know you will," said Anastasia, and there was a generous cheer from all present.

"Rawrr!" shouted Death Rage, showing her teeth and twirling her needle. The cheering devolved into some boisterous chaffing, and then died down.

"Now," said Anastasia, "we've been attacked by a weasel, and we've been attacked by coyotes. The weasel we pushed back with the help of our heroes." She looked around the room and touched noses with Grégoire, Holly, Wendy, and Coriander. "And Freddie," she said.

"And Freddie," echoed the others.

"But the coyotes ravaged us. Seven rabbits and five mice were Glorified that day." There were some sniffles in the room, and then silence. "I blame myself," said Anastasia. "I dithered when one thing is perfectly clear: We need more weapons."

"Bah," growled Wendy. "Why we need these toys? We have weapons here." She tapped her teeth. "And here." She tapped her skull.

Anastasia turned to her. "Your weapons are mighty," she said, "and you didn't even mention the burps." There was a small chuckle. "If we had a thousand Wendys, no Blessed would dare to come near us. But alas, all we have is one. And ourselves."

"Ya," said Love Bug. "And some of us only have one tooth. If I had more to fight with, I'd use it. I'd give anything to have a Claw." There was a general murmuring of assent.

"I'm with you, friend," said Anastasia. "But so far, it seems like only one is on offer."

Grégoire stepped forward. "What about your friend, Nicodemus? You speak of him often."

"Probably too often," said Anastasia.

"It sounds like he has skills. And he might be persuaded to bring some moneystones."

"We'd be asking him to give up his secure position as Reader at the most successful warren in this area, and steal the rest of their moneystones besides," said Anastasia. "That's a hard ask for an elderly bunny."

"Starting over is working for me," said Grégoire, "and I'm old enough to be your grandsire." There was a small chorus of cheers.

"I'm willing to ask," said Anastasia. "The Blessed are throwing everything they have at us. We need to gather everything we can to protect ourselves."

"What about the straightstone burrow?" asked Love Bug. "I've heard about it, but never been there."

"Freddie is there now," said Anastasia. "He sent me word that it looks promising. Of course, even with money from Nicodemus, we don't have money to pay for raw elements there to be made into weapons. We'll have to barter. And Bricabrac has his own loyalties." She intended to smile, but it came out as a grimace. "We won't be getting a friendly rate. And who knows who he'll be telling about it."

Coriander stepped forward awkwardly. "Loving Auntie," he mumbled, "as you know, I was once a second Remembering acolyte. So I feel I must say ..." he trailed off.

"Go on," said Anastasia.

Coriander looked at the floor. "Going against the Word of Yah ..." He chewed his paw.

"Spill your guts, stupid," said Wendy. Then she belched, and several nearby rabbits moved a few steps away.

Coriander placed one paw directly in front of him, and then placed the other paw on top of it. "It can be dangerous."

"To who?" asked Wendy.

"Going against Yah how?" asked Anastasia.

Coriander looked straight into Anastasia's eyes. "More weapons," he said quietly. "Harming more Blessed. Is this what Yah wants?"

Anastasia sat up very straight. After a moment, with

one paw, very slowly, she drew a circle around herself in the earth. "As long as I am helping Yah's people," she said. "I know that I am doing right by Yah."

Coriander rubbed his temple with his right front paw. "Not everyone will agree with that," he said, in a barely audible whisper. "Powerful people might—"

Anastasia stepped forward and touched noses with him. "I hear you, brother," she said. "We have had to learn how to live in the world with Blessed. And now they have to learn how to live in the world with us."

Coriander turned away. Anastasia stepped into the center of the group. "Let's go to the underhall," she said. "They're all waiting for us. Don't forget to bring the stones."

As Anastasia and her council entered the underhall, they each set down a small stone on the floor. Dozens of furry faces turned to look at them. Anastasia stood in the center, under the shaft of light that came down from the small hole in the ceiling.

"Friends," she said. "Always before, you have been told that when someone has been Glorified by the Blessed, the right thing to do is to let their memory slip away and fade quickly, because that is what Yah wishes. I have prayed about this, and I think our Rememberers may have gotten this wrong." There was a confused murmur in the crowd. "They do the best they can, but sometimes, errors can creep in." The murmur grew. She spoke over the noise. "*Yah loves all His children.* He would not want us to forget our friends who have crossed over and gone to be with the Loved One. He wants us to remember them, and love them, always."

Anastasia picked up a black pebble, studded with shiny gray flecks, and said, "Our beloved friend Chervil, just six months old, was Glorified two days ago. I remember the day he came with his sister Juniper to live with us in a small burrow that had no name. He had just lost his mother, but he was brave, and he comforted his sister. He loved to help others, and we loved his bright spirit."

The sound of a young rabbit crying softly slowly filled the room. It was Juniper. Anastasia moved to stand near her, pressing against her flank. "Whenever we gather in the underhall, and we see this shiny stone, we will remember our young friend." Anastasia turned and pressed the stone into the earthen wall. "Chervil, you are loved. And not forgotten." The congregation of rabbits stamped three times together, slowly, in affirmation. When Anastasia turned, she saw Coriander staring at her from a far corner, his eyes dark and worried. She held his gaze for a moment, then looked away.

Holly stepped into the light. "My beloved friend, Hyacinth, was Glorified two days ago," she said. And so continued the first rabbit memorial service in the history of the world.

NICODEMUS

Nicodemus had been around a long time. During his years, he had learned, among other things, the ironclad rule of bureaucracies: When they start having meetings without you, your time is almost over.

Nicodemus sighed. It was clear Aiden wanted to be close to the seat of power and saw him as an obstacle. Rotten luck. Nicodemus cared nothing for power. Olympia's quirky affection for him only made him nervous. His idea of a perfect day was finding a new type of lichen for his collection, having a good chew on some fresh lavender, and dispensing some chamomile to a rabbit with a fever.

But the meetings with just the Warren Mother, the Prime Buck, and the Rememberer were getting more and more brazen. He couldn't help hearing about them, although he had no idea what was said there.

Did he have any leverage? Not really. His first and second apprentices were both strong. The warren could be rid of him without suffering any damage.

Would Aiden trump up some charge to get him unwarrened? Readers almost never got demoted. They died in office, or else they were exiled for some crime. Of course, the obvious crime here was the theft of the moneystones. *Drat that girl.* But maybe it would be all right. He just wanted to be eased through his final year or two and then into the arms of Yah.

Nicodemus left his chamber to head outside for morning feed. He ran into Aiden in the main passage. "What's up, Honored Reader?" asked Aiden brightly. "Looking a little stiff this morning, old friend. Have you tried chewing some willow bark?"

Nicodemus did his best to keep his gaze mild. "Just thinking about what I can do for the good of the warren," he said pleasantly. "Nothing that would interest you." As Aiden moved away, he murmured, "Look, there's a hawk. O, what a tragedy. Rememberer seized in his prime."

"What was that?" asked Aiden, turning.

"Nothing," called Nicodemus cheerfully. "Just thinking about safety."

"You senior rabbits are so funny," said Aiden.

Nicodemus stepped outside and spent a few minutes munching on the questionable Kentucky bluegrass that grew near the entry. A bee bumbled by. He lolloped toward a dewy patch of clover under an ancient cherry tree. He was lost in the tender leaves and thinking about a tawny doe he had loved when he was a young buck, when he realized the squirrel overhead was speaking actual words instead of the usual squirrel gibberish.

"Message to the Reader Nicodemus from the Terror of Foxes, Disciplinarian of Hawks, and Mangler of Coyotes," said the squirrel. "Do you read me?"

Nicodemus looked up and squinted at the squirrel. After a long moment, he found himself smiling. "I do," he said.

"Show me the scar on your chest," said the squirrel. Nicodemus did so. "Ah, chek chek chek chek chek chek chek," said the squirrel.

"Understood," said Nicodemus.

"First," said the squirrel. "You are strong."

Nicodemus nodded. He felt like laughing or crying, and didn't care which.

"Next, you are cordially invited to come join me, old friend," said the squirrel. "Bring whatever you can. We have a soft landing for you."

"Got it," said the old Reader.

"Oh, and this is for you," said the squirrel, and dropped a roomy backpack made of fresh leaves. "For the moneystones."

"Message to She Who Dances in the Blood of the Blessed," said Nicodemus. "I'm coming."

"Ah, chek chek chek chek check chek chek," said the squirrel, and whisked away into the neighboring trees.

Nicodemus went back into the warren, and strolled down to his chamber. He filled the backpack with all the moneystones he had. Then he took the five ancient pages leaning against the wall and folded them up. He winced a little as he heard the brittle paper crack, but he put them in the backpack anyway.

Then he used both paws to pick up a small piece of graphite he had inherited from the Reader before him. He had used it sparingly to take some notes on observations he had made about the position of the sun. Now he used it to write on a piece of dried leaf that he left leaning against the wall. It was his last jab at Aiden.

"Fool takes a hike," he murmured, as he scratched out the characters: "IOU $8.27."

LOVE BUG

Love Bug was taking a shift as Door Warden. A storm was blowing up, and the smell of rain was strong and sweet in the warm night air. The gibbous moon was creating shiny highlights on the surfaces of the rocks. A young doe showed up out of the night. In the center of her face was a white triangle, and the sides of her face were black. She wore a small circlet of tiny baby's breath blossoms around the base of each ear.

"Hey, girl," said Love Bug.

"Hey, yourself," said the doe, who had dark, witchy eyes. She smelled like snapdragons.

"Is it beautiful out here or is it just you?" asked Love Bug.

The other rabbit smiled. "It's just you. I could see your fine, white coat glowing in the moonlight a hundred yards away." She lowered her voice. "Just like the Blessed."

Love Bug had a little unpleasant chill run down his spine. "Thanks for the ... tip," he said.

The doe bowed deeply. "I bring tidings from Tumble Stone Warren." She touched noses with him. "I'm Mabel, second Remembering acolyte."

"I'm Love Bug," said Love Bug. "That's the new warren on the other side of the hill, right?"

"Ya, we were north of the Shandy," said Mabel. "We crossed over a few months ago because the Blessed were pouring down on us like rain. Now that we've been here awhile, we see that they're almost as bad over here."

"Ya," said Love Bug. "These are hard times for a bunny."

"But you've been fighting back," said Mabel. "Who gave you permission to do that?"

Love Bug was taken aback, but then remembered he was talking to a Remembering acolyte. "We love Yah," he said evenly. Anastasia had coached all the Door Wardens on the official warren line. "And we know Yah loves us. We're just acting as though we really believe that."

Mabel came close enough that Love Bug could feel her whiskers tickling his face. "You're cute when you're saying things you don't believe."

Love Bug took a step back. "Nice flowers," he said, finally.

Mabel giggled. "Don't worry," she said. "I won't tell anyone."

"Um … thanks?" said Love Bug.

Mable sat up and adjusted her circlets of baby's breath. "Anyway, I'm here on official business. We want to join you."

"You mean move here?" asked Love Bug. "We welcome everyone, although we are getting a little big to take on a whole warren. How many are there of you?"

Mabel smiled. "No, silly. We want to stay in our warren. And learn from you. Fight with you."

Love Bug was surprised. The rabbits at *Sans Gloire* saw their own warren growing, but they had never thought of this. "That's a … new idea," said Love Bug. "But a good one. I'll gather up some people, and we can talk."

"That would be glorious," said Mabel. She licked his forehead. "Well, aren't you a tasty boy."

Chapter 9

Chek chek chek chek chek,
Chek chek chek chek chek chek chek,
Chek chek chek chek chek.

—*Classic squirrel haiku*

SUMMERDAY CLAN

At the northern end of the Million Acre Wood, a thick layer
of soft sandstone topped with hard basalt had weathered over
aeons into a forest of stone columns. A team of Dead Gods
had once come to survey and claim this geologic wonder, but
their venture had faded into the dust, leaving only an indus-
trial-sized roll of *aluminum d'or*[38] 9-gauge fencing wire.

---

[38] Golden aluminum.

These days, they were called the Spires by the animals living in the North Shandy, and the Summerday wolf clan had for many generations made this their home base when they were not roaming. In the upper reaches of the Spires lived a murder of crows.

In the center of the Spires was a place where several columns had collapsed, many thousands of years before, and the rubble had weathered into a stony hill. On late summer afternoons when the sun was low in the sky, the wolves liked to gather on the spot, which they called the Hill of Voices.

On this day, one of the wolves appeared and slowly climbed most of the way up the hill. It was an older female, the kindly Second She, her golden coat flecked with black. She lifted her head, and quietly a low growl rolled out of her throat. It raised in pitch, gliding upward in a velvety glissando, and slowly built into a long, low howl.

Then a younger male nosed forward out of some overhanging brush where he had been dozing, and climbed a few steps up the hill. His coat was mostly golden down the center of his back, but his legs and belly were gray. As Fifth He, the wolf stopped well below the female, and raised his own head. A lighter howl grew in his throat, and climbed until it was near the female's howl in pitch, but still deliberately dissonant.

An injured male, Third He, was next to appear. His jaw

had been broken by a kick from a stag a year earlier, and he could no longer bite with any strength. That meant he could no longer join the hunt, and had to rely on his packmates to provide for him. In a bid to prevent his status from falling to that of Least Wolf, he turned to the role of Shaman, learning everything he could about the heavens, so he could predict the seasons of the hunt. His howl was less controlled, more splintery, and dissonant from the other two.

Aliyah trotted in eagerly from a side path. As a two-year-old, she was bursting with energy. And as a full-blooded gold, she was huge, larger than many of the males. Her size and bravado had earned her the position of Third She and Lead Striker. It was a dangerous job: The Striker was the wolf who made the move to bring down the prey after a long run. It meant going in close, tearing open the throat or belly, taking a chance on injury from sharp hooves or sweeping horns. The injured wolf had been a Striker. She took a place near him.

Wolves were appearing more quickly now. Second He, a lone who had joined the pack as a yearling, loped quickly up the hill and settled near the top. His coat was gray and black, without a trace of gold in it. Then Least Wolf approached the hill timidly and stayed near the base.

Alaric, Fourth He, who had a splendid golden coat and yellow eyes, came in through the side path, and nipped the Least Wolf, who yelped and rolled onto his back in submission. Alaric then bounded up the hill like the climber he was. In the next few minutes, most of the rest of the pack arrived, and one by one, added their voices to the howl.

But the space at the top of the hill was still empty. For several minutes, the wolves of the Summerday Clan created music together, holding a still space at the center.

Then Micah and Sephora Summerday appeared, walking side by side down the wide avenue between the tallest Spires. Their lush golden coats burned like fire in the long low rays of the setting sun.

Micah Summerday was larger than any wolf a Dead God had ever seen. The mutation that made the Summerday clan golden in color had also added heft and muscle. He had the canine teeth of an alpha killer and the aquamarine eyes of an otherworldly lion. Sephora Summerday was larger than most half-gold males. The muscles in her long legs moved with careless power under her tawny skin as she strode. Her leaping ability and the murderous effectiveness of her canines were legendary throughout the Million Acre Wood. And her evergreen eyes shone with a cool intelligence.

They climbed the hill together, and settled onto the flat space on top with easy familiarity. Then they each raised their heads, and with unhurried joy, lifted their voices to join the family howl and weave the many dissonant voices into harmony.

Together the wolves' voices rose and fell, drifted from

side to side, developed cascades of harmony, stretched into broad dissonance, returned to intimate consonance, then resolved into slow and tender diminuendo.

At last, they were done. Sephora Summerday looked at Micah, and he looked out over the many upturned faces and began to speak. "Wolves are a kindly people. When Kiskari Highsummer killed my father and united the two golden packs into the Summerday Clan, he could have killed me and my brother and sister, but he did not." He paused, "Instead, he raised us as his own children, because, as has been known since time immemorial, the wolf is a creature of love."

Several ratifying howls lifted into the warm air.

Sephora Summerday stood and spoke. "As we all know, we have taken in many lones over the past three years. And they have brought us much joy."

The Second He, the highest-ranking adopted lone, yipped in support.

Sephora Summerday continued. "We've been privileged to have a mother and young cubs join us. And we love them well."

The Fourth She, with a fierce black and taupe ombre pelt, raised her dark face. "The privilege is all mine, Clan Mother."

"Golden is as golden does," said Sephora.

The other wolf growled in assent.

Micah Summerday resumed speaking, his voice heavy

and sad. "We know the Icewind Clan has recently moved into the Million Acre Wood. They used to be an upland pack, but the Municipal Wolves of Oom have driven them out, since the bears are now claiming all the upland territories."

Sephora Summerday broke in. "We owe them no ill will. In another time, we would happily embrace them as fellow travelers in this vale of tears."

Micah continued. "But game is scarce and times are hard. I look at you here today and see wolves who have been going hungry. How many days has it been since we've seized the gift of a deer's warm self-offering and said, *"Turn your face from me, Hunger Mother"*?

There was a general groan with a sad, flatted third.

"I say we can no longer afford to say to every wolf who comes a-walking, *'You are my family.'* What say you, wolves?"

Fourteen wolves howled in a woebegone minor that rose and fell, then climbed again to a ragged crescendo.

"I hear you," said Sephora. "We will ask the crows to tell them we offer them three days' grace in our lovingkindness. After that, Blood Father will awake."

NICODEMUS

It was late in the day when Nicodemus arrived at Warren *Sans Gloire*. The coins in his backpack had a tendency to jingle as he walked, which made him nervous. So it had been a very slow hike. Then he arrived and saw all the rabbits out at evening feed, squirrels bustling overhead, mice streaking by just under the grass, chatting about seeds. The poplar tree stood up straight and strong, and he saw a beautiful white buck acting as Door Warden by the front entrance. A thrush was singing high in an old oak tree. In the golden afternoon light, the greensward looked warm and beautiful, like the Lucky Fields, where the Glorified rabbits went to play for eternity.

He stood still for a moment and inhaled deeply. He could smell their joy.

Then he saw Anastasia come out the front entrance. He squinted. *Is that her?* The yearling rabbit he had known, the anxious mumbler, the shy misfit, in just a few months had grown into someone else. This rabbit didn't stand in a protective hunch. She stood tall. Her eyes were bright. She spoke to other rabbits and they listened, some ran off to do things. But they weren't afraid of her. The rabbits near her stood close to her flanks. A group of kittens played nearby, taking turns running over for a quick nuzzle.

His eyes moistened. *She's doing all right.*

Then Anastasia caught sight of him. "Nicodemus!" She bounded toward him, indulging in a *bink*, waving a "give us a minute" gesture to the other rabbits. As she approached, he could see the metal tube strapped to her front right foreleg. The Dragon Claw. It glinted as she ran, a sober reminder. His strong and beautiful friend was dangerous. A killer.

She came near him and licked his forehead. Her scent was very alpha. He pulled away. "No, it's I who should kiss *your* forehead. You have your own warren. You're the Warren—" he stopped suddenly.

She nuzzled his cheek. "They call me Loving Auntie," she said into his ear.

He pulled back to look at her. "That is beautiful. You are beautiful."

"You saved my life," she said.

"No," said Nicodemus. "I was weak. I didn't do anything when the time came."

"You saved my life long before that moment," said Anastasia.

"How?" asked Nicodemus.

She turned and sat side by side with him, pressing against his flank as they looked out over the grassland and scrub toward the blueberry patch. "You listened to me," she said. "When everyone else said I was crazy, you listened."

"You were a brave little point of light," said Nicodemus. "I didn't want you to flicker and go out." He felt himself tearing up, so he sat up suddenly and shrugged off the backpack. "And, I come bearing gifts," he said brightly. The backpack jingled as he opened it. "Eight dollars and twenty-seven cents. All yours. If your mother doesn't send an army to come take it back."

Anastasia laughed. "I think Mommy owes me this, don't you?"

Nicodemus nodded. "Yeah. Yeah, I do."

She touched noses with him and nuzzled his shoulder. "Thank you, old friend. And welcome to Warren *Sans Gloire*."

"So happy to be here. And don't worry about me," he said. "I may be an elder bunny, but you're not going to have to look after me."

Anastasia sat up and looked at him in surprise. "Look after *you*?" she said. "*You're* going to look after *us*. I've been telling everyone what a genius you are." She dropped down and looked at him very intently. "You may not realize it from looking at this happy scene, but every Blessed out there wants to kill us. We are at war."

FREDDIE

Freddie and Death Rage stood close together under a sweet pepperbush near the entrance to the straightstone burrow. Freddie lay on his belly so he could look Death Rage in the eye. "Thank you for having this talk with me. Anastasia asked me to do this."

"My rapier is ready," said Death Rage, drawing her

needle from its fine pineapple leather scabbard. "I'm calling it the Kiss of Death." She tapped it twice on her Canada Dry helmet and dropped into a fighting stance.

"Nice," said Freddie, and smiled. "I'm glad you're on our side, fiercerina."

Death Rage twirled and caught a falling leaf on the point of the Kiss of Death. "I'm on the side of honor," she said.

"I see that," said Freddie. "So I have a very fierce mission for you, from the one who wields the Dragon Claw."

Death Rage settled in to listen. "I live to serve her."

"You know that Bricabrac is going to be doing some work for us. He is a very talented craftrat, and Anastasia believes he can create all the weapons the warren needs, now that we have the stuff the Dead Gods left in this burrow."

Death Rage nodded, then adjusted her bottlecap helmet.

"He's going to need an assistant—an army of assistants, really—to make this happen," said Freddie. "I know he thinks the world of your abilities and the other mice of Musmuski Wood. The most logical lieutenant for Bricabrac is you, and the best crew would be your buds from back home."

"True," said Death Rage, as she polished the Kiss of Death with the fur of her left underpaw.

"Now," said Freddie, "Bricabrac's payment for all this would add up to far more than the moneystones we have available, so he will get to keep one out of every six weapons he makes. That way, it doesn't cost us anything."

"Very smart," said the mouse.

"Here's the issue," said Freddie. "Bricabrac is a fine rat, but he has his own loyalties. So Anastasia wants you to keep an eye on him. If he takes more than he's supposed to, let us know. If he does something weird, let us know."

Death Rage sheathed her sword. "This is not the kind of mission that suits me," she said. "Show me a coyote and I will take him on." She held out her hands, palms up. "Spying on a friend, meh."

"I hear you," said Freddie, very seriously. "But Bricabrac is an ally, not a friend. And this will be a war, not a skirmish. We will all have to do things that are not our favorite."

Death Rage looked at him for a long time. "I hear you, brother," she said, finally.

"Thank you," said Freddie.

"So I'll do it. But let me just ask you this. Save a mission for me that has some honor."

"There will be many," said Freddie. "You won't be short of opportunities to prove your valor." He licked Death Rage's forehead. "Bricabrac isn't here yet. This is an exploration for *Sans Gloire* friends only. Let's go in."

They passed through the small entrance hole into the straightstone burrow. The smell of dust and rot filled the wide, low space, just as Freddie remembered. They saw Nicodemus crouching over a piece of paper. A piece of graphite lay near him on the hard-packed earth. He nodded at them. "Death Rage, would you mind sketching? Your hands are so skillful."

Death Rage smoothed her brown fur and picked up the graphite. "How may I serve, Wise One?"

"Just draw out a quick map of *Sans Gloire*," said Nicodemus. "Front entrance here, underhall here, main run here, cross runs here and here." Death Rage sketched rapidly with the chunk of graphite.

"And there are entryways here, here, and here," said Freddie.

"So ... weasels are definitely the first priority," said Nicodemus. "We have to keep them out."

"Ya," said Freddie and chewed his lip. Death Rage, who was standing next to him, saw him tremble.

"Have you dealt with weasels before?" asked Death Rage.

"No," said Nicodemus. "We didn't have a problem with weasels at Bloody Thorn. Just lucky, I guess."

"Everyone's lucky, until they're unlucky," said Freddie darkly. "Fallen Oak Warren was lucky for a long time."

"True," said Nicodemus, who then touched noses with him. "And I'm so sorry." Freddie looked down at his front paws. Nicodemus turned back to the map. "How about this? We make a grating, a mesh of small branches. Green ones, so they're still pliable. Put them across the entrance runs to stop the weasels from getting in."

"Coyotes could dig them out," said Death Rage.

Nicodemus sat back on his haunches. "We could place them about three feet inside the entrances, so the digging would be a hard slog."

"We'd have to be able to open it, though," said Death Rage.

"Need some kind of hinge," said Nicodemus.

"Maybe green twigs, bent double, pushed into the floor?" said Freddie. "They could hold the lowest bar of the grating in place. You could dig them out, but it would take awhile."

Nicodemus looked at him appraisingly. "Good idea," he said. "You sound like a Reader, my boy."

Freddie felt a warm glow from the praise, but he made sure to keep on his most serious face. "We could have the gratings open outward, so they'd be hard to force. Use agave twine to hold them closed. Twine is on the inside, so the weasel can't just bite through it."

"I like it," said Nicodemus.

"Now," said Death Rage, "all we need is something to stab through the grating at the weasel, so he can't just stand there and gnaw through the branches." She twirled her needle. "Something like the Kiss of Death, but longer."

"The Dead Gods have left some useful gifts for us here," said Freddie. "Let's go and take a look."

They pushed along the edge of the foundation into a larger area where more of the ancient floor had collapsed, allowing more items to fall down from above. Some were large hardstone shapes, which Nicodemus said were "tools." Among the detritus, Death Rage discovered a small rectangular object lying on the ground. She picked it up and examined it.

"What is this?"

"Pencil sharpener," said Nicodemus.

"What's a pencil?" asked Death Rage.

"Some kind of weapon, I guess," said Freddie.

Nicodemus laughed. "Not exactly."

"If it's not a weapon, then why does it need to be sharpened?" asked Death Rage.

"It was a very special kind of weapon," said Nicodemus. "But I think you're onto something, Death Rage." He picked up the pencil sharpener between both his front paws and turned it over several times. "We could use this to sharpen stout twigs. It would turn any strong twig into a spear."

"We could push those through the gratings!" said Death Rage.

"Great idea," said Freddie.

Nicodemus chuckled. "Pencil pushers. The most powerful force on earth."

They fanned out to look around the larger space. In one area was a tumbled heap of metal cylinders covered with faded paper labels showing images of plants and animals. These had burst open and dried out centuries ago.

Another section of the planks above their heads had collapsed under the weight of heavy metal implements, which now lay rusting in the earth. Death Rage scampered over to them quickly. "Hardstone, sharpstone," she said. "Way too big for us. But some of the sharpstone bits might be useful."

Freddie nosed around the place where had found the fragments of books earlier. He turned up something new, a few large pages, still flat and orderly. The dust made him sneeze. Nicodemus came over to look. "That's a magazine," said Nicodemus. "*EarthKid.* I've seen a couple of pages of this before."

Freddie turned a page with his teeth. It fell open to an ad. A big piece of the corner had been torn away on the left side and some of the text was gone. The remaining large letters across the top of the page said, "…oga for kids." Under that, smaller letters said, "Be calm. Be happy. Move like water." Nearby were small pictures of animals in special stances, labeled, "Tree Pose," "Mountain Pose," and "Downward-Facing Dog." The animals included a rabbit, a squirrel, and a mouse.

There was more writing on the page, about breathing

deeply and being centered. *Hmmm,* thought Freddie, *this could be good for Dingus. He's kinda getting on my nerves the way he jitters around the warren.* Freddie pulled the page out, folded it up, and slipped it into his backpack.

"Hey! Look over here!" Nicodemus was looking into a scratched bin of faded plastic. It was lying on its side, more than half-filled with pointed shiny metal objects.

Death Rage scampered over and clambered into the bin. She caught her breath. "Hundreds of them," she murmured. "Maybe a thousand."

"A thousand what?" asked Freddie.

"*Nails,*" said Nicodemus. "An army waiting to happen."

ANASTASIA

The night was hot. Anastasia awoke in Holly's chamber, with a squirmy mound of kittens snuggled in between her and their mother. One of the kittens was pressed against her, trying to nurse. She gently turned the baby around and got her headed toward Holly.

Anastasia got up and paced down the hall. Even the usually cool passages of the warren felt warm. She had fallen asleep with the Claw on her foreleg, fresh in from another recon trip. Now she felt the weight of it as she walked.

She came up to the entrance to her own chamber. She so rarely slept there now, preferring the cozy domesticity of moms and kits. She nosed up against the stick smeared with dried fox blood that stood outside her doorway. The scent was long gone, but the authority it conveyed remained.

As she moved along the passages, she looked in on Yasmin and her kits. She noticed that Juniper had taken to sleeping in Yasmin's chamber since her brother Chervil had died. She kissed them all, one by one, as they slept.

She observed that Grégoire had moved out of the nut room and was sleeping in the communal sleeping chamber that many of the unattached bucks shared. Coriander was there. Love Bug was not. He was probably bunked with one of the many does who had joined the warren in the last few weeks. She touched each rabbit as she walked through the chamber.

She passed the rough chamber where Wendy slept alone and saw her sprawled out with her huge back feet extended into the hallway. The reek of her uncured raptor claws filled the close space. A low rumble that sounded like a cross between a growl and a snore drifted down the passage. Anastasia smiled and laid her paw on the pads of Wendy's enormous foot. She shifted in her sleep and rumbled quietly, "Bah."

There was some noise as she passed the nut room, now grown to accommodate the nut hoards of the many squirrel sentries. She looked in to see Dingus inside, restacking his acorns and counting them as he went.

"May all your nut dreams come true," said Anastasia.

"Don't make me lose count," said Dingus, sharply. "Seventy-eight. Seventy-nine ..." She kissed the back of his head. "Stop touching me," said Dingus.

When Anastasia passed the guest chamber they had built, she looked in and saw Mabel, the visitor from Tumble Stone Warren, fast asleep with a pair of leafy sage twigs crossed on the wall above her head. And there was Love Bug, snuggled up beside her. Anastasia smiled and lightly touched the tips of their toes.

Finally, Anastasia reached the front entrance. A young doe she did not know was on Door Warden duty, and she snapped to attention when she saw the Loving Auntie come out. Anastasia touched noses with her and then stepped into the night.

It was just a few months ago when she had been pushed out the front door of Bloody Thorn Warren, alone and terrified. Now she walked easily through her own space, a night watch on guard, Blessed Ones respectful of her perimeter.

And now another warren had asked to join forces with *Sans Gloire*. Her council had had a long talk about it. They decided to share everything they had: ideas, weapons, techniques. Why hold back? The more creatures freed from the Blessed Ones' yoke of fear, the better. This generous decision also held a healthy dose of *realpolitik*: It would mean that *Sans Gloire* wasn't the Blessed Ones' only target.

The first-quarter moon cast a dim light. A strangely familiar smell came to her in the still night air. The woody tang of thorns. But there were no thorn bushes near *Sans Gloire*. Then she saw a steel-gray rabbit with a slash of white across the face, standing framed between two jagged agave plants. Her breath caught in her throat. "Mother!"

Olympia did not move. "Hello, beloved daughter." Her ocean blue eyes shone in the moonlight.

Hot rage flooded Anastasia's body. She moved toward her mother, and as she came near, her foreleg twitched, as though of its own volition, and the Claw flicked out. Even in the dim moonlight, the blade shone. But Anastasia did not raise her paw, and the blade dragged through the dry earth.

Olympia stood still as a statue. "You are my sweet girl," she said.

"You pushed me out and gave me to the Blessed Ones," said Anastasia. Her breath came fast.

"I gave you into the care of Yah," said Olympia, her blue eyes steady. "I knew that He could care for you better than any Earthly mother."

Anastasia stared at Olympia. "What if Yah had let me die?"

"He didn't, because you are important to him," said Olympia. "He loves you."

Anastasia came close to Olympia and nuzzled her cheek. "What about you, mother?" she asked, softly.

"I always loved you," said Olympia. "You were special."

"You said I was crazy," snarled Anastasia. Then she stalked away, Claw dragging through the leaves and dust.

"You were the bright one. The smart one. You asked questions," said Olympia. "Those are dangerous qualities." She followed Anastasia, her voice soothing and insistent. "You could see how dirty and dangerous the world is."

Anastasia turned around. "And what did that get me?"

The slash of white across Olympia's face gleamed in the half-moonlight. "I always thought you would take over the warren after me."

Anastasia stared at her in silence for several seconds. "The barren one? So I would be the Warren Mother with no children? Tell me more lies, mother."

Olympia pressed close to Anastasia's flank, her scent warm and accommodating. "Children don't matter. After me, there would have been a whole warren of souls in need of a bright spirit like yours to help them find their way." She shifted her body so she could look into Anastasia's eyes. "And to make the hard decisions."

A cool, tickly feeling ran down Anastasia's spine. She took a step back. "Why are you here, mother?"

Olympia sat down and washed her face. Anastasia watched her gray paws scrubbing her cheeks in the dim light. When she was done, she said, "Nicodemus took all

the moneystones that Bloody Thorn owned and vanished."
She looked up at Anastasia. "I know he's here."

Anastasia was silent.

"He's not bad," said Olympia, as she groomed her
forepaw. "He's just old. And a little … confused." As she
spoke, her long front teeth shone in the moonlight. "I want
him back. And my moneystones."

Anastasia heard a noise and glanced back at the entrance to *Sans Gloire*. The Door Warden was changing
over. A sturdy spotted buck had come out to relieve the
young doe. She turned back to Olympia. "Nicodemus is
my friend. As to the stones, I'll take them as blood money."
She polished the Claw's blade with her left forepaw. "It's
the least you can do, mother."

Olympia laid her chin on her forepaws. "I could send
an army to collect what is mine, but let's say I don't, because of my great love for you." Her ear twitched. "You
would owe me a favor."

Anastasia flicked her forepaw and retracted the Claw.
"What kind of favor?"

Olympia smiled. "Do you know what it means to be
Presiding Spirit of the Shandy Vale Conclave?"

Anastasia shrugged. "The Rememberers from the
local warrens get together and elect one of the Warren
Mothers."

"Do you know why it's important?"

Anastasia stared at her. "You got elected recently. So ... now you're a star?"

Olympia smiled. She began walking toward Anastasia very slowly, one step at a time, backing her toward the oak tree. "I'm going to tell you something that only two other rabbits at Bloody Thorn know." She took a step. "Something that only a few rabbits in the Shandy Vale know." She took another step and stood eye to eye with Anastasia. "Can you handle a hard truth?"

Anastasia swallowed. "Yes."

Olympia nodded. "If you're elected Presiding Spirit, the Blessed Ones don't attack your warren."

Anastasia's eyelids quivered slightly, but she did not blink. She did not allow herself to blink. Finally, a single interrogative ripped its way out of her throat. "*What*?"

Olympia's eyes, suddenly night-ocean dark, did not glance away. "They don't attack your warren."

"They attacked *me*." Anastasia spat the words into the warm air.

"You went beyond the Ring of Love," said Olympia. "How many times did I tell you not to?"

"Why would they do that?" Anastasia's voice came out in a whisper.

"It's a sign of their respect for the office," said Olympia, her voice sweet and reasonable. "They need an opposition leader to communicate with."

Hot tears filled Anastasia's eyes. "You *negotiate* with these killers? You're *cozy* with them?" Her right forepaw came up, and the Claw came out, singing its hungry song. "They killed *your* children! How could you do that?" Anastasia buried the Claw in the oak tree's trunk next to Olympia's head.

Olympia did not flinch. "I did it for *us*. I did it for the *family*." She nuzzled Anastasia's cheek. "Presiding Spirit is a free pass for the whole warren. Can't you imagine how hard it is to get this?"

Anastasia stared. "You're making deals with the people who killed the brothers and sisters I lived with in your womb."

"Don't you think it wounds me that I could not save all my children?" Olympia's eyes were wet. "But that's in the past now."

Anastasia pulled the Claw out of the oak tree and snapped it shut. "Why are you telling me this?"

Olympia kissed Anastasia's forehead, tenderly. "I want you to be happy, my love. Whatever you do, I will be happy for you." She sighed deeply. "But the Conclave … they're going to see this as heresy."

"See what as heresy?" said Anastasia.

Olympia tried to lick her forehead again, but Anastasia pulled away. "Attack the Blessed. Hurt the Blessed. Heal the Blessed," said Olympia. "That is not Yah's plan for us." She sat up, and her eyes were soft and kind. "We are granted an unknown number of days. Every one of them a gift. And one day our number of days is known, and we are Glorified, and we go to be with the Loved One."

"All I want," said Anastasia, her golden eyes shining, "is that we count, too."

"We do count, baby," said Olympia. "Yah loves us." She came toward Anastasia.

Anastasia backed up. "I believe Yah loves us," she said. "So I ask Him for more."

"You can't do that," said Olympia.

"Why not?"

Olympia stood up and dropped her front paws in a gesture of helplessness. "Because if you're a heretic, it casts a stain on our family. And the Shandy Vale Conclave will vote me out as Presiding Spirit."

Anastasia felt the implications of this rushing over her, so she stepped away and nibbled some dandelion.

"And then Bloody Thorn Warren might be cleansed," said Olympia. "Remember what happened when the Warren Mother at Fallen Oak was voted out." A small whine crept into her voice. "All your sisters and brothers. All your friends. Your dad. Me."

Anastasia turned. "Mother—"

"It's always weasels," whispered Olympia, her scent small and helpless. "Because only weasels can get in. You don't want that to happen to us, do you?" Her wheedling voice made Anastasia's skin crawl. "We'll all be Glorified. Every one."

"Shut up!" shouted Anastasia.

"Angel, it's only because I love you—" began Olympia.

Anastasia flicked out the Claw. "Get away from me, mother."

Olympia looked at her with big sad blue eyes. "I know you'll make the right choice," she said, finally. Then she turned and vanished into the dark.

Anastasia looked after her for a full minute. Then she found herself pressing the sharp point of the Claw against the first pad on her left paw. She held it there until a drop of blood appeared as a neat bead around the point. Then she moved the blade to her second pad and waited for the blood to appear. Then the third. Then the fourth.

In the dim light of the quarter-moon, the drops of blood falling to the ground looked black as poison.

Chapter 10

The bestest treats,
Have tiny feets.

—Weasel proverb

DINGUS

"You take me for a fool?" shouted Dingus at the little group standing in a line on the large oak branch overlooking the front entrance to the Warren. He stamped in a rage. The group of five squirrels, two chipmunks, and three wood mice looked around in mild alarm. "What?" asked one of the chipmunks, finally.

Dingus stood with his arms outstretched and his fine fingers in jazz-hands mode. "Admission to the *Amazing Glorification & Resurrection of Foxes, Terrible Punishment of Hawks, and General Spanking of Weasels By the Rabbit*

Without Antecedents is three nuts, as is clearly stated in my jingle. And staying on my hotel branch is a further two nuts." Dingus grabbed a shell out of the hands of one of the wood mice. "This is a peanut! It is not a true nut!"

The wood mouse began to stammer apologetically about protein equivalencies, but Dingus threw the shell at him. "I will not be disrespected in this way. Now get out!" The wood mouse looked at him for a long moment. Then he shouldered his peanut and began to walk away, muttering that a certain somebody definitely was a "true nut."

Dingus overheard the muttering and drew himself up to his full height of several inches. "No show today," he announced. "All of you, out." There was a general chorus of protests. Dingus turned his back on them. "I'm an artist," he said. "I don't work like this."

As the ex-customers grumpily filed down from the oak branch, Dingus noticed Freddie watching him from below. "Hey," called Freddie, "I got something for ya, buddy."

Dingus skimmed down the trunk and stood near Freddie. "What?"

"I found this at the straightstone burrow," said Freddie, taking off his backpack. He took out a piece of paper and unfolded it. It was the magazine ad for "…oga for kids" that Freddie had found earlier. "Look," he said, indicating the pictures of animals in special poses. "Some kind of animal dance thing from the Dead Gods."

"What are 'kids?'" asked Dingus.

"Young goats," said Freddie.

The squirrel's eyelid twitched. "Why are you giving this to me?"

"Thought it might help you feel better," said Freddie, with what he hoped was a disarming smile.

"I feel fine!" snapped Dingus, as he started a round of stampy dance.

"Well, maybe it'll help *me* feel better." Freddie touched some of the pictures. "*Be calm. Be happy.*' And look, there's a squirrel doing it. Sounds pretty good, huh?" Freddie indicated the rest of the text on the page. "And there's lots more, too."

Dingus eyed Freddie as he continued stamping. "Thank you, Comrade Freddie," he said, coolly. "I shall take this and put it in my house and review it at a later time." He stopped stamping and picked up the page and folded it up.

"Okay, great," said Freddie, "and just let me know if—"

"Good day," said Dingus.

"—you need any help reading it," finished Freddie.

"I said, good *day*!"

DEATH RAGE

"Okay," said Death Rage to the small group of rabbits gathered at the front entrance of Warren *Sans Gloire*. Her bottlecap helmet gleamed in the sun. "I've been working with Freddie and Nicodemus on the gratings idea, and Anastasia asked me to tell you all about it. But, first, I've sent for some help. So let me introduce, fresh from Musmuski Wood, a crafting genius, Throat Punch." A sinewy mouse with a light gray body and a head dark as death stepped forward. "She's a genius with wood," said Death Rage.

"Welcome," said Yasmin. Throat Punch smiled and bowed.

"And this fabricating wonder: He cut his teeth on wooden blades, and now he's ready to shape all the sharpstone we've just discovered, Moody Loner," said Death Rage. A trim mouse whose coat was the color of cast iron speckled with rust stepped into the open space. "Afterwards, you'll all say, 'He was such a nice guy.'" All the mice guffawed at this ancient mouse joke. The rabbits looked confused. Wendy picked her teeth with an owl talon.

"Aaand, the winner of this year's Musmuski Young Fiercemaker Award, a new friend to me as well as you," said Death Rage. She gestured to a youthful mouse with an ombré coat that began as a dusty rose around her feet, and faded to a summer-pink as it rose upward. Elegant sumac juice designs adorned her shoulders. And in the fashion of young mouse does, she wore dandelion floaties woven into the fur around her ears. This made it look as though she were wearing a crown of starlight. "Please welcome, Exit Wound."

Exit Wound curtsied. Then she reached over her shoulder and unsheathed a steel greatsword that had begun life as a novelty key-ring in the gift shop at the Metropolitan Museum of Art. As she held it aloft, the sun gleamed on the shiny blade. The other creatures *ooh'd* and *aah'd.*

"This is *Belle Lumière.*[39] She has been in my family for twenty-nine generations," said Exit Wound, stroking the bright blade. "She will now fight for freedom."

The mice and rabbits all clapped and cheered.

"I've never seen an angel fly so low. Welcome, Exit Wound," said Love Bug, and he gallantly leaned forward to lick her forehead.

"Careful," said Throat Punch. "She can rip your tongue out with one hand and use it to clean your ears."

Love Bug stopped in mid-gesture. His eyes flicked toward Throat Punch.

"Just kidding," said Throat Punch. "It takes both hands." There was a general chuckle. Exit Wound stepped forward and bowed her head. Love Bug patted her forehead—gingerly.

"Now let's get on these gratings!" cried Death Rage.

---

[39] Beautiful Light.

ALIYAH

Aliyah was with her mother Sephora in her favorite niche in one of the largest spires. The clan was restless and prickly as the sun beat down. They were waiting to hear back from their message to the Icewind wolves. Down below, her brother, Alaric, was playfighting with some of the other young males. It was a jittery moment, filled with waiting.

"You know, I had the weirdest conversation about rabbits the other day," began Aliyah. "It was with that sweet little coyote from South Shandy. 'Member him? The crippled one? He came up for the Shaman thing last year. Anyway, he said that down there, rabbits were attacking foxes—"

Suddenly, a large black crow swooped around from the side of the pillar, alighted on the smooth stone, and cawed loudly.

"Grammy Kark," said Sephora, and bowed respectfully. Aliyah bowed as well.

The crow stood on one foot and looked at Sephora with her midnight-black eyes. "We did as you asked, golden child."

Sephora ended her bow. "Thank you, Grammy."

"We found the other wolf pack. They're hunting near the Boreal Cliffs. Probably came down from the uplands on the Midsummer Path."

"What did they say?"

The crow fluttered up to a mini-spire and stood a few feet above the wolves. *"As Landlords, it is your right to close the gate. We have been driven out of City of Oom's demesne. We claim asylum with our teeth and claws. Sisters and brothers, we await your warm embrace."*

"Thank you," said Sephora. "It is as I had thought."

"Is it?" asked the crow, hopping a few steps nearer Sephora and pecking at the ground near her feet.

Sephora's eyes flicked over to Aliyah and then back to the crow. "Tell me all that you have seen, mother of my mother."

"It is well not to assume," said Grammy Kark. "There are twenty-two wolves in the other pack."

Aliyah felt the fur on her back stand up. *And we just challenged them.* There were fourteen wolves in the Summerday Clan, and two were cubs less than a year old.

A low growl rolled out of Sephora's throat. "Are you sure?"

Grammy Kark flapped her wings. "I took Cacao with me. He's the best counter in our murder."

"Must have been two packs that recently joined," said Sephora, lightly scrubbing the stone with her paw.

"How many adults?" broke in Aliyah.

Grammy Kark turned to look at her, amusement in her midnight-black eyes. "Already this one wants a seat at council. I did not speak to my mother until I was five years old."

Sephora laid her muzzle on her paws. "She's impetuous, Grammy. But she can tear the throat out of a fourteen-point stag before you can say, 'Jackdaw Robinson.' I think we'll keep her."

"You are a sweet shiny puppy," said Grammy Kark.

"And you are an angel by other means," said Sephora. "How many adults?"

"Nineteen," said Grammy Kark.

Sephora was silent. Even big golden wolves are not anxious to rush into a fight against almost two-to-one odds. Aliyah watched her anxiously.

"Take your time laying your killing plans," said the crow as she beat her wings and took to air. "Call me when the carrion's ready."

"Wait," said Sephora, "I have an idea."

AIDEN

Aiden was out at evening feed, looking for tender shoots of sweet pea. A nightingale was singing. Now that Nicodemus was gone, the first Reading apprentice had been promoted to take his place. That meant the warren's other key officer was a very junior rabbit. The field was wide open for Aiden the Rememberer to become the Indispensable Bunny at Bloody Thorn. Or the mess with Anastasia could drag him down. It was a delicate moment, and had to be played just right.

Then he saw a lean, long-legged rabbit loping toward him through the chest-high grass. *Ugh.* The huge ears, one with a notch of flesh missing, telegraphed who it was, even at a distance. With everything going on now with Anastasia, the Lord Harmonizer Tobias was the last person he wanted to see. Still there was no getting away from it. He ran to find Olympia. Soon, the three of them were in the thorny meeting room above the warren, just finishing the ceremonial greetings while Briar ran out to find nasturtium leaves.

"Tobias," said Olympia. "It is so *good* to see you again. How are things at the Known World Symposium?"

Tobias pulled an ear down and washed it, slowly. Finally, he said. "Oh, we are doing what the old ones always do, little one: studying, studying, studying the Word of Yah. Rooting out discontinuities, revealing the truth that has always been there for us to see."

"That is the good work," said Olympia. "The rest of us are simply living day to day. Your work is rooted in eternity."

Tobias did not answer. Aiden wasn't sure whether he should say anything or not. Finally, he murmured, "Yes, we are so grateful."

Briar hustled in with some fresh nasturtium leaves and laid them out near Tobias. Then he bowed and retreated.

Tobias picked up a leaf and munched it, slowly. "As you might imagine, at the Known World Symposium, we are constantly listening to all our children: The Shandy Vale Conclave and all the other local Conclaves. The work of remembering is so important, and it's easy for errors to creep in."

"And so terrible when that happens," said Olympia.

Aiden looked at his toes. Was this about Anastasia? Was he about to be demoted for lack of vigor in wrangling the heretic? Surely, the Known World Symposium had heard the stories about the strange rabbits by now, but did they know Anastasia was a daughter of Bloody Thorn Warren? Maybe he could survive this crisis. He racked his brain to think of something to say that sounded vaguely penitential, yet energetic and ready to fight as needed.

Tobias put down the nasturtium leaf and said, "In the Book of Creeping Sedge, chapter three, verse seven, we find the line, *And the Loved One said, Like you, when I see the Blessed, I feel a rupture in my heart. And I am rooted to the earth.*"

"Yes," said Aiden. "I know it well."

"You recall that we learned there was uncertainty about the authenticity of this verse, so we solicited the learned opinions of all our brothers and sisters."

"Yes," said Olympia. "I believe our majority opinion was *there is a rupture in my heart.* And our minority opinion was *I find a rupture in my heart.*"

The Lord Harmonizer closed his eyes and put his paws

to his temples. "We have discovered, in collating the many different memories of all the Rememberers in the Known World, the true text of this verse. Praise be to Yah." His scent was heavy with authority.

"What is it, My Lord?" asked Olympia, as she crept slowly toward him.

Without moving, Tobias said, "The true text is this: *When I see the Blessed, I feel a rapture in my heart. And I am rooted to the earth.*"

Olympia stepped back and growled, in spite of herself. "*Rapture?*" Her claws raked the earth. Then she laughed. "Oh, you're joking! You are quite the card, Tobias."

Aiden felt his eyes bugging out with surprise. Usually, corrections were about things like how many plums were in the plum-monger's basket during the Miracle of the Stone Fruits.

Tobias shook his head. He did not take his eyes off Olympia. "The finding of inauthenticity is the essential mystery of the Conclave. Yah moves in mysterious ways."

"This … correction will seem strange to people," said Aiden. "They are naturally afraid of the Blessed. Even though, of course, we know that the jaws of the Blessed are the gateway to paradise."

"We serve a living god," said Tobias. "Corrections may be surprising, but they are always gifts."

"Yes, yes, of course," said Olympia, faintly.

"Now," said Tobias briskly. "As the Presiding Spirit of the South Shandy Conclave, it is your responsibility to propagate this correction and new teaching. And I'm sure your sturdy Rememberer can help you make this happen." He touched noses with Olympia. "You haven't lied," he said, smiling. "Bloody Thorn Warren still has the finest nasturtium in Yah's creation."

DEATH RAGE

It was late at night at the straightstone burrow. The mice had been working all day on making nail-tipped wooden spears that could be handled by creatures with hands, like mice, rats, and squirrels. And they had been creating the sharpened wooden stakes that would be stored near the gratings protecting the warrens, so they could be shoved through the openings at any weasel attempting to chew through the cords holding the gratings together.

Throat Punch and Moody Loner lay curled up among the other mice. Exit Wound was nestled in between Freddie and Nicodemus, the dandelion floaties woven into her fur glimmering in the moonlight.

Death Rage could not sleep. She tossed and turned, her mind filled with plans for weapons. She threw herself on her back, sighing irritably. Her eyes opened a little, and she saw Bricabrac slipping quietly along one wall, avoiding the sleeping animals. He reached the entrance, took a last look around, and vanished into the night.

Instantly, Death Rage was on high alert. She seized her helmet and the Kiss of Death, and quietly buckled them on as she scampered toward the entrance and slipped through. Once outside, she saw Bricabrac scuttling along under an azalea. In the bright moonlight, she could see that he was carrying something that shone. It was round and looked heavy, maybe a moneystone.

In a few minutes, Bricabrac had reached the edge of a field. He paused and scanned the sky for a minute. Death Rage waited under a laurel bush and watched, her hand resting on the hilt of the Kiss of Death.

Suddenly, Bricabrac headed out into the meadow. When he was about seventy-five feet out into the grassy area, he began to stagger, as though he were injured. One of his legs appeared to have gone lame, which gave his whole body a jerking motion as he moved.

Death Rage stared. Why would he do that? Just being in the open was asking to be snatched by a raptor, but looking wounded was a virtual guarantee of an attack. Had he lost his mind?

Sure enough, within a minute she saw a blunt feathered form leave the tree line and sail out across the meadow. Two feathered crests adorned the head, and it was as silent as death. Owl. Within a few seconds, the owl was approaching Bricabrac. Death Rage closed her eyes. She did not want to see the tiny shape struggling in the two great claws, and hear the small distant cry of terror.

But there was no cry. At the last second, she could hear Bricabrac yell, "*Olly olly oxen free!*[40]"

Astonished, she looked up to see the owl veer off suddenly and land roughly in the grass near Bricabrac. The owl looked none too pleased, but still, they seemed to be having a conversation. At one point, Bricabrac tugged his left ear and his copper earring shone in the moonlight.

Then Bricabrac proffered the moneystone to the owl. The owl grasped it with surprising delicacy in its huge, heavy claws. Then, with a few heavy wingbeats, it took to the air. In a few seconds, it was lost against the dark wall of trees at the edge of the meadow.

AIDEN

Olympia, Darius and Aiden arrived at the apple tree a hundred yards from Bloody Thorn Warren in the early afternoon. Fufu was fluttering after them. The cool, fresh scent of growing apples hung in the warm air.

"This is far enough," said Olympia. "No one will bother us here at this time of day." Darius fell to nibbling a twig.

---

[40] A term of truce from children's games.

"Fufu, there's a good chickie," said Olympia. "Just circle round once in awhile and keep an eye out, will you?"

"Want wormy," murmured Fufu.

"And you shall have wormy," said Olympia. "Just keep your little eyes open, darling." Olympia turned to Aiden and reclined on the grassy sward. "Give me your thoughts."

Aiden sat up straight and did his best to look wise. "So, the pressing issue is the revision to the Word of Yah that changes foundational teachings—"

"That is one issue," said Olympia. "But the more pressing problem is the potential coming special election that could see me lose my office as Presiding Spirit of the South Shandy Conclave." She paused. "And everything that goes with that."

"Yes, yes," Aiden stammered. "That is a sticky problem." He scratched his ear. "But … perhaps one of these can be the solution for the other."

"I'm all ears," said Darius, as he munched on a windfall apple.

"This—" Aiden struggled to find the right words. "—newly revealed truth about the Word of Yah can be a great distraction from people's concerns about Anastasia's heresies. And who can fault the Presiding Spirit if she is very visibly wrestling with a new challenge from Yah Himself?"

Olympia moved toward Aiden and lay down with her

deep-water-blue eyes on him. "How would that work, counselor?"

"The teachings about fear of the Blessed Ones have always been the hardest," said Aiden. *"Everybody runs.* And everyone knows that. Even we, the Rememberers, talk about embracing Glorification out of one side of our mouths while we murmur expiations for the sin of fear out of the other side."

"I've run many times," said Darius.

Aiden felt a warm buzz starting to flow through him. "We could take this revised teaching and treat it as something remote and arcane," he said. "Or we could treat it as very real and immediate. Something that's going to change all our lives."

Olympia got up and settled down near Aiden, her warm flank touching his. "Tell me more."

"We could drop a challenge into the laps of the Rememberers of all the warrens in Shandy Vale," he said. "Give them a real problem to worry about, so that the peccadilloes of tertiary daughters suddenly seem a million hops away."

"Keep talking," said Olympia. "It pleases me." Her scent was friendly, almost intimate.

"Old rabbits can't change," said Aiden. "So, we start a cadre of youngsters. Not even yearlings, six months old. And we train them not to run. *Ever.* They will be the elect,

Yah's special children. And it will be every warren's responsibility to do this."

Olympia was very quiet for a long moment, and then she began to speak in the rich and kindly tones she usually reserved for addressing public gatherings. "Your children. Yah's chosen ones. Marching toward Glory in perfect stillness. *When I see the Blessed, I feel a rapture in my heart. And I am rooted to the earth.*"

Smiling, Aiden leaned toward her, and licked her forehead, murmuring, "*I shall meet them in the jaws of the Blessed Ones, and we will be with Yah in Paradise.*"

Olympia giggled and nuzzled his ear. "Will you come by my chamber tonight?"

A bright buzz roared through him. His eyes darted toward Darius. "But—"

She lowered her head, so she could look him in the eye, smiling. "*It shall be under Yah's eye, and not just well, exceeding well.*"

Aiden closed his eyes. "Yes, Honored One."

WOLVES

Aliyah was playing keep-away with some of the other young Summerday Clan wolves, using an old deer skull. They were tumbling and leaping in the dust among the Spires when Clan Mother Sephora's voice rang out.

"Icewind Pack is crossing the Delf at Breakwater Rapid. Summerday, gather!"

Aliyah looked up to see Grammy Kark flapping her wings as she rose up from Sephora's favorite afternoon niche in the old spire. Suddenly, all the wolves were in motion. They came together at the foot of the little hill, milling around in a jittery swirl. The crows saw what was happening, and one by one, they lifted off from their nests at the top of the Spires.

This was the opportunity that Sephora had been waiting for. The Delf River was a fast-flowing river that fell from the top of the Boreal Cliffs a few miles from the Spires. It flowed brutally fast and cold, and any pack that came down from the uplands on the Midsummer Path would sooner or later have to cross it in order to reach the more extensive hunting grounds south of the river.

Micah Summerday entered the swirl and touched noses with each wolf in turn, his aquamarine eyes bright. Then he opened his throat and roared, "Blood Father is awake! Summerday, run!" The wolves took off at a dead run for the Delf River. Only the Shaman with the injured jaw and the two yearling cubs stayed behind.

The Summerday Clan flowed over the land like droplets racing down a windowpane. Sephora and Aliyah were the fastest, their long golden legs flying over the ground. The other females were close behind. Micah, Alaric, and the other full-golden males, heavier and slower, were in the next wave. And the half-golden and lone males came a few yards after. The entire murder of crows from the Spires flew low and fast behind them, silent and black.

In less than half an hour, the wolves reached a copse of trees on the top of a hill overlooking the Delf and stood panting. The crows settled down on bushes close to the ground, so as not to draw attention from afar. Down at the river, they could see the wolves of the Icewind Pack struggling to cross the icy white water. Several had successfully crossed and were milling around on the bank not far from where the Summerday Clan stood. Many were in the midst of the crossing, with some having been swept a hundred yards or more downstream. And the rest were on the far shore, calling and yipping.

Micah faced them all, breathing heavily. "On this day, we are defending our home. On another day, *we* could be the refugees. It is not their fault, but it *is* their time. What say you, wolves?"

"Blood Father is awake!" growled the other members of the clan.

Micah raised his head to the sky for a long moment, his eyes closed and his enormous canine teeth shining in the sun as a low rumbling note poured out of his throat, so quiet it could just barely be heard. All the other wolves growled a drone harmony in the same hushed tone, the males sounding the third of the chord and the females singing on the fifth.

Then Micah lowered his head, opened his eyes, and whispered, "Summerday, kill!"

The clan burst out of hiding and streaked toward the wolves on the riverbank, running in complete silence. The slower and heavier males ran in the center of the line. The faster females ran on the wings, casting a wide net. The Icewind wolves looked up, and suddenly a slew of barks and growls poured forth. Four large males stood their ground, several other Icewind wolves retreated toward the river. The wolves on the far bank plunged into the water.

The eleven Summerday wolves hit the four standing wolves like a wave hitting a sand sculpture. The Icewind wolves disappeared under a sea of teeth and claws, and a terrible storm of cries and howls poured forth. The Summerday females circled around and closed the net. The fight was fierce, and fought with lightning speed. In less than a minute, one of the Summerday wolves lay still and bleeding on the ground. And two minutes later, the four Icewind wolves lay with their lifeblood draining into the sandy soil.

The Summerday killing scrum moved on to the Icewind wolves struggling at the edge of the river, some backing into the water, others trying to climb out. One by one, they were dispatched, ruthlessly, quickly. Soon, more than half the Icewind wolves were dead. The others in the river were retreating toward the far bank.

The Summerday Clan, familiar with the river, ran to the best crossing spot where a line of boulders broke the worst of the current. They picked their way across quickly, and only Least Wolf was swept downstream.

As they reached the far bank, the Icewind Clan was scattering, racing away from the river in ones and twos. The crows from the Spires divided into groups and followed them, cawing loudly, "Here! Here! Here!" so the Summerday wolves could easily follow them.

The Summerdays broke up into smaller groups to chase the stragglers, and Aliyah and Alaric found themselves running south after a pair of Icewind wolves who were trying desperately to lose themselves in the wood.

Grammy Kark, along with some of the other older crows from Spires, settled down on the carcasses of the dead Icewind wolves, emitting a torrent of greedy and excited croaks. "Thank you, golden child," she said as she plunged her beak into the exposed liver. "Your mother would be proud."

CORIANDER

It was late in the evening, and the sound of cicadas filled the air. When Coriander arrived at Bloody Thorn Warren, he found Olympia and Aiden in the *al fresco*[41] thorn chamber. They were lying side by side, munching on strawberries. Coriander noted that Darius was absent.

Olympia arose as he entered the chamber, the moonlight calling out the slash of white across her face and down her back. "Our beautiful boy," she said. "So hardworking. Do come and have a strawberry."

Aiden looked none too pleased. "Welcome, brother. Holy day."

"Every one a gift," said Coriander as he lolloped forward. "I have something to tell you."

"Speak," said Olympia.

"Another warren is joining with Anastasia's group," said Coriander.

"Oh, Yah … this is a *cancer*," said Aiden. His eyes flicked toward Olympia. "I mean, your beloved daughter is a … challenge. She has a lot of drive and a lot of smarts … like her mother."

"Mmm-hmm," said Olympia coolly. She lay down next to Coriander and nudged him with her hip. "What warren is it?"

"Tumble Stone," said Coriander.

"Never heard of it," said Olympia. "Is it around here?"

---

[41] Open air.

"It's new," said Coriander. "They came across the Shandy a few months ago."

"Why are they doing this?" asked Aiden.

"They're afraid of Blessed," said Coriander. "People from *Sans Gloire* are helping them fortify right now."

"Loved One protect us," said Aiden. "We've got to take action *now*. Before this … challenge … spreads across—"

"Could be an opportunity," said Olympia.

Aiden dropped down beside her, casually touching her outstretched foot. "How, Honored One?"

"*Sans Gloire* is pretty well fortified now. Hard to get in. If this other place is just starting—Rumble Bone or whatever—"

"Tumble Stone," said Coriander.

Olympia looked at him for a long moment without speaking.

"Sorry I interrupted, Warren Mother," said Coriander humbly.

"If this other place is just getting started now, it'll take them awhile," said Olympia. "If something bad happens to them, it could scare off anyone else who might be thinking of joining."

"*Could* something bad happen to them?" asked Aiden.

Olympia got up and lolloped over to the strawberries. "Who can plumb the depths of Yah's terrible pleasures?"

Chapter 11

During the last days of the Dominion, the Dead Gods worshipped raccoons. Every night, they put out offerings of food for their raccoon overlords, sealed in altars of precious chewystone.

—Thimble Thimbalian, History of the Known World

DEATH RAGE

It was dawn at the straightstone burrow. Bricabrac was choosing the best twigs to use for the nail-tipped spears. A large crew of Musmuski mice was grinding the rust off the nails using flat pieces of sandstone. Death Rage, Exit Wound, and another group of mice were busy splitting the tips of the twigs, inserting the butt ends of the nails, and then binding the split twig tips tightly with agave fiber to hold the nails in place. The sharp tang of newly-sharpened metal hung in the air with the aromatic scent of worked wood.

Bricabrac glanced over at the mice. "You don't need to spend too much time on that," he said. "Just make the nails snug."

Exit Wound, now with bright-red spider lily stamens entwined around her tail, cast a quick glance at Bricabrac. "Weapons should be beautiful. I'm using the same braid on this agave fiber that I use on my spider lilies."

"It doesn't need to be beautiful. It just needs to work," said Bricabrac.

"She *wants* to be beautiful," said Exit Wound, her fine fingers flying around the spear she was making. "She wants to feel pretty when she punctures a vital organ of my enemy."

Bricabrac took a long look at Exit Wound. "You're scaring me," he said, good-humoredly.

"That's because you're not a fighter, you're a craftrat," said Exit Wound. "It matters to me how my enemies die. I want to show them the respect of killing them with a beautiful weapon."

"You are bad, grrl," said Death Rage.

Bricabrac chuckled. "Remind me to stay on your good side."

Freddie and Nicodemus were examining the gyrfalcon claw that Freddie always wore around his neck. Both were intent and focused, ears forward, speaking quietly. Death Rage crept in between them to see what they were talking about.

"Anastasia told me that this claw worked well as an improvised weapon during the weasel attack," said Nicodemus. "I think you may have stumbled onto a real principle of weaponry here."

"How?" asked Freddie.

"Since rabbits don't have hands, we can't hold weapons," said Nicodemus. "So we can make spears and whatnot for rats, mice and squirrels, but not for ourselves. That's unfortunate, since they're small-fry."

"Small what?" said Death Rage.

Nicodemus ignored her. "A rabbit could use a much bigger weapon, and apply more force, but we can't carry it. Only something with complex mechanics like Anastasia's Claw works for a limb-based weapon."

"But something held in the mouth ..." said Freddie.

"Opens a whole new class of weaponry. And wearing it around the neck, as you were with the gyrfalcon claw, keeps it always available. It was a brilliant improvisation, Freddie. You're a natural fighter."

Freddie glowed with pleasure, and the rabbits went on to discuss a new kind of sword, which they could make from all the exploded steel cans. They dubbed them *bite blades*.

Death Rage, a little hungry, scampered out into the gray dawn to look for something to eat. She found nothing near the doorway, so her steps led her toward the meadow lined with trees in hopes of turning up some grass seeds.

As she foraged, nosing under leaves, she continually glanced up, scanning the sky for raptors. Suddenly, she saw a gray hawk drifting over the tree tops. She immediately scuttled under a nearby thistle, peering out cautiously between the spiky leaves.

It was early for a hawk to be out hunting. The sun had not yet risen. This was really owl time. Death Rage watched as the hawk assumed a landing glide path. With a start, she realized it was holding a little creature in its claws. She stared. Why was a hawk landing with prey in its talons? Then she noticed the creature was not struggling. As the hawk got closer, she could see the long naked tail drooping down. So, likely a rat. And since it wasn't struggling, a dead rat.

The hawk came down within fifty feet of her, and opened its claws. Death Rage was amazed to see the rat stand up, say something to the hawk, and scamper away. *What the—?* The hawk took off, and banked in a tight circle, heading back the way it had come, toward the Boreal Cliffs.

The rat was heading in the general direction of the straightstone burrow. Something about her dark-brown top-fur and reddish-brown underbelly looked familiar. Within a few seconds, the rat was near the thistle and noticed Death Rage hunkered down under a leaf. As she scampered over, Death Rage saw she was wearing a copper earring in her left ear.

The rat ran straight to Death Rage and flashed a friendly smile. "Have you seen a rat around here who looks like me? Goes by the name 'Bricabrac.'"

COYOTES

It was now many days since the coyotes of Clan *Paresseux* had made their attack on Warren *Sans Gloire*. In spite of their enthusiastic beginning, and Gaetan's plan, they had not gone back to hit the rabbits again the next day. Or the day after. They didn't say it, or even really think it, but they were afraid. They had been injured by rabbits, and that threatened to bring their whole worldview down. So every day, they found reasons not go, and hunted unarmed rabbits instead. But for animals used to a steady diet of deer, with smaller animals as an occasional garnish, it was thin going.

So they found themselves here, at the edge of Stranglethorn, looking hungrily through the ring of thorn trees at the apple grove within. Lilou sidled forward, wearing her most pleasant expression. Her eye was almost healed from being stabbed, but it was still partly blurry. At last, she caught sight of a raccoon she knew, sorting apples under a copse of Mangrove Jacks.

"Hey, Pam!" she called. "Can I ask you for a favor?"

Lorazepam looked up from her fruit piles and ambled toward the ring of thorn trees that surrounded the precious apple orchard with a protective wall. She recognized Lilou as one of Clan *Paresseux*, enthusiastic customers of her fermented apples.

"What do you need, honey?" she called.

Lilou dropped down in a casual bow. "Sorry to bug you," she said with an embarrassed half-smile, "but hunting is so bad now, and we're a *little* hungry. Most of the fruit won't be ripe for another month. So ... the boys and I are wondering if we could have some of your leftover apples?"

"Aw, sorry to hear that," said Lorazepam, wiping her hands on the grass.

"Just whatever you're not going to use. They're too proud to ask, of course," said Lilou, with a little eye-roll.

"Aren't they always," said Lorazepam, with a wheezy chuckle.

"Yeah," said Lilou, joining in the laugh. "So ... would you have any?"

"I'm just sorting the midsummer crop," said Lorazepam.

"Pulling out the ones that aren't sweet enough. I'll bring some over."

"Thank you so much," said Lilou. "I really—well, *we* really—owe you one."

A few minutes later, Lorazepam was threading her way along the twisting path through the thorny hedge that made it hard for any creature larger than a raccoon to enter. Behind her, she was a pulling a *travois* half-full of yellow and brown apples.

When she came out into the open, she spilled the apples out on the grass, and Lilou fell on them eagerly. At that, Benoit, Edouard, and a dozen other coyotes came spilling out of the scrubby oaks where they had been loitering.

As they trotted forward, Benoit, still favoring his front left paw, called out, "Pam, those Yellow Bellies we got from Wellbutrin were *magnifiques*.[42]"

"Thank you," said Lorazepam, flashing her snaggle-toothed smile.

Edouard shouted. "Pam, Pam, Pammy! The flavor of your Mangrove Jacks: *J'en ai l'eau à la bouche*.[43] Like summer stars in rich organ fat."

"Now you're just buttering my bickies," said Lorazepam. She winked at Lilou. "But I like to see my

---

[42] Magnificent.

[43] My mouth is watering.

coyboys enjoying their food. Don't forget to thank Lilou for doing the sweet-talking." She picked up her empty *travois* and headed back through the thorn hedge.

A few minutes later, the coyotes were still gorging on the apples when Gaetan appeared from behind a patch of northern chaparral.

"Well, looky here," he called, smirking, as he limped toward them. "I believe I see a bunch of killers enjoying—what?—a fresh fruit salad? How fierce of you."

"It's cool," said Edouard around a mouthful of apple mush. "They screamed when they died."

Gaetan touched noses with his sister, and nuzzled her neck. Then he picked up an apple and lay down to crunch it. "Guess what, you *crottes*?[44]" he said. "You know those rabbits that gimped you out? Now there's going to be twice as many of them."

Benoit jerked his head around to glare at Gaetan. "What?"

"You heard me," said Gaetan. His eyes flicked down to Benoit's front paw, still not healed after being savaged by a brown rabbit with a blade. "They gave you a little taste of being a crip like me, didn't they? Well, now there's going to be more. A lot more."

---

[44] Turds.

Benoit's eyes narrowed and his lips curled. A low growl rumbled out. "What are you talking about, *blaireau?*[45] "

"A second warren is joining up. That means they're gonna have all the same weapons. Soon."

"Holy crap, it's happening," said Edouard. "What if all the warrens do this?"

"That's why we need to act fast," said Gaetan. "If we don't shut this one down, there's gonna be another one. Then another one. No more rent, *ever*. We need to hit this new warren *now*. I got the dope on what and where."

Benoit eyed him. "Where'd you get all this info?"

Gaetan sucked his teeth. "Friend of a friend."

CORIANDER

Coriander had spent the night at Bloody Thorn Warren. When he awoke, he heard singing coming from the under-hall. He made his way into the chamber to find Olympia, Darius, and Aiden presiding over a ceremony. The whole warren was gathered around Sunbeam and five other beautiful little kits, each about four or five months old.

Sunbeam radiated joy as she sang proudly with the others in her bright, girlish voice:

---

[45] Literally, "badger." Figuratively, "Jerk."

"Oh, how I love my Blessed One,
My Blessed One loves me,
Together we shall live in love,
And I will never flee."

Then the whole congregation joined in:

"The Flowers of our loving Yah,
Shine brighter than the sun,
We hold them in our hearts with love,
And they will never run."

Startled, Coriander scanned the crowd of rabbits. Briar and others were beaming. Sweet Leaf was looking at the kits with an "aww" expression. Other rabbits looked uneasy. A few looked distraught.

The singing came to an end and Olympia stepped forward. "Thank you, everyone, for joining us here as we celebrate the corrected teaching of Yah with our first class of novices being inducted into the new order of Yah's Flowers!"

The triple-thump of affirmation filled the underhall. Olympia embraced the new flowers one by one. She hugged Sunbeam last. As Coriander approached, he heard Olympia whisper to her, "Remember, darling, don't go beyond the acacia trees."

"Yes, Honored Mother," said Sunbeam sweetly.

Then Olympia noticed him and laid her chin in the earth so he could kiss her forehead. "What new wonder is this, Warren Mother?" asked Coriander.

Olympia rose and shepherded him toward her private chambers, with Aiden and Darius following. When they were alone, she and Aiden explained the new teaching about the Blessed that had come recently from the Lord Harmonizer, and the reasons for their creation of Yah's Flowers.

Coriander was shocked. "But ... these beautiful babies ... will ..." he couldn't finish the sentence.

Aiden leaned toward him. "Don't question the Warren Mother," he murmured. "She and I know things that you don't."

Olympia nuzzled his cheek. "It's okay, it's okay," she said. "As long as they stay inside the Ring of Love, they'll be perfectly safe."

"But the Flowers at the other warrens ..." Coriander began.

Olympia clucked sympathetically. "Yes, that's sad. This is the world that Yah has made. We live in a sad, sad world."

"That's why we need our faith to sustain us," said Darius cheerfully. "Say, did Briar bring in any of those midsummer figs?"

TUMBLE STONE WARREN

Tumble Stone Warren was filled with rabbits and mice from Warren *Sans Gloire*, building gratings, sharpening sticks, and demonstrating the use of bite blades to the local bunnies.

Bricabrac trotted down a main passage, his arms full of supplies. Death Rage came out of a side passage and fell into place alongside him, carrying the pencil sharpener. "Hey, I wanna ask you something," said Death Rage. "Recently I was out early, and I saw an owl come by and land. And then he drops off a live rat, who then asks me if I've seen you. What is that? How …?"

"Oh, that's my sister, Frippery," Bricabrac chuckled. "I've gotten so overloaded with work I asked her to come out from Oom. It'd take her forever to get here on foot. I had the money, so I brought her out on Raptor Air."

"What is that?" said Death Rage.

"Got ten cents? You can hire a raptor," said Bricabrac. "If you have one of these." He flicked his copper earring. "That's your pass."

"Why don't they just eat you?"

"My earring says I'm a craftrat, from City of Oom. So I have protected status," said Bricabrac. "The hardest part is calling them down without getting killed. You can't just yell at a hawk half a mile up. They can't hear you. So you have to go in the open and act injured. Then they'll dive for you. At the last second, you yell out the password." Bricabrac smiled. "Then you give them a dime."

"You … make deals with Blessed?" stuttered Death Rage. "But they … live to kill us."

Bricabrac stopped and looked at Death Rage. "Don't go all country mouse on me," he said, not unkindly. "There's a lot that goes on in this world that doesn't fit in with lunchmeat religions."

"Lunchmeat?" said Death Rage.

Bricabrac looked embarrassed. "Oh, that's what the Blessed call us." He shrugged. "Ya, I guess it's kind of harsh. You didn't know that?"

"No," said Death Rage. She put down the pencil sharpener and sat on it. "But how can we do business with killers who murder our friends? How is that honorable?"

"We do what's needed to survive," said Bricabrac. "And then we move on. There's honor in that."

"Really?" said Death Rage.

"It's a tough world," said Bricabrac. "Rats is for rats. That's good enough for me."

Dingus passed them going in the opposite direction. He had just finished putting the final touches on the deep warren nut storage areas. He had been running around so much, he had left his spear somewhere. Now he was going to do the final tidying on the nut room at the other end of the warren. It was a temporary storage space, more of a cupboard, really. Easy to miss from the main passage.

Dingus jogged down the passageway. *Where's that dang spear?* The tiny room was near one of the open entryways. He arrived, slipped through the low doorway, and started cleaning. *I'll find it later.*

For a few minutes, he was lost in thought, thinking about nut sizes and stacking patterns. Then there was an odd motion in the corner of his eye. He ignored it. And then there was another. Then another. *That's weird.* He turned to look, and realized why it seemed strange. Animals were going past. Animals that didn't move like rabbits or mice. Or squirrels. He froze, and when the next creature went by, he saw the rolling shimmy, and the deadly reek hit his nose. *Weasel.*

His heart dropped into his toes. What to do? He did not even have his spear, little good that would do against an army of weasels anyway. In the distance, he heard screams and yells begin. Then he realized no weasels had gone by for a good many seconds. He stole a peek into the hallway. Empty. The light of the entryway was so bright and inviting. What was he doing down here anyway?

The screams were louder. He thought he could hear Freddie and others shouting orders. He should go help with the fight. But what could he do? He had no spear. Plus, he was a tree-dwelling animal. A lookout, really. If he had been up in the trees where he belonged, he could have given warning. This whole tragic disaster had been caused by a squirrel being out of place.

He darted into the passage, and a few seconds later was out in the bright sunlight, on the grassy area in front of the warren. He was still dazzled by the sudden transition when a huge shape loomed out of the brightness like a dirty gray-brown cloud, and he realized he was looking at a set of jaws larger than he was, and they were coming right at him.

In the instant between life and death, all four of his hands gripped the grass stems under him and he jerked himself sideways. The jaws slammed shut just inches away from him, but he was already gone, skimming like a speed racer over the patchy ground toward the nearest tree. And then he was forty feet up, heart pounding like a hummingbird's wings, and breath coming in ragged gasps.

As he caught his breath, he stared downward, and he could see there were eight or ten coyotes, running from hole to hole, excitedly calling to each other and digging at the holes. There were also two foxes standing in ready position by one of the entryways. He saw a white weasel back out of one of the holes and then dart over to another hole.

A large brindle rabbit came bursting out of one of the open entryways and ran as hard as he could for a nearby patch of thorny scrub. Dingus recognized him as Dogwood, a Tumble Stone buck that he had come to know. His eyes were wide and white. A coyote wheeled to intercept him and was within a few feet when Dingus looked away.

He started for the safety of his own oak tree above Warren *San Gloire*, keeping to tree branches the whole way. As he ran, angry half-coherent thoughts banged in his mind. *What is squirrel doing on ground? Tree is place for squirrel. Ground is death. Tree is life. Stupid stupid stupid!*

After a few minutes, this had coalesced into a chant that he yelled in his head as he raced through the trees toward home.

> *"Squirrel on ground?*
> *Why why why?*
> *Ground is where*
> *Squirrel go to die."*

At last he reached his tree, and plunged into the darkness of his hole in the trunk. He crouched there, surrounded by the cozy clutter of his familiar things, soft moss, nuts, leaves, pieces of fruit, shiny stones, some twigs he was gnawing on, and the page that Freddie had given him that said "… oga for kids" on it, leaning against the wall.

He was in agony from the receding adrenaline burn, and so angry at himself for leaving the trees that he swore he would never leave them again, over and over. *Fie on those stupid rabbits.* And as he hunkered down, hot and panting, the page of "oga" slowly leaned down and enfolded him in a cool and comforting embrace.

Chapter 12

It was the rats who first learned to read. And the first word they learned was 'poison.'
—Rattus Rattus, Book of Gnawledge

ALIYAH

Aliyah Summerday and her brother, Alaric, caught up with the first of the Icewind wolves they were chasing in less than two hours. The fight was short. When the newly dead wolf lay still on the grass, the Summerday wolves gathered white roses and scattered them on the body.

As the ranking wolf present, Aliyah spoke the funeral words as the light floral scent wafted upward. *"The death of any wolf is a sad day for all wolves. We fought as adversaries, but we bid you farewell as cousins. May your hunting be fine in the Forever Forest."*

"*Blood Father turns his face from you. Hunger Mother forgets you,*" said Alaric. Then he lifted his head and let a long, sad howl pour out. Aliyah joined him, and their voices entwined in a soaring *pas de deux*[46] of the mourning cry. Every creature within miles knew that a wolf had died.

That done, they touched noses and took up the hunt again, still heading south. And the crows circling overhead descended on the body.

After a few miles, they were very far down the Million Acre Wood, and were within sight of the Shandy. They lost the trail at the river's edge. "It doesn't matter," said Aliyah. "Icewind is over, and the lones will disperse. We've completed the dance."

Alaric's yellow eyes drifted along the river bank until he saw something unusual. "Look," he said, "a scruffy little coyote is coming this way. Looks to be injured."

Aliyah glanced down the bank. "O that one. He always limps. Born with it or something."

The coyote spotted them and started to jog toward them, awkwardly, ears high and happy. Aliyah noticed he looked thinner than the last time she had seen him.

"Running with a limp is so sad," said Alaric.

---

[46] Literally, "step of two." A ballet dance for two dancers.

The coyote came within earshot. "Hey, what luck seeing you here," he called. "I was coming up north in hopes for running into you." He arrived at the hillock they were standing on. "My Lady Aliyah Summerday," he said, with a deep bow. "My Lord Alaric," said the coyote, and bowed again. "A message from Clan *Paresseux*."

"Do I know you?" asked Alaric.

"Yes, my Lord," said Gaetan. "I was at the Shaman's Conclave last year. We talked about the best times to hunt, as revealed by the night sky."

"Right, right," said Alaric, vaguely.

"I've come with important news that the Summerdays should know, as Landlords of the Million Acre Wood."

"Yes?" said Aliyah, already feeling a little bored.

"A new rabbit warren joined the rabbits who have been attacking Blessed—"

This again? thought Aliyah. Seemed like this crippled coyote was always excitedly delivering "messages" about trivial topics. *Bit of a stalker, this one.*

"As your agents, when the rabbits' rental payments were clearly in arrears, Clan *Paresseux* launched a disciplinary action. We brought weasels with us to serve the collection notice, on behalf of the Summerdays—" Gaetan paused and bowed deeply. "And what we discovered would make your hair stand up."

"Okay, what?" sighed Aliyah.

"The rabbits had sharpy-cutty things in their mouths," said Gaetan, the words rushing out. "They had mouse allies with long pokey-stabby things. Most of the entrances were blocked with sticks woven together. The weasels could not get in, and the lunchmeat hurt them with pokey-stabbies that they pushed through the stick gratings, so the weasels couldn't tear them down."

"Whoa, slow down, boy," said Alaric.

"Sorry, my Lord," said Gaetan. He took a deep breath. "Finally, some of the weasels found a way in. And when they did their sweep, *the lunchmeat attacked them.* Some of them were injured. They were driven back."

"Weasels? Preposterous. They were *born* to serve collection notices," said Alaric.

"My Lord, my Lady," said Gaetan. "I know this is hard to believe. That's why I brought you this." He ducked his head into his carrying pouch that he usually used for moneystones, and pulled out a shiny new blade that had just been made at the straightstone burrow a few days before.

The curved blade gleamed in the sun as Gaetan held it between his teeth and turned it this way and that. Aliyah and Alaric were stunned into silence.

The long silent moment dragged on. After many seconds, Gaetan lay the blade down on a nearby rock, and all three of the canids looked at it intently.

Finally, Aliyah spoke. "A *rabbit* made this?"

"Yes, Third She."

"How did you get this?" asked Aliyah.

"A weasel brought it out of the warren when they retreated."

Somewhere in the distant recesses of Aliyah's mind, an alarm bell was beginning to sound, very faintly. *The luncheon meat are arming themselves.* The fortunes of many a noble house have turned on whether or not they could hear this bell when it rang. She was just about to speak when Alaric chuckled.

"Their god Yah gave them no weapons, so now they're making their own," said Alaric. "Cute." He laughed. "Rabbits, weasels, what did you say, mice? There's a lot going on down there, six inches from the ground."

"My Lord," said Gaetan. "These rabbits have managed to injure coyotes as well."

"Well, that *is* a shame," said Alaric, not unkindly. "I'm sure you do the best you can with what you have, but, let's face it, coyotes don't—"

"Hush!" said Aliyah, sharply. Alaric looked shocked, but as he was outranked, he held his tongue. To Gaetan, she said, "Clan Summerday thanks you for this important information. With your leave, I will take this weapon and present it to the Clan Mother and Clan Father. They will know what to do."

"Yes, yes, certainly," said Gaetan, doing his best not to

wag. His scent was suddenly much brighter. "Thank you so much for your kind words, My Lady. It means a lot to a hungry coyote."

Aliyah stepped forward and touched noses with him. Alaric watched stonily. "Thank you, Gaetan," she said. "I'm sure I'll see you again."

Gaetan bowed deeply. "Thank you again, Third She of the Summerday Clan and Golden Spirit of the Million Acre Wood—"

"Good *day*, boy," interrupted Alaric.

Gaetan began to turn, and then remembered his manners. "And thank *you*, my Lord," he said, bowing to Alaric. Then he headed out at a brisk trot, head held high.

Alaric lay down and smirked at Aliyah. "Well, aren't you the ministering angel," he said. "The golden girl with the common touch."

Anastasia

It was another busy day at the straightstone burrow. Among the tools of the Dead Gods, the animals had found a pair of metal shears. With much effort, they had managed to wedge the shears among the foundation stones in such a way that they could cut and shape pieces of the exploded cans into bite blades for the rabbits. Freddie had even rigged up a rather ingenious counterweight so that it could easily be operated by the mice. So the cramped space under the floorboards of the collapsed building was beginning to take on the look of a medieval machine shop.

Anastasia came through the doorway, having just arrived from *Sans Gloire,* and took her place in a circle with Freddie, Nicodemus, Love Bug, Wendy, Death Rage and Bricabrac. An elegant young water rat with dark-brown fur and a reddish-brown underbelly approached from the shadows where she had been working. Like Bricabrac, she wore a copper earring in her ear.

"Have you met my sister, Frippery?" said Bricabrac. "I brought her out from City of Oom on Raptor Air."

"So I heard," said Anastasia, who stepped forward and touched noses with Frippery. "That takes some nerve, trusting your body to a raptor."

"It has its downsides," said Frippery, with a tinkling laugh. "But if you're a craftrat, you're trained to do it from an early age. Gotta go where the customers are." She looked at Bricabrac. "Am I right?"

"Rats is right," said Bricabrac, and then they did a complicated hand thing that included a mixture of high-fiving, patty-cake, and finger snaps.

"Welcome," said Anastasia. Frippery bowed and returned to her work. "Now," Anastasia continued, "be sure you do the memorial service tomorrow with Tumble Stone Warren. And keep up the training with bite blades for their rabbits, as fast as we can make them. They need to know that we are helping them, not just bringing Blessed down on their heads. And, Love Bug, be sure to tell them how sorry I am."

"Yes, *Femme Avisee,*[47]" said Love Bug.

Nicodemus nose-bumped Anastasia's flank. "I'm not sure this trip is a good idea, little one," he said.

Love Bug looked at Nicodemus. "The word from Tumble Stone is that weasels were asking for Anastasia *by name,*" he said. "She needs more protection."

Bricabrac said, "I need the tools and materials on my ship to make this new gear for her."

"I know," said Nicodemus. "I'm just worried."

"A small party is best to avoid notice," said Bricabrac. "We'll travel fast and light, and she'll come back safer."

Anastasia nuzzled Nicodemus' cheek. "Thank you for all your loving care, old friend. I'll be back before you know it."

Nicodemus nodded. "I just … don't want the world to lose you," he whispered, and walked away into the shadows.

"Okay," said Bricabrac, tightening the straps on Anastasia's backpack, and then his own. "I think we're ready."

---

[47] Wise Woman.

"Sorry I don't have more time to make arrangements," said Anastasia, touching noses with each of them in turn. "I'll be back in a few days. *Sans Gloire* is in your hands."

TUMBLE STONE WARREN

The underhall at Tumble Stone was packed with rabbits from both warrens. Mabel, the second Remembering acolyte, stood in the center, a wreath of dark funeral flowers on her head and a piece of orange and brown striped sandstone between her front paws. "Dogwood was not just our Door Warden, he was my friend," she said. "He fought bravely against both weasel and wolf, and died with honor."

She stopped and looked down, eyes wet. The sweet scent of her flowers wafted through the chamber. Everyone could hear the sound of a young rabbit crying on the far side of the hall.

Mabel held up the smooth piece of sandstone. "Whenever we gather in this hall, and we see this brindle river stone, we will remember our friend." She turned and pressed it into the earthen wall. All the rabbits did the slow triple-thump of affirmation.

The other Tumble Stone rabbits then said their memorial words and pressed stones into the wall of the underhall. Each time, all the rabbits in the room offered their affirmation through the heavy triple thump.

Then Love Bug rose. "Warren Mother, Prime Buck, friends, allies," he said. "Our Loving Auntie, Anastasia, wants to share her deepest sorrow at this tragedy befalling your warren."

The Tumble Stone Warren Mother nodded. Then she asked Mabel to lead the group in song. So Mabel lifted her voice and led the congregation of rabbits through the ancient rabbit end-of-life hymn.

> *"Now then rabbit, rabbit in the morning,*
> *Strong and bold and bright are you,*
> *Now then rabbit, rabbit in the noon time,*
> *With your children, sweet and true.*
>
> *Now then rabbit, rabbit in the evening,*
> *Kind and patient, wise are you,*
> *Now then rabbit, rabbit in the night time,*
> *Soon you'll sleep ..."*

Her voice soared here on a long and intricate melisma.

> *"...and the world begins anew."*

After the singing, a long silence descended. Then Wendy's voice rumbled through the room. "Sad for dead bunnies," she said. "Now time to fight for live bunnies."

The Tumble Stone Prime Buck growled and sat up straight, his tortoiseshell fur glowing a sullen orange. "All these new ... ways," he said. "That's what brought down the Blessed Ones down on us like earthfall after a heavy rain. Many friends have died. Now you want to stir the hornet's nest even more?" There were many murmurings of assent. "I've got half a mind to dump this alliance and go our own way."

Wendy sat up as well, her claw necklace jangling. "How many raptors you see fight?"

"What difference does that make?" growled the Prime Buck.

"How many?" barked Wendy.

"None," said the Tumble Stone Warren Mother. The Prime Buck started to speak, and she laid her paw on his.

Wendy turned and looked at her. "Why?"

The Warren Mother hesitated in answering, so Death Rage piped up, "Because we beat the crap out of a gyrfalcon."

The Prime Buck looked irritated. A silence fell. Wendy shambled out into the open space in the center of the room. She turned in a circle and her gaze swept the room, then her obsidian eyes settled on the Tumble Stone rabbits. "Want live?" she rumbled. "We need make ground killers fear us."

"We hurt some of the coyotes when they attacked *Sans Gloire*," said Freddie. "We've showed them we can do damage."

"Not enough," said Wendy. "Time put fear in their hearts. *Le bhith a 'marbhadh.*[48]" She stood up, stretching out her hind legs and reaching up to press her front paws against the roof of the underhall. With her long ears and loose skin, she looked like a huge, baggy rabbit scarecrow from another world. Her scent was like dust and ashes, and her rumbling voice filled the room. *"We need kill a coyote."*

There was a long moment of shocked silence, then Coriander said, "No. *Totally* against the Word of Yah."

The Tumble Stone Prime Buck bristled. "You're not listening to me. I said we need to do *less* stirring up of the Blessed, not *more!*"

"Is that even possible?" asked another rabbit. "I've never heard of that happening, even in stories."

"Yah's teeth," said a fourth rabbit, all his fur standing up. "Why are we listening to her? She's not even a rabbit."

"Silence!" shouted Freddie. He ran into the center of the room and stood directly under the skylight where the beam of light shone down and picked out the gray in his fur and made it gleam. He raised his paws. The room quieted. "There's no argument here," he said, his voice quiet but penetrating. "The main reason not to do this is that Anastasia would *not* want us to. And you know that." He turned to glare at Wendy. "You *know* that."

---

[48] By killing.

Wendy looked back at him, her dark eyes unreadable. For a few moments, her rumbling breathing was the loudest noise in the room. "She very nice lady," said Wendy, "but she not here now. Lives of rabbits in *our* hands."

"This is the world that Yah has made. Anastasia wants us to find a way to live *with* the Blessed," said Freddie. "She gave us hope. Showed us we can fight back at the right time, in the right way." He came close to Wendy, his eyes locked onto hers. "Don't destroy her work just because you think killing is always the answer."

Wendy sucked her teeth, nodding her head a little. "You very good boy," she said. "I like you." Then she shook her head, flapping her huge ears. "Killing Blessed wrong? Let's ask these bunnies."

Her gaze raked the room. A hush fell over the group.

There was a long pause. Finally, Holly spoke up. She took a step forward, so everyone could see that her front leg had been bitten off below the shoulder. "Blessed took my leg," she said, her voice small and shaky. "If they had the chance, they would take my kittens and crush the life from them. I love Anastasia, but ... I would kill a Blessed One if I could."

Her words fell like stones into a big, empty space. They made a splash, then receded to silence. Then Juniper stepped forward. When she spoke, her voice was sweet and girlish. "Blessed Glorified my mother, who kissed me to sleep at night. Blessed Glorified my brother, Chervil, who was my last family in the world. I loved him. I would … I want … to kill a Blessed One."

Death Rage drew the Kiss of Death and stepped into the center. "If you are a mouse," she said, "you've seen whole families murdered in a few moments. For us to Glorify a coyote will be hard. It will be an honorable fight." She somersaulted over her rapier and landed on one knee in front of Freddie. "Like you, Anastasia is my hero. So it is with sadness I speak this truth. I want to kill a Blessed."

Mabel stepped into the light. Coriander, a fellow Remembering acolyte, glared at her. "Blessed Glorified my friend, Dogwood," she said. "And I will say this: There is *no* verse in the Word of Yah that forbids rabbits from Glorifying Blessed." She performed an elaborate shrug. "I guess it never came up." A gasp and a shocked, nervous chuckle ran through the assembled rabbits. The Tumble Stone Prime Buck stared daggers at her. Mabel looked away from him. "It's time to kill a Blessed One."

The Tumble Stone Warren Mother sat up and spread her forepaws. "All my life, I've lived in terror of the Blessed Ones. These new ways are dangerous, and ya, the Blessed hit us hard. We've got two choices—lay down or fight back. Anyone who knows me knows which one I'll do." She chewed her foreclaw. "Let's kill a Blessed."

Then it was Love Bug's turn. He was sitting next to

Mabel. Freddie looked at him with beseeching eyes. Love Bug avoided looking at him. "*La Belle Dame* saved my life. And I'll never forget that. But I was the first one to speak to the rabbits at Tumble Stone Warren." Mabel's ear tip softly caressed his ear as he spoke. "The Tumble Stone rabbits are now our family. The Blessed attacked them because of their connection to *us*. And many a noble rabbit was Glorified that day. If we don't fight for them now, we are not worthy of the name of 'ally.'" His eyes flicked over to Freddie. "I don't know how, but we are going to kill a Blessed One."

AIDEN

It was meeting day for the Shandy Vale Conclave. The thirty-seven Rememberers of the warrens in the Shandy Vale area were gathered in their accustomed meeting spot. It was a collection of blackberry bushes that grew together in a spiky tangle with a cleared area in the center. A loud buzz of conversation filled the space, and a blue dragonfly flicked through the thorns. The sweet smell of berries hung in the warm air.

Aiden was among them, trying not to look nervous. He greeted his colleagues in a steady stream of "Holy day. Holy day. Holy day. Every one a gift."

Olympia strode into the space, wearing her badge of

office as Presiding Spirit: a woven crown of forget-me-nots. Her scent was bright and cheerful.

She called the Conclave to order, and immediately the Rememberer of Grackle Beach Warren asked to speak. He had a patch of gray around his eye that made him look like he was wearing a monocle. She recognized him, and he stood. "Ahem, fellow keepers of the Word. We've been hearing about rabbits doing things that are truly terrible," he said. "Harming the Blessed. Desecrating their bodies. Fraternizing with squirrels."

"And *rats*," said the Rememberer of Warren *Frêne Rouge*.[49]

"All directly contravening the Word of Yah," harrumphed the Grackle Beach Rememberer. "This is heresy, plain and simple. We must find out *where* these rabbits came from, and trace the heresy *back* to its source. All heretics *must* be driven out, root and branch." He slapped his right paw onto his left as he spoke.

Aiden scanned the circle of rabbits. A lot of heads were nodding.

Olympia raised her paws for quiet. "My learned colleague," she said, "I agree with you completely. That is why the Shandy Vale Conclave has launched an investigation. We have planted spies in those despicable … warrens,

---

[49] Red Ash.

if that's what you want to call them. Soon, we will know the truth. And then we will take action with the full support of the Known World Symposium."

Aiden started the triple-thump of affirmation. At first, no one joined him. But by the second time through, most of the rabbits were on board. And by the third time, everyone was thumping, and there was some desultory cheering.

"Thank you, thank you all," said Olympia, smiling gravely.

"But what is happening right *now*?" persisted the Grackle Beach gentlebunny.

"Excellent question. Let's come back to that," said Olympia. "But first, I must tell you that the Lord Harmonizer himself has been here on an urgent mission that concerns all of us."

There was a smattering of "oohs" and "aahs." Everyone thought Tobias was very cool. Many of them wanted to *be* Tobias one day. Aiden focused on gazing at Olympia intently.

"Recall that the Known World Symposium asked our opinion recently on a certain verse," said Olympia. "The Lord Harmonizer let it be known that the true text of this verse has been discovered."

"Praise be to Yah," called Aiden.

"Our Rock and our Protector," answered the congregation, as one.

Olympia stood up tall, raised both her paws, and spread

her forelegs wide. "The true text is this: *And the Loved One said, Like you, when I see the Blessed, I feel a rapture in my heart. I am rooted to the Earth.*"

There was a long, stunned silence. Then, the Grackle Beach Rememberer spat the word, "*Rapture?*"

Immediately, a cacophony broke out as thirty-six rabbits all began talking at once. Aiden ducked his head and smiled to himself.

Olympia held up her paws for silence. "This harmonization is very … challenging. The implication is that there can be no running from Blessed. Ever."

There was more angry chatter and a smattering of groans from the crowd.

"So I worked with the Lord Harmonizer as to what the exact interpretation should be. We agreed that this teaching is *aspirational*. It will apply to a new generation of bunnies, not to old fogies like you and I."

The group noises sounded somewhat mollified.

"So rabbits in your warrens, under six months old, should be formed into a group called 'Yah's Flowers,' and trained to never run. We've started a pilot program at Bloody Thorn, and it's going swimmingly."

The crowd chatter took on a distinctly positive tone. Aiden half-smiled and half-rolled his eyes. *That was easy.*

"Praise be to Yah," said Aiden, behind his paw. "Praise be to Yah." Other rabbits started to pick up on it.

"Praise be to Yah!" called a few others in the group, as they slowly realized that they themselves were not going to be expected to offer their warm bodies to the jaws of the Blessed. "Praise be to Yah!" By the end, even the gentle-bunny from Grackle Beach had joined the cry. "Praise be to Yah!"

NICODEMUS

Mabel was leading the effort to integrate the Tumble Stone Rabbits into the *Sans Gloire* ways. So Nicodemus and Freddie were showing her and a delegation of Tumble Stone rabbits around the straightstone burrow, which had now become a large workshop. They gawked in astonished silence at the sight of so much organized industry.

Dozens of mice labored at tiny workstations, scaled to their size, and they sang lustily as they worked.

> *"Sing, hey, for the sword at the break of day!*
> *Sing ho, for the spear that you've come to know!*
> *Sing hi, for a blade in an enemy's eye!*
> *Sing hoo, for a rapier that's fine and true!"*

Nearby, other mice were weaving agave fiber gathered by rabbits into strong cords. Some were fashioning cured pine-apple skin into grips. A team of fifteen sturdy mice were cutting the steel cans into blades with the metal shears. Others were assembling these materials into bite blades, spears, and swords, which gleamed in the morning sun. The warm wispy smell of mice filled the air.

The Tumble Stone rabbits nudged each other and pointed. "What *is* this place?" asked Mabel.

Nicodemus nodded. "We had that question for a long time. There are a lot of pages here, and we've been going through them. Some are still bound into their original form. Books."

"Whole books?" said the Tumble Stone second Reading apprentice. "Are you serious? I thought they had all gone extinct."

"We have some," said Nicodemus, gravely, "and we've been reading them as best we can, although it's hard to understand what everything means. For example, here's a page that came from a book called *The End-of-the World Alphabet.*"

"C is for Climate,
Those idiots broke it,
Welcome to hell,
If you got any, smoke it."

"What does that mean?" asked Mabel.

Nicodemus shrugged. "We're not sure. Something bad was happening. This place is a 'cabin,' built by a Dead God who moved out from one of their cities. The upper part has long since collapsed. We're standing among the foundations, under the ruins of the lower floor." He cleared his throat. "Here's another page."

"D, Dengue Fever
Is now in Toronto,
Skin burning? Gums bleeding?
Well, say your prayers, pronto."

"We think Toronto was ... a major river," said the Reading apprentice.

"This is all new," said Mabel, as she turned around slowly, her forepaws indicating the whole space. "I'm a Rememberer, and I've racked my brains. The Word of Yah says nothing about anything like this. We are making new memories right now. One day, other rabbits will remember what we are doing here today."

"If we're lucky," said Nicodemus.

Next Freddie led the group outside. There was a small army of mice busy braiding the agave fiber cords into a still-thicker rope.

Wendy and Exit Wound sat huddled together, speaking quickly and making measurements with agave twine. Bricabrac's sister, Frippery, was standing near the center of the area, wrestling a length of rope into a knot. Her copper earring gleamed and her delicate hands fluttered around the ungainly knot like helpful butterflies.

Nicodemus looked at the Tumble Stone rabbits searchingly. "And here's where everything changes." He pulled down an ear and cleaned it. "Frippery!" he called. "Tell them what you're doing."

The rat raised her head, her look of concentration replaced by a ready grin. "Working on a sliding knot. We found half a picture in a Girl Scout Handbook. The other half was eaten by beetles."

Mabel hopped forward and sniffed at the rope. "Why do you need a sliding knot?"

Frippery looked at Nicodemus, who nodded. She stopped working, wiped her hands, and leaned against the coils of rope. "Sometimes, when you invite someone to dinner, you don't want them to ever go home."

ANASTASIA

It was a hot afternoon, and Anastasia and Bricabrac were resting under an azalea bush on the way to Bricabrac's ship on the Shandy River. The azalea blossoms smelled sweet, Bricabrac was asleep, and Anastasia's eyes were almost closed. Some mosquitoes buzzed nearby. It was a soothing, afternoon-y sound. She was close to dozing off when she noticed a strangely-shaped stump twenty yards away.

Immediately, she felt the *thrum* pulling her toward it. She tried to ignore it, but it was insistent, like an itch. Like an ache. She tried to push it down, but could not. She sniffed the air. No threats nearby. "Okay, okay, okay," she muttered to herself. "I'll go. Might learn something."

Anastasia looked around carefully, and then crept out from under the azalea and made her way to the stump. Just as she touched it, a hazy golden mist tickled her peripheral vision on her right. She swung her head just in time to see a massive gleaming shape come crashing through the scrub. From downwind. Her nails were already digging in, turning her body and launching it into flight when it became clear that the shape was a golden wolf, jaws open, accelerating forward.

Anastasia bolted back the way she had come. In a few seconds, she would be at the azalea, where Bricabrac lay sleeping.

"Bricabrac!" she yelled, breathless, as she sprinted. "Bricabrac, wolf!"

Then she was rushing past the azalea, with the wolf gaining ground on her at every step. Now she could feel the breath on her back. Should she turn and use the claw? Pointless. The wolf was too big. In its world, the Claw was a gnat. Just a few steps more and the jaws would be closing around her. It was all so sudden, she didn't even have time to grieve. She just felt sad and angry.

Ten yards behind her, she heard a little ratty voice yell, *"Olly olly oxen free!"*

The wolf immediately turned its head to the side, as though listening, and it slowed from a sprint to a trot. Bricabrac shouted again, *"Olly olly oxen free!"*

The wolf nodded now, slowing, turning. "Got it," she said. "Sorry, didn't see your pass." Anastasia continued sprinting for the horizon. In a few seconds, she would be out of earshot.

Bricabrac shouted out, "Auntie! It's okay! Come back, Auntie!"

Anastasia slowed and sat very still for a moment, under a spray of gorse, her breath coming in gasps, her heart pounding.

"Auntie, it's safe! I have my pass!" Anastasia remained frozen. And a few seconds later, she saw something she would remember for the rest of her life. The huge golden wolf came bounding through the scrub with Bricabrac *sitting on her back.*

As soon as the wolf caught sight of Anastasia, she stopped and bellied down. Bricabrac jumped down and ran over to Anastasia. He petted her head and stroked her neck to calm her down, then fiddled with the straps of her backpack, looking for all the world as though he was fussing over his mount.

"She's a little simple," Bricabrac called cheerily to the

wolf. "Auntie Slowpoke, I call her. Her mother had fever when she was in the womb. Very nice, gentle bunny. I use her to help me carry supplies. She just knows a few words," he slapped the back pack. "But she can carry ten times the load I can." Bricabrac turned to look at Anastasia. "Isn't that right, Auntie?"

Anastasia, her head whirling, managed to get out, "Mmm-hmmm."

"Okay, all good," said Bricabrac. "What can I do you for, Miz …?" He held out a hand toward the wolf.

The wolf laid her chin down on the ground like a friendly dragon. "Aliyah Summerday," she purred. "Third She and First Striker of the Summerday Clan, Landlords of the Million Acre Wood."

Anastasia started, but did her best not to show it. Her mind was racing. *A Summerday wolf!* Practically in her own backyard. And just as the stories said, she was golden. As golden as a late-summer chrysanthemum. And her eyes were as green as a spring leaf. But she was not killing her. She was *chatting*. Death Rage had told her about Bricabrac using a magic phrase to travel via raptor. Maybe this was something like that?

"Aliyah Summerday!" gasped Bricabrac. And he immediately started to do a complicated genuflection that included kissing the ground, syncopated knee-slapping, and tapping his ears with the tip of his tail. "It is my honor to meet you, Third She and Scion of the storied Summerday Clan."

"Oh, stop," said Aliyah, not very convincingly. "You don't have to make a fuss."

"No fuss at all," said Bricabrac in a muffled voice, since he was laying fully prostrate with his face pressed into a buttercup. Then he sat up. "Just wanna do as my saintly mother told me I should do in the presence of royalty. Bless her heart." He stood up and made a deep bow. "Name's Rummage," he said. "Junkrat from the southern swamps. Although I do get into the city now and then, chasing the Almighty Penny." He flicked his copper earring. "I deal in low-end stuff, for the not-too-discerning client. Mostly whipsydoodles and calabashes. Of course, I'm sure you're *very* discerning—"

"Thank you," interrupted Aliyah, a trifle impatiently. She sat up, which meant she was suddenly looming over Bricabrac and Anastasia like a golden tower. "I came down for a visit because we feel, as the Landlords, that it's important to stay in touch with our residents."

Bricabrac nodded. "Yes, yes."

"We've been hearing that there are some rabbits getting out of line," said Aliyah. "Starting trouble. Attacking innocent Blessed. Injuring mothers. Corrupting other rabbits. Fraternizing with other ... luncheon meat." Her eyes flicked toward Anastasia. "Sorry, there's really no other word for it."

"No, no! All good. Understood," said Bricabrac, as he steepled his fingers. "Wow, those are really terrible things. And you know, I have kind of heard of that going on, but I haven't really seen any of it myself."

"Where have you heard this was happening?" asked Aliyah.

"Oh, over there in the … wooded area," said Bricabrac, waving his arm vaguely toward a horizon that was a solid wall of trees.

"Do you ever make weapons, Rummage?"

"Oh, well, I'm more of a gewgaw-maker, myself," said Bricabrac, shuffling around and doing his best to look lazy and dimwitted.

"And do you know the name of the leader of these renegade rabbits?"

Bricabrac rubbed his chin and looked skyward, then folded his arms and squinted hard into the middle distance. "Lessee, I wanna say … Lotta?"

"Last name?"

Bricabrac frowned. "Crabgrass?"

Aliyah looked at Bricabrac impassively as the breeze tousled her golden fur. At last she said, "Thank you, Rummage. You have proved yourself a true friend of your realm and your Landlords today."

"Well, thank you very much, Your Highness, I'm sure," said Bricabrac as he tugged his forelock. He looked around for a moment. "Welp! I guess we'll be on our way." He bowed again. "By your leave, Your Honor."

"Be well," said Aliyah.

Bricabrac walked over to Anastasia and slapped her flank. "Okay, girl. Let's get 'er done," he called amiably. "Northward, ho."

Anastasia set out toward the Shandy at a slow lollop, with Bricabrac walking beside her with his hand on her haunch. When they were out of earshot, Anastasia let out an explosive sigh and realized she had been holding her breath this whole time.

"Oh, my Yah," she said in an intense whisper. "*Thank* you, Bricabrac." And she turned and licked his forehead with such force and emotion that he staggered sideways.

"I go the extra mile for my clients," whispered Bricabrac, as he scraped her saliva off his head. Then he touched his ear. "Oh, no."

"What?" asked Anastasia.

"My pass is gone," whispered Bricabrac. Anastasia looked and saw that his copper earring had indeed disappeared. "Stay here," he whispered, and then turned and darted back the way they had come.

Anastasia hunkered down, feeling very exposed. After several minutes, in the distance, she could faintly hear Bricabrac and Aliyah talking, although she couldn't understand them. They talked for a minute or two, then

Bricabrac came bounding back, his copper earring in his hand.

"Found it!" he said, as he put it back in his ear. "Now let's get the heck out of here."

WARREN SANS GLOIRE

Nicodemus sat at the edge of a sandy spot by the creek. On the banks near him, a group of volunteers had gathered. Yasmin, Love Bug, and seven other rabbits were sitting together, all with bite blades around their necks. They were surrounded by forty warmice armed with swords and spears. Death Rage and Exit Wound sat among them. Wendy sat on the far side of the sandy patch. Freddie was conspicuous by his absence.

Frippery stood in the middle of a sandy patch, holding a large twig.

"We've found a good place," said Nicodemus. "A place in a dried-out stream bed where there's an eight-foot-high waterfall with a deep pool at the bottom, and an outflow that squeezes between narrow rocky banks." Frippery sketched rapidly in the sand while the old rabbit talked. "With the water gone, it creates a narrow hallway that dead-ends into a small chamber with walls too high for anyone to jump out. Even a coyote."

The mention of the Blessed caused a riffle of unease to

run through the audience. A glance from Wendy's dark eyes quieted them.

"The banks of the stream are overgrown with trees and brush, and vines hang down the walls. There is a sapling growing on the bank here." Nicodemus leaned out and indicated a spot. Frippery drew furiously. "We've done some tests. If you tie a rope to the top of the sapling and pull it down, it's strong enough to lift a forty-pound weight a couple of feet. That's an adult coyote."

A murmur rumbled through the watching rabbits and mice, interspersed with a few nervous chuckles. Here they were, talking about something so crazy, killing a Blessed that *towered* over them, and Nicodemus was droning on about it as though he were talking about a colorful mushroom he had seen that morning.

"The rope from the sapling top leads down to a loop with a sliding knot, concealed in the overhanging greenery. It's at the right height for a wolf to put its head through. A length of cord attached to the rope above the sliding knot runs over to a tree root here," Nicodemus indicated a spot on the other side of the stream from the sapling. "That's what holds the rope taut."

"Coyote sees the bait here," said Nicodemus. Frippery drew an X in the streambed. Upon hearing herself referred to as "bait," Wendy started cleaning her left ear with elaborate carelessness. "Bait runs under the overhanging foliage.

Coyote runs after. Puts its head through the loop. A team of mice, stationed here, will bite through this cord as soon as the coyote has it around its neck. The sapling will pull upward, pulling the loop tight."

Frippery drew a coyote being pulled into the air.

"All goes well, the loop of rope will dispatch it," said Nicodemus.

"And if it doesn't go well?" asked a tiny mouse voice.

"Then we will need to assist in dispatching the coyote ourselves," said Nicodemus. "On behalf of the Free Warrens, thank you for being Plan B."

Chapter 13

This I promise you, devoured one: You shall be added unto me. And in my sinew, in my bone, and in my breath, you shall walk again into the evening wood.

—*Wisdom of Hunger Mother*

BRICABRAC

Bricabrac was scampering around his catamaran that he had tied up under the protective cover of an elephant ear on the banks of the Shandy River. Now down in the hold, now rummaging through supplies lashed to the deck, he kept up a running commentary to himself and Anastasia, who waited patiently on the shore.

"See, the thing is," Bricabrac was saying, "traditional

armor doesn't make sense here, because you're not going to be sword-fighting with other rabbits. Most of your enemies will be bigger than you—much bigger. Always excepting weasels, of course." Bricabrac spat out the word *weasels*. "You're going to have jaws that are trying to crush your skull and rib cage, and puncture your skin with teeth the size of your forepaw."

Anastasia fidgeted uncomfortably. "Mmm-hmmm."

"So I'm looking for ..." said Bricabrac, trailing off, as he dug into a pile of items on his rear deck. "Aha! Here it is. He jumped off the boat and ran toward Anastasia, trailing some fabric behind him. "This stuff's great, and look! This piece still has the original tag on it."

'*Baby Safe!*' trumpeted the three-hundred-year-old plastic tag. '*My First Kevlar Onesie. Now with Lycra for extra comfort. Perfect for trips to the mall. Active shooters, who cares? Pew-pew-pew!*'

"What does that mean?" asked Anastasia.

"Damfino," said Bricabrac. "This stuff is super-hard to penetrate. But because it's already pretty much your size, I think I can adapt this as kind of a jacket. Cover your back, your sides. It'll come down onto your legs a little. Not too much because you need to be able to move freely."

"Sounds pretty cool," ventured Anastasia.

"Yup, yup," said Bricabrac. He dropped the fabric and sprinted back to his ship and disappeared down the hold.

A few seconds later, he popped up carrying several metal rings and parabolas. "Aaaand, I have some of these *aluminum d'or* machine parts, from the old Tesla rocket engines, in a few different sizes. Strong as heck, very light, and if we're lucky, some of them may fit you." He ran up to Anastasia, measured her head with his hands, then quickly flipped through the jangle of parts. He took a ring and slipped it over her ears and down onto her head. It fit snugly around the back of her skull, resting on her forehead just above her eyes. "This one looks kinda good," said Bricabrac. "It'll be like an …open-air helmet. Great for skull integrity." He chewed his foreclaw meditatively. "And maybe some of these parabolas around your middle can be like … ribs."

He fell to sorting and stacking the metal pieces. Anastasia lolloped down to the river to see what she looked like. She found a still patch of water and gazed at her reflection. The gleaming golden circlet looked quite handsome resting on her forehead, shining in the sun.

ALIYAH

Sephora and Micah Summerday were resting in a shaded bower in the Spires when Aliyah found them. Micah's huge, golden head was lying on his forepaws, and several of the junior crows were grooming him, picking parasites out of his fur. Sephora's eyes were almost closed in the afternoon heat.

"Oooo, that's good," said Micah, rolling over to let the crow have better access under his left foreleg. "Be sure to thank Grammy Kark for this kind gesture."

"Grammy Kark thanks *you*," said the crow, hopping forward a few steps, "for the wonderful feast."

"Yes," said Micah, as he rolled over onto his back. "A feast for crows. A sad day for wolves. Circle of life."

Aliyah bowed low. "Mummy. Daddy."

Sephora opened her eyes and gestured for Aliyah to come close for a nuzzle. "How are you, darling? We haven't seen you in ages. I was starting to get worried."

Aliyah stepped forward, exposed her throat in submission, and pressed her nose against her mother's shoulder. "We ended up chasing that Icewind wolf way down near the Shandy. So I went across to investigate the rumors."

Sephora wrinkled her brow. "What rumors?"

"You know, I told you awhile back. About rabbits attacking Blessed."

Sephora's eyes started to droop. "Right, right."

"I have this to show you." Aliyah nosed into her carrying bag and came out with the bite blade from Gaetan between her teeth. She laid it on the ground.

Sephora frowned and came forward, sniffing it. "What is this?"

"Rabbits use this to fight. They hold it in their jaws."

Micah opened one eye. "Look how tiny it is. Who are they fighting, squirrels?" A couple of the crows chuckled.

"Rumor is that they're doing real damage," said Aliyah. "To canids. People like us."

"Impossible," snorted Micah.

"That's what all the songbirds are saying," said Aliyah.

"Songbirds are ninnies," said one of the crows. "They'll say anything that rhymes."

Sephora stretched and yawned, then came fully awake. "This could not hurt us," she said, tapping the bite blade. "But it's not good news if the rabbits are doing something new. If they're doing this today, they might be doing something else tomorrow."

"There's one other thing I wanted to mention," said Aliyah. "While I was down there, I ran into a craftrat. Says he doesn't know much about weapons himself, but he could set us up with a craftrat who could. They could come up by Raptor Air."

"Why would we need weapons?" scoffed Micah. "We already have the best weapons. Wolf teeth and claws. And our pack members by our sides."

"Those are great, but we still have enemies," said Aliyah.

"More importantly, we have our honor," said Micah. "We will not take unfair advantage. Hunger Mother and

Blood Father have made wolves perfect, just the way we are."

"But, daddy—" began Aliyah.

"No," said Micah firmly. He yawned and sleepily declaimed:

"The strength of the pack is the wolf,
And the strength of the wolf is the pack."[50]

He closed his eyes again. "A great wolf said that once."

"*You* say it, daddy," said Aliyah.

"I would never say I'm a great wolf," said Micah, lying down on his side and allowing the crows to return. "Others might say it, but I would not."

Sephora drew in the dust with her paw. "I don't like new things, but I know that doesn't keep them from happening," she said. She looked up at Aliyah. "Let's talk about this later."

"They already are happening," said Aliyah. "At first, there was one warren in arrears, but now they've gotten another warren to join them. It's not just one group having a bad month and going over the grace period. This is planned. I think this may be a rent strike."

---

[50] From "The Law for the Wolves," Rudyard Kipling, 1895.

"Huh? Whuzzat?" said Micah. He shook himself, and a small cloud of crows rose up.

"Darling, *language*," said Sephora, glaring at Aliyah.

"Rent strike?" said Micah, grunting as he began to rise. "But mother—"

"Not in the sanctity of our home bower," said Sephora.

"*Rrrrrrrrrent strike*," growled Micah, a twitch running down his foreleg. His scent was beginning to roil.

"We talk about business where business is appropriate," said Sephora. "Not at home. We don't want to get anyone all excited about something that may not even be a problem." She fixed her eyes on Aliyah and nodded her head sideways toward Micah.

"Yes, mother," said Aliyah, as she laid her muzzle on the earth.

"It's nothing, my love," murmured Sephora, nuzzling against War Leader's massive golden head. "Our little girl's just growing up. She doesn't want to sit at the kid's table anymore."

Micah relaxed back into his afternoon snooze. "Well, be sure she gets a nice helping."

NICODEMUS

It was going remarkably well. Nicodemus stood on the streambed at the foot of the dry waterfall and squinted up at the bag of stones hanging down. Exit Wound stood next to him, shading her eyes as she peered up. Her greatsword was strapped to her back. And she had tiny blue lobelia blossoms twined around her ears.

The bag was attached to a rope tied to the top of a maple sapling on the bank, and the weight of the bag was bending the small tree over the stream. A steady procession of rabbits was approaching the bag and tossing pebbles into it. As each stone was added, the tree bent further and the bag sank a little lower.

When the bag reached the optimal position, they would tie the rope in a loop with a sliding knot, disguise it in the overhanging brush, and anchor the rope in place with a cord tied to a tree root. Then cut off the bag of stones.

Death Rage was slated to be the leader of the team of mice who would bite through the cord and spring the trap. She stood on the stream bank across from the willow, her Canada Dry bottlecap shining, trying to judge whether or not the bag of stones had reached the best position. "How about this? Is this good?" Death Rage called down to Nicodemus.

"Not quite," he replied. "The rope needs to be centered over the streambed."

"When's the next batch of stones arriving?" Exit Wound called up to Love Bug, who was supervising the bag.

"Gonna be a few minutes," shouted Love Bug. "We've

used all the nearby rubble. Wendy took a team upstream to find more."

"Fine, no hurry," said Nicodemus. "But no more yelling, please. People can hear you a hundred yards away."

He sat down to rest for a bit. If this worked, it would be striking a tremendous blow for freedom, but the reality of managing this project was making him tired. There was no escaping the fact that he was an elder bunny. Exit Wound snuggled up next to him, and soon the afternoon heat had them both in a fitful doze.

EDOUARD

Edouard was out scouting for prey. The afternoon was hot and sticky. He was so hungry that even a mouse would have been a find. He stood on the edge of a ridge and scanned the ravine below. It was narrow and choked with brush, and there was a dried-out stream running through the middle. As he stood, stock-still and scanning for any sign of motion, he suddenly noticed something odd. A maple sapling was bent over at an odd angle, as though it were leaning over the streambed, and as he watched, it seemed to dip down a little, and then rise up.

He tilted his head sideways and his ears pricked up. Then the sapling did it again. Edouard glided down the side of the ravine, taking care to move quietly. In a few minutes, he had reached the dry streambed and was looking up it, still gazing at the tree. The tree twitched a little, then bent a bit further down.

Edouard trotted up the streambed, and came to a place where the sides began to rise up. A marvelous scent came to his nose. *Rabbit.* He froze and inhaled again. *Fine, fat rabbit.* The rabbit was upwind, so it could not smell him. His salivary glands kicked on. Without moving a muscle, Edouard scanned the area. The scent was coming down the streambed. Must have something to do with that strange tree.

He went into slinky mode and carefully walked upstream and slipped in between the high stream banks. The vegetation was thick. The rabbit smell got stronger and stronger. He could tell now that it was an older bunny. All the better. An easy *casse-croûte.* Soon he smelled mouse. That gave him pause. Could this be another one of those sharpy-stabby gangs? He stepped very carefully, as only a hungry coyote can.

Soon he could see, through a screen of hanging vines, an old gray rabbit resting on the stream floor with his eyes half-closed. It looked like there was a steep surface of stone behind him, although it was a little hard to tell, since there was so much vegetation hanging down.

Edouard started to breathe faster. *Just grab it and go. If there are sharpy-stabbies on the upper bank, they won't be able to get down in time.* He took a last look around. *Okay, old-timer. Your lease is up.*

Edouard lunged forward, burst through the hanging vines, and seized the rabbit in his jaws. It screamed and struggled feebly. He was just lifting it to give it the death shake when he felt a burning sensation in his left foreleg.

Startled, he dropped the rabbit, who scuttled away stiffly. Then he dropped his head to bite the little creature who was bothering him. By the time he registered that it was a mouse with a shining sword, he was already opening his jaws. The mouse leaped upward and slashed at his lip. More annoyed than hurt, Edouard flicked the creature away with his forepaw. It went tumbling over the stones and crashed into the rock wall, where it lay still.

The sound of multiple yells and screams penetrated Edouard's consciousness, and he glanced up briefly to see several rabbits and a dozen mice scampering around on the stream bank eight feet above. And they were armed. *Where was that rabbit?* His head snapped around angrily. It had disappeared into the foliage covering the rock walls. Best find it and get out before the whole crew of *voyous* showed up.

ANASTASIA

Anastasia and Bricabrac were about half a mile from Warren *Sans Gloire*. Anastasia was wearing her new Kevlar jacket, reinforced with *aluminum d'or* ribs. It was hot, but she liked the feeling of protection, and wearing it on the long hike back from the Shandy River was helping her get used to moving in it. Bricabrac had also just cleaned and sharpened her Claw, and had adjusted the sleeve to make it fit better.

Bricabrac was singing a little ditty about a rat who falls in love with a quail's egg.

> *"Oh, what an egg, what a fine speckled egg,*
> *So bright in the morning dew,*
> *It would make any rat want to cry and beg*
> *'Let me spend my life with you!"*

Suddenly, Anastasia's long ears perked up. She shushed Bricabrac. From a distance came the sound of screaming. She bolted forward, crested a small ridge, and looked down to see a dried streambed with several rabbits and many mice running around on the high banks, panicked and yelling. Some of the mice were throwing their spears at a target on the streambed below. She ran down the slope and in a few seconds she was there, looking down into the deep basin where a large sandy-gray coyote was ripping apart the heavy, hanging vegetation. From her vantage point, she could see a rabbit hiding in a nook behind the thick strands of ivy. In another instant, she realized who it was. *Nicodemus.*

Her heart spasmed. Looking around wildly for some solution, she noticed the bag of stones, bobbing gently on the end of its long rope, a couple of feet below the level of the bank. A plan flashed into her mind, and there was no time to think of a better one. The coyote was getting closer to Nicodemus with every second, yellow eyes glaring.

She took a few steps back, then lunged forward and made a flying leap toward the bag of stones. She landed on it, just barely, and clung to the rope. Her weight made the bag sink, and then bounce upward, like a diving board. As the stones rose, she pushed off with her powerful hind legs, in a trajectory to take her high above the coyote. A wordless cry burst out of her, so filled with rage at the Blessed and fear for her old friend that it cut through the rest of the noise.

The coyote looked up, saw a rabbit falling toward him, and instinctively leaped to meet it, jaws aimed at the sky, opening wide. A second later, Anastasia fell between the rows of pointed, grimy teeth, which gripped her around her mid-section.

A joyful, murderous whine burst from the coyote's throat, and the jaws began to close. Anastasia's brain was on fire with alarms, and her limbs burned with adrenaline, but she forced herself to stay with her plan. She flicked out her Claw, but did not use it.

The teeth were pressing into her, but they could not pierce the Kevlar. And once the jaws met around the *aluminum d'or* ribs, they could not close any further. Enraged, the coyote tried to bite harder, but the ribs did not bend. Now confused, the coyote lowered his head, and loosened his grip to try and get her in a better position.

Anastasia took advantage of that moment to squirm forward, so that the coyote's jaws were now clamped around her lower abdomen, and she was hanging head downward. She knew she had only a few seconds before the coyote resorted to his other means of destruction, the killing shake that would break her neck.

As the coyote applied all his force to his jaws, Anastasia swung her hanging upper body toward his neck, and found she could just reach. She punched the gleaming point of the Claw through his fur and skin, and then pulled it across his throat with all her strength. The three-hundred-year-old precision-manufactured blade moved through his flesh like a steel whisper.

For a moment, it seemed like the coyote had not even felt it. Then, the arterial blood gouted from his wound in a shining stream. The bright smell of copper filled the air. Anastasia felt the jaws loosen their grip, and the coyote coughed and shook his head. She was thrown across the chamber, and had the breath knocked out of her as she hit and rolled across the stones.

Anastasia scrambled awkwardly around to face the

coyote. He took a halting step toward her. Then another. After a moment, he sat clumsily and looked at the stream of crimson running down his chest. His yellow eyes drifted up to Anastasia's face.

"Qu'est-ce que je t'ai jamais fait?" he asked. *What have I ever done to you?*

Then his eyes rolled back in his head and he fell sideways across the stones.

Anastasia lay quietly for a few seconds, feeling the adrenaline burn start to recede. The noise from above diminished as the rabbits and mice ran down the bank to where it was lower, so they could run up the streambed toward the waterfall basin.

Anastasia got up and crawled toward Nicodemus. He came slowly out from under the vines and they touched noses, then lay down side by side, breathing fast.

"Thank you," whispered Nicodemus. Anastasia patted his side.

A few seconds later, Love Bug, Yasmin, and some other rabbits burst in to the space, all talking at once. They gathered around Anastasia and Nicodemus. Right behind them came a group of mice, led by Death Rage. They ran to Exit Wound, who was just starting to regain consciousness, and surrounded her with many soft hands and anxious murmurings.

Anastasia pulled herself erect, finding the adrenaline

rush still lingered. She felt exhausted and jumpy at the same time. And she was also feeling the beginnings of a dull throb of rage.

The rabbits stared at her, agog at her Kevlar jacket and the *aluminum d'or* circlet on her head. She held up a paw for silence and gestured for Love Bug to come close. He sat down facing her. She stared at him. "What are you doing, Love Bug?" she asked, finally.

Love Bug spoke softly. "Loving Auntie, the Tumble Stone rabbits really got hammered, because of *us*. Many rabbits there were hurt, some were Glorified." He covered Anastasia's forehead with humble kisses. "I think the alliance could have been in danger. We needed to do something to show them ..." He trailed off.

"Show them what?" asked Anastasia. Her voice was quiet, but her scent was hot and spiky.

"Show them we friends worth having," grunted Wendy. Everyone looked up to see Wendy just entering the waterfall basin with Coriander and several other rabbits behind her. She came close to Anastasia, her dark eyes unblinking. "Nice crown."

Anastasia stood and looked around at the rabbits and mice gathered there. "I'm trying to make a space for us. A place where we can live where there is no killing. Don't you understand that?"

The other animals looked down, with the exception

of Wendy. "And now we've killed a Blessed One," said Anastasia, her tone steely. "*You made me do that.*"

"*Och!*" said Wendy, her eyes black as the night sky. "We kill walking Blessed. Make them fear." She stepped up to Anastasia. "Make them fear *us*."

Anastasia pushed up close to Wendy's face. "You ignorant lump of half-rabbit. It is *Yah* who makes the rules. It is *Yah* who decides when the Blessed come. If we break His rules, if we anger Yah, there will be no peace."

Wendy did not move back at all. "What is Yah?" she rumbled.

Anastasia stamped the ground in frustration. "Did you fall from the sky? Are you brain-damaged?" She threw her front paws in the air. "Yah began everything. Yah created the world. Yah created the animals. Yah created the Dead Gods. And when he was done with them, he killed them." Her voice dropped to a whisper. "And when he's done with us, he will kill *us*."

Wendy shook her head. "No," she said. "Everything began when Elsie MacGowan mortgaged her house to buy world."

"*What?*" shouted Anastasia.

"What does 'mortgaged' mean?" asked Yasmin.

"This God, stupid," barked Wendy. "No questions."

Anastasia stared at her. "You don't know who God is. You're … you're a …" She racked her brain for a concept almost completely unused in rabbit society. The words came out slowly. "You're a … barbarian."

Wendy snorted contemptuously. "Elsie MacGowan began world with all rabbits like me. Water all around. She love rabbits. Rabbits love her. Then one day, she sleep. Rabbits very sad. They live on as best they can without God." Wendy sat up straight. "We stay strong. We train. We fight hawk. One day, Elsie MacGowan will wake and need us. We will be ready."

Wendy belched, and the stench clouded the warm, still air. Anastasia refused to step back.

"One day I fall off world," said Wendy. "Float many day on log. Now I here. I hate this place. I want go back."

"I've heard of this." It was the voice of Nicodemus. He pulled himself into a sitting position. "During the Dominion, the Dead Gods often gathered animals together to torment and kill them. But sometimes, one or two Dead Gods would gather animals and take care of them. No one knows why. They called these places 'sanctuaries.'"

Nicodemus stood and hobbled over to Wendy. He laid his paw on the side of Wendy's massive head. "You came from an island, my dear," he said kindly. "There must have been a sanctuary there. Maybe one day we can help you get back."

Nicodemus turned to Anastasia and kissed her forehead. "My brilliant spark of light," he said. "We are learning as we go. You left us with no instructions, and you gave your power to no one." He rubbed his face. "There was a crisis. We took counsel as equals." He took her forepaw between both of his and raised it to his lips. "We did our best to preserve what you have built," he said quietly.

Anastasia pulled her paw away and stared at him sullenly. "Yah will punish us for this. If I know anything about Yah, I know that."

Chapter 14

You were born a prey animal, but you don't have to die as one.

—Anastasia Bloody Thorn

GAETAN

The coyotes had been hunting since dawn, and killed only three mice and one rabbit between them. Now Gaetan and Lilou were resting near the stream in the hot afternoon, their paws lying on the cool mud. Gaetan noticed that Lilou's ribs were showing through her fur. Nearby, Benoit and some of the others sporadically gnawed on some weather-worn bones they had found. The sweet vanilla scent of a nearby cluster of heliotrope was heavy in the air.

"You know," said Lilou, as she licked her paw. "we should head down to the southern marshes. The Summerdays almost never go that far south."

"Mmm-hmmm," said Gaetan. He was making a small pile of mud between his front paws.

"There's really only foxes and weasels hunting there. Maybe more lunchmeat to be had." Lilou smacked her lips. "We could head down there tonight, after it cools off."

Gaetan rolled over onto his back. "I've heard it's worse than it is here."

"Well—" began Lilou.

Suddenly, they heard from a ways off a shrieking, sobbing noise. Their heads all snapped up, and Benoit got to his feet. The sound came closer. Now they could tell that it was a coyote crying and coughing. They all stood, looking from one to another, anxiously.

"Hey," called Gaetan, his voice a little higher than usual. "Hey, friend. Are you—"

He broke off as the weeping coyote broke through the scrub and came in sight. It was Lucien. His eyes were red, and tears and mucus were dripping from his muzzle. His scent was a hot wave of panic and rage.

They all ran to him and surrounded him, nuzzling him and pressing against him. "What is it? What is it?" said Lilou, softly. "Lucien, what *happened*?"

Lucien stared at her with bloodshot eyes. "It's Edouard," he whispered.

"What? Tell us," said Lilou tenderly.

A deep groan pushed its way up out of Lucien's body. *"They killed him."*

All the coyotes winced as though they had been struck. "What?" hissed Gaetan. "What are you saying?"

Lucien turned his red eyes to him. "They cut his throat. *They cut off his claws.*"

Gaetan felt a sudden rush of bile in his mouth at the thought of Edouard's mutilated body.

"Who?" Benoit shouted. "Who did it?"

Lucien stalked stiffly toward Benoit. "Who do you think?" he shouted. *"The rabbits."* He coughed these words out with such hate that Benoit flinched.

"Are you sure?" asked Lilou.

"Of *course* I'm sure," groaned Lucien, an on-rush of rage making his body jerk like a marionette. "I could *smell* them." He coughed. "Look at me." He went slowly through the pack and touched noses with every coyote there. "We are going right *now* to execute those killers and leave their heads on sticks as a warning to anyone else who dares raise a tooth to Clan *Paresseux.*"

The other coyotes stared at him without moving.

"We are Summerday agents!" shouted Lucien. "We *collect* rent. We don't *pay* it!"

No one moved. They could not meet each other's eyes. Now it was in the open. The proud, lazy coyotes of Clan *Paresseux* were afraid. Of rabbits.

And soon everyone would know.

Brave New World

The news that rabbits had killed a coyote was electrifying. It burned through every social network like a lightning strike. Rabbit to rabbit. Squirrel to squirrel. They were giddy with it. The wonder of it. The artful, aphoristic beauty of it. The hunter hunted. The killer killed.

And, of course, once the songbirds heard, everyone knew. Their mocking couplets flew far and wide.

"Coyboy sleeping by the maple tree,
One less Blessed for you and me.

Little brown bunny, flying high,
Kissed that coy and made him cry.

Gray coyote, on a stream bed,
All the stones are red, red, red."

In truth, it was the other shoe dropping. The release of the tension initiated all those months ago when Anastasia killed the foxes and then brought them back to life. The death made it real, and made it final. It was time for the amazing victory lap.

And so they came. By the dozen, by the score. Rabbits, squirrels, and mice, coming to fete the Blessed-killers and join the throng in celebration. Warren *Sans Gloire* became a city unto itself, until finally they had to say "No more." The *Sans Gloire* council put the word out: Stay in your warren and join with us. Become one of the Free Warrens. If you're a squirrel or mouse, go to one of the Free Warrens near you. There's a place for you. There's a place for everyone.

Love Bug was in his element, the boy-band bunny with long eyelashes and the gift of gab. He greeted newcomers, returners, inquirers, seekers. Representatives from other warrens arrived on an almost daily basis. Bright Shoal Warren near Musmuski Wood sent an emissary. Hoodoo Heights Warren near Boreal Cliffs sent a decorated ambassador. Warren *Feu de Lune*[51] sent a full delegation to negotiate terms, accompanied by a squad of Reader apprentices to take copious notes. Love Bug greeted them all, swept them off their feet with sweet words and courteous kisses,

---

[51]   Fire of the Moon.

connected the movers to the shakers, and suggested the occasional moonlight *tête-à-tête* with lively does wanting to kick up their heels on a business trip.

Within a few days, more than a dozen warrens had joined *Sans Gloire*, each bringing along their complement of local mice and squirrels. Of course, there weren't enough cans and nails in the tumbledown cabin near *Sans Gloire* to give everyone a steel bite blade or a metal-tipped spear, so most of the new warrens were armed with weapons of wood and whatever else they could find. But the real thing that *Sans Gloire* exported was not metal blades but an idea: *You can fight back*. And even the warrens that didn't join watched closely.

New warrens were schooled in the defensive technologies of gratings and sharpened sticks by Freddie. He walked them through the creation of bite blades from found objects, like washed-up fishbones and macadamia shells, edged and sharpened with sandstone. He showed them how the pointed leaf tips of agave and other succulents made excellent spear points, both sharp and pliable. He introduced them to the torch plant, a variety of aloe with saw-like spikes along the edge of every leaf, which could easily turn a bite blade into a ripping instrument.

The newcomers saw him as a frosty assassin, the precision designer of death-dealing tools, focused, relentless, implacable. And if he still sometimes cried at night for the

warmth of his mother's touch and the laughter of his favorite friend, no one knew.

Wendy set up platoons to patrol the frontiers. Each was
made up of ten rabbits armed with bite blades, their claws
sharpened each morning, plus twenty warmice with spears
who fanned out, traveling under the grass. Squirrels accompanied each platoon as mobile lookouts. On the long warm
afternoons, Wendy could be heard drilling her teams, putting them through complex war games with blunted weapons, her long brown ears flapping as she barked orders.

Yasmin often worked as her second-in-command, her
copper-colored, white-streaked fur flashing in the sun as
she took on the role of opposing captain, sending the platoons under her command to test Wendy's defenses. She
soon earned a reputation as a cool commander, unruffled,
unhurried, finding the winning angles while she kept her
troops safe.

They constructed life-sized models of weasels and
foxes with sticks covered by pineapple leather. The platoons would practice coordinated attacks, some going for
the throat, others for the eyes. They even built a model
coyote, with the mice focusing on dealing damage to the
legs, while the rabbits concentrated on powerful leaps to
lift their bite blades high and drive them home.

Death Rage proved herself a marvelous teacher of the
arts of combat. She developed an acrobatic style based on

her ability to leap and tumble, with the goal of placing her rapier tip on any given object at a moment's notice. Many mice came to study with her in the cool of the day, soaking up her techniques and her dedication to honor, all delivered with considerable *élan*. Even a squirrel or two was seen on occasion, using six-inch honey locust thorns as rapiers and taking Death Rage's airborne fighting style to *cirque d'écureuils*[52] heights.

Exit Wound gained her own acolytes, dedicated to the artful murder. She usually dressed to match her greatsword, and her aesthetic became influential among the young female mouse and rabbit warriors. The *beau meurtre*[53] was the goal, and one offered respect to one's enemy by choosing beauty in all things. Wendy scoffed the first time a squad of mice showed up for drill with purple lavender blossoms twined around both their spears and their tails. But when she saw the skill and vigor with which they swarmed the model Blessed, spears rising and falling like murderous pistons, she granted them a short, curt upward nod by way of salute.

Coriander was much in demand as a warrior. His muscular physique made him an excellent fighter. He was adroit with a bite blade, and his intelligence made him a

---

[52] Circus of Squirrels.

[53] Beautiful murder.

fast learner and good improviser. And the iridescent sheen of his copper agouti fur and the kindness in his teal blue eyes turned the head of more than one doe. But there was a sadness that clung to him, and he was endlessly quoting the Word of Yah.

Grégoire, whose extensive knowledge of plants made him a natural healer, had been named the master of the new healing hall. A few months in the safety of Sans Gloire, together with a new purpose in bringing healing to his community, had put a new spring in Grégoire's step. His coat was thicker and darker. And even though he could see little, he knew much, and could often diagnose a sick bunny by scent.

Juniper had appointed herself the apprentice healer. Her bright eyes missed nothing, and her warm, empathetic touch brought comfort to those who came seeking help. She pored over the pages of medical information that Nicodemus had gathered from Bloody Thorn Warren, the tumbledown cabin, and other sources. She could only read a little, and relied mostly on the pictures, but these days there enough Readers and apprentices visiting from other warrens that there was always someone available to help her puzzle out the texts. And Grégoire made a point of sending medical emissaries to other warrens to share healing knowledge, both oral and written.

The healing hall was new because traditional rabbit culture accepted suffering as natural, immutable, ordained. Encounters with Blessed were mostly fatal, and lesser injuries were given scant attention. Sick animals were driven out to protect the group. The Readers in most warrens gleaned and gathered what medical skills and plants they could, but it was a scattershot effort, just a small part of their job. A new idea was growing at *Sans Gloire*. The pain and suffering of individuals *mattered*. Those who were sick or injured should be helped, not exiled as liabilities.

Holly was the prime embodiment of this idea. She reached out to newcomers, offered kind embraces, found them places to stay, showed them where eat, made sure they met the right people. And since she talked to everyone, she knew everything about what was happening at *Sans Gloire*, and much about the other Free Warrens. It was her joy to use this information to help others, and she was constantly finding a snug nook here for a mouse family in need, or a relationship opportunity there for a bedraggled soul who needed a second chance. Anastasia was the Loving Auntie, but Holly had become the unofficial mommy-at-large. Sometimes she could be heard conducting welcome-aboard sessions with new arrivals in her own chamber while she nursed her kittens.

Nicodemus was everywhere, more Regent than Reader, for Anastasia was scarcely to be seen. One morning, he might be meeting with a delegation from a new warren, discussing a mutual protection arrangement sweetened with a promise of trade in dried mangoes. That afternoon, he might be meeting with Freddie, Bricabrac and the craftmice, ironing out a wrinkle in a new weapons idea. If someone was needed to add gravitas to a ceremony, it was Nicodemus they called. And if there was a particularly knotty doctoring case, you would see Nicodemus hurrying on an errand of mercy, murmuring the names of medicinal herbs as he went.

And where was Anastasia? For all that her footprint on *Sans Gloire* was heavy, the Loving Auntie was scarcely to be seen. Many who came wanted to meet the Rabbit Without Antecedents, Killer of Blessed. And Killer for real this time. No healing. No backsies. The rabbit who carried death in her hand. Nicodemus did his best to make some quiet apologies for the absence of Anastasia, and then quietly steer them toward someone else.

The Loving Auntie herself was a fleeting shadow. For days, she sulked in her chamber, or spent long hours roaming the lands around *Sans Gloire*, her mind grinding through a sullen list of grievances. She had saved them all. Lifted them up. Peopled a metropolis of little animals far greater than Bloody Thorn Warren would ever be. She had armed them. Trained them. Loved them. And how did they thank her? By going against her will the second she was out of sight.

For the first time in her life, she felt a kinship to Olympia. *After all I've done for you, ungrateful, disappointing children.*

BLESSED ONES

For the Blessed Ones, there was a new element in their world. Since time immemorial, their fear had been the unconsummated hunt, coming home with no rent collected, hungry mate, hungry cubs. They raised up a god to this fear, the primordial, unblinking Hunger Mother.

Their lives were games won or lost in broad strokes. A single unsuccessful hunt meant nothing. Hunger was something that happened *eventually*. The whole game did not turn on a moment, the way it did for the rabbits. Most predators were like company men. You get up and go to work every day, and over time you were certain to catch a renter, and collect payment in full.

Until now.

Now there was fear of death. So you weren't just playing the odds, doing your bit and coming home once in awhile with warm bellyful. Now there was a killer out there. A small killer. Wily. The unBlessed One. Someone who had no business killing you, but might do so anyway.

The weasels felt it the most. *Yuh try sixteen holes, and whaddaya get? A rabbit who's armed and your throat's all wet.*

Most weasels, like the smirking Saskatoon, kept up a brave front. Lunchmeat could never be dangerous. Unless there was too much horseradish in the mustard. But when it came time for her to slip into a rabbit warren, she suddenly felt shy. More recon was in order. A more appropriate warren was needed.

Yes, she was a god of death, but she preferred victims who knew their place. There was a chill in the air. Something whispered in her ear that the Age of Weasels was passing. But that was ridiculous. She was a mighty hunter of tenants before the Lord.

The foxes did not keep up a brave front. The mauling of Juliette, Isadore, and Desdemona had been echoing through the fox community for weeks. And Anastasia's efforts at healing only made it worse. Were the foxes *toys*, to be harmed or helped at whim? This could not be a rabbit. Just possibly it could be a nonrabbit shaped like a rabbit. A rabbit with a tumor. A freak of nature. But when whole groups of murdering rabbits appeared, attacking innocent foxes without so much as a by-your-leave, it was clear this was no old dam's tale.

Foxes are solitary hunters, bidding even their mates farewell when they go out collecting. And now the scent of rabbit was no longer a simple, unbridled joy. It came with caution. Was this the right sort of rabbit? The foxes tried to learn the smell of steel. The redolence of worked wood. It was hard. It was new. They worked at it, like foxes do.

But when they realized *mice* could be dangerous, they knew it was the end of the world. A mouse, not even real lunchmeat, a *snack*, could suddenly pierce your throat with a sharpy-stabby and send a trickle of your own blood into your lungs. The world was so dark it could no longer be mapped. Let alone understood.

By now, dozens of foxes had met the rage-filled Juliette, obsessed with revenge, a stranger to her cubs. The melancholy Isadore looked after his children the best he could. And the crippled Desdemona, no longer a proud vixen, recited the tale of her injuries over and over again.

Hundreds of foxes heard the rumors, more fantastical with each retelling. In some versions, Anastasia was a chastising spirit, created by Hunger Mother to punish foxes who no longer offered prayers at the beginning of every hunt. In others, Anastasia was a new rabbit god, cruel and merciless as rabbits are, placing liens against property at will. In the shadowed corners of fox dens, it was whispered that she was a necromancer, practiced in the dark arts of the *clawback* and the *hostile takeover.*

The dark music of these eldritch terms shook the foxes to their core. And more than one fox mother could be heard singing to her cubs:

"Sweet, tiny babes,
Stay close and warm,

Inside is safe,
Outside, the storm."

The gyrfalcon who had lost a talon to Wendy's sharp teeth had told the other raptors that he'd been attacked by a group of rabbits with rabies. So they heard the continuing reports of aggressive rabbits as confirmation of the spread of this disease along the southern banks of the Shandy River. Raptors can range over hundreds of square miles, so it was easy for them to drift away, some toward the southern end of the Million Acre Wood, some north toward The Spires, and some to the uplands above the Boreal Cliffs.

Coyote packs are casual groups, not the intimate families that wolves create. So Clan *Paresseux*, the sometime alpha predators south of the Shandy, began to break apart. Some of the coyotes crept up the Stone Stair toward the uplands, hoping to find a little space to live and hunt where the bears' reach had not yet extended. Some scattered south to the swamps. Only a few stayed together, including Gaetan, Lilou, Benoit, and Lucien, bound by their shared horror at what had happened.

The fact that one of their own had been killed by rabbits was bad enough, but the unnaturalness of it made it worse. Edouard's body, killed but uneaten, with his claws cut off, seemed a harbinger of new terrors to come. Animals don't kill like that. If he had been savaged by a bear, his torn and half-devoured corpse would have been less frightening. As it was, they knew that something alien was coming into being, right in the middle of the Wood they called home. They had been traumatized by murderous rabbits, and now they cowered while the renters laughed at them, in verse.

The golden wolves of the Summerday Clan had ridden for generations on a cushion of their own inevitability, and even the most alarming news could not easily puncture that. They ignored the songbirds, of course, but one day Grammy Kark sent Cacao to share news that he had heard from some South Shandy corvids. Rabbits had killed. For real.

Even Micah Summerday registered some genteel annoyance at this. And amid a pack gathering with much *tsk-tsking* on the Hill of Voices, the wolves discussed the problem of the felonious rabbits.

"It's Clan *Paresseux,* they're not up to snuff as agents," said Micah. "That's what happens when we do business with people who aren't quite…our sort. Didn't get into the best schools and all that."

"Sad, really," said Alaric. "And overly familiar as well."

"What if it's more than that?" asked Aliyah.

Sephora Summerday looked at her. "You find good people and put them in place, and then you don't micromanage them," she said. "If the *Paresseux* can no longer do this job, the South Shandy franchise will have to go to someone who can."

Aliyah looked around at the other wolves. "What if this is the beginning of a general rent strike?"

Micah sat up tall with a jerk and the hair on his shoulders rose. "Then we would take *immediate* action," harrumphed the War Leader.

Sephora fought down an irritated glare and instead stretched and yawned. She kept her scent cool and careless. "The issue with defining this operations problem as a rent strike," she said, "is that the bears in City of Oom would want to get involved. They'd be afraid of the strike spreading to their demesne. So they would be *here*. Micromanaging *us*." Her gaze drifted around the circle of wolves. "And believe me, being micromanaged by a bear is no trot in the park. The performance evaluations alone can be fatal."

The other wolves found this to be a very persuasive argument. The day was coming when the Summerday Clan would sweep through the Million Acre Wood like a shining scythe, but that day had not yet come. Instead the golden wolves came up with the classic senior management solution: Fire some junior people.

ANASTASIA

Anastasia was in her chamber, chewing the nails of her left forepaw, when Nicodemus came in and dropped down next to her. He looked exhausted. His gray coat was thinning. "I can't do this anymore," he said.

Anastasia looked at him without speaking.

"Your job. My job. Everybody's job." He double-bumped her flank. "Look, you won the war, don't lose the peace."

Anastasia looked at him steadily. "The war's not over. You know that."

Nicodemus dragged his claws through the earth. "I know this isn't how you wanted it. But it's good and it's what we have. Seize this and run with it."

She got up and paced the length of her chamber, then turned and looked at him. "Yah could take this away at any time."

Nicodemus came over to her and sat down, nose to nose. For the first time in her life, Anastasia heard him sound angry. "Yah could take *me* at any time. Yah could take *you* at any time. Who knows what God will do? I'm old. I'll be dead in a year. Or two at most. Let's grab this and go." He pulled down his right ear and cleaned it. "Speaking as a friend, Loving Auntie."

She gazed at him, and he saw her golden eyes fill with tears. "I'm a killer," she said.

"You killed an enemy," said Nicodemus.

"A Blessed One," said Anastasia.

"He would've killed me," said the elder bunny.

"I know," said Anastasia. She drew a complicated shape on the floor. "Do you believe in Yah?"

"I believe in rabbits," said Nicodemus.

"Rabbits don't kill," said Anastasia.

"Until now," said the old rabbit.

Anastasia was silent.

He came close to her and kissed her forehead. "Yah may not forgive you," he said, "but I do."

FREE WARRENS

The word went out from the Warren *Sans Gloire* Council, "This is the day that we have made. Rejoice and be glad in it. Come and celebrate. BYODill."

The *Sans Gloire* rabbits spent the whole day gathering the freshest yummies and the most succulent nibbles. And of course, they did not stint on the blueberries that *Sans Gloire* had become known for. These treats were scattered around the greensward outside the front gate of the warren in little snack 'n chat stations that invited bunnies to do their two favorite things.

A team of rabbits from Fuji Warren, located not far from the apple orchard tended by Wellbutrin and Lorazepam, showed up around mid-day with a travois of fermented apples. They scattered them in amongst the treats, engaging in some sampling as they went.

In the late afternoon, just as the sun's rays were leaning toward gold, the first few squirrels began to show up. One brought a pair of walnuts that rattled in their shell. Two others carried a bean pod as big as themselves, balancing it between them.

A group of squirrels brought an abalone shell from the beach. They set it down near a flat-topped boulder that commanded the area and began to rake over it with a twig in a sturdy 4/4 rhythm. At this sound, the walnut and bean pod squirrels gathered nearby and started to add their own rhythmic commentary. The bean pod proved an excellent off-beat accent, seesawing back and forth between its two players. And the squirrel with the walnuts shook and tossed them in a casual but infectious polyrhythm that drew animals from around the greensward.

One of the abalone squirrels looked up and noticed something. It was Dingus, climbing out of his hole in the old oak tree. She elbowed her neighbor, who then tossed a nutshell at his neighbor. And soon all the squirrels were watching as Dingus walked with eerie certitude and precision along the main branch near his hole.

He did not scamper. He did not scold. He did not move quickly. Nor did he move unquickly. He reached a fork where the branch spread out and made a wide platform. He sat down with his legs crossed in the lotus position, and rested his left hand in his lap with the palm facing up. His right hand lay on his knee, and he reached down with one finger and touched the living wood beneath him.

"Ah," he said. "*Chek.*"

All the squirrels looked astonished for a long moment. Then they broke into a loud cheer.

Soon after, the mice began to gather. Craftmice and warmice both appeared, most of them originally from Musmuski Wood, and they considered each other two hands of the same mouse. They greeted each other with many affectionate nuzzles, talking excitedly about the Free Warrens as they noshed on the treats and dirty apples. The main vibe from the warmice was, *Finally, a cause worth fighting for.* And from the craftmice, *My fingers sing for freedom.* Over the last several months, they had come to see how valuable hands were in the animal world. And if they carried themselves with a bit of extra swagger, they can be forgiven that.

A few minutes later, Throat Punch appeared, carrying her double flute made for her by her father, a craftmouse of some renown. Her light gray form swayed as she lifted her flute to her lips, and a sinuous melody began to reel out, drifting across the greensward. The squirrels in the midst of their percussion jam lifted their heads, eyelids drooping for a moment in approval. Some of the rabbits noticed and wandered over. Throat Punch played on, tiny fingers flying as she warmed up her instrument and showed that

Musmuski fingers could be used for something besides making weapons.

Soon after, Moody Loner showed up. In the afternoon sun, his coat was dark like cast iron flecked with rust. He opened his small, finely-crafted bag and pulled out a set of pipes made of reeds, an octave and a half wide. When he put the instrument to his lips, the sound of his close intervals leaping hither and yon around Throat Punch's melody was like a cool rain falling on a hot afternoon. More animals came near. And soon representatives of the other Free Warrens began to appear.

The Bright Shoal Warren rabbits brought tender watercress from the banks of the Shandy River. A group of bunnies from Warren *Feu de Lune* brought a fine selection of golden, late-summer pears, carrying them in their backpacks. And a boisterous bunch from Warren *Orléans* showed up, rolling their big stomp drum. It was three feet across, a construction of small branches and pineapple leather, built by craftrats hired by the warren. Around the rim were five seats, and when they laid it on its side, five rabbits immediately clambered up to take the spots, their back feet resting on the skin of the drum.

They looked at each other, making eye contact as their ears began to move together, forward and back, *flik, flak, flik, flak*, synchronizing into a single beat. Then, a nod traveled around the group, and an instant later, their powerful back feet hit the drum in unison, launching a lively 2/4 dance rhythm that seized the attention of everyone in the area, and could be heard half a mile away.

Immediately, rabbits came pouring out of *Sans Gloire*. Juniper came bounding out, with Holly's young kittens running after her and laughing. Since the death of her brother Chervil, she had become almost a second mother to them, and they tumbled with her on the grass, giggling and amazed by the sound of the drum. Yasmin came right after, her copper-colored fur shining in the golden sun as her kits frolicked near her.

Freddie had come from the workshop that morning, and he still had traces of sawdust on his thick gray-and-white fur. The weeks of steady work and developing a valued skill had made him more self-assured. He cut a handsome figure as he lolloped across the greensward, deep in conversation with Bricabrac. The water rat adjusted his earring and smoothed his fur as he walked, wearing his usual *I'm here for the networking* smile.

Coriander came out, leading Grégoire by pressing against his flank as they walked. He found a nice spot for Grégoire near a mound of strawberries, and left him trading tips on poppy seed storage with the Reader from Bright Shoal. Then Coriander sauntered toward the big drum, head nodding in time to the beat.

Nicodemus appeared, chatting with some visiting

Reader apprentices and looking happier than he had in months. He made a beeline for the fresh watercress and pear extravaganza.

Wendy stepped out of the main doorway and stood for several seconds, rocking slightly on her feet and blinking. It looked like she'd been doing some early sampling of the dirty apple supplies. She caught sight of Love Bug a few feet away, bantering with a spotted orange doe from a nearby warren, and ambled over, swaying to the beat.

"You busy boy, Bug of Love," she rumbled. "So so busy."

Love Bug looked over at her, surprised. "What?"

Wendy stretched and farted. "Busy with little does. Busy, busy, busy." The orange doe's eyes flicked back and forth between Love Bug and Wendy. "Don't mind me," chuckled Wendy. "Just friend. Go way back."

The doe smiled blandly and began to drift away towards a nearby group. Love Bug looked annoyed. "Thanks a lot."

"Sorry," said Wendy and took another big bite of dirty apple. "You very nice boy."

"Go home, Wendy. You're appled," said Love Bug. He lolloped off.

A moment later, he appeared on the flat-topped boulder, leaning into the big drum's insistent rhythm as he glided effortlessly through a series of moves that included the stomp 'n thrust, the hoodoo shuffle, and a set of simple but strangely beguiling gestures that some of the Dead Gods would have identified as the *macarena*.

Mabel laughed as she moved through the crowd, a gorgeous crown of purple fairy foxglove twined around her ears. "Hey buddy," she called up to Love Bug. "Don't get thirsty." She tossed him a piece of dirty apple. Love Bug caught it in his mouth and waggled his ear tips at her.

Anastasia came out of the main entrance of *Sans Gloire* wearing the Kevlar armored jacket Bricabrac had made, and she looked splendid. As a surprise, the craftmice had been working on the jacket all week, plying all the tricks of their trade. It was now reversible. One side was a muted pattern of greens and browns, shaped like leaves, sticks, and earth: The perfect camouflage for a bunny sitting still under a bush. The other side, which she was wearing today, they had colored with turmeric root so it was an earthy gold, perfectly set off by the *aluminum d'or* fittings, gleaming in the afternoon sun.

Freddie lolloped toward her. "Haven't seen you in awhile," he said, kissing her forehead gently. "I brought this for you." He held up a succulent piece of dirty apple wrapped in a mint leaf and sprinkled with vanilla bean chips.

"What is it?" asked Anastasia.

"A little gift for the Loving Auntie who is remaking the world," said Freddie, smiling. "From her old friend."

Anastasia stared at him for a moment, then kissed him sweetly on the forehead. She took the fragrant *hors d'oeuvre* between her claws and held it under her nose, closing her eyes as she was enveloped in the aroma. "It's wonderful." She took a bite and then held it out. "Share it with me, friend." Freddie took the other half in his mouth and for a moment, their eyes were locked together.

Then she nose-bumped his shoulder, turned, and leaped nimbly up onto the flat boulder. The musicians quieted the beat, but kept it going softly. Love Bug bowed and hopped down. Anastasia turned to face the crowd.

As soon as they saw her, the animals began chanting, *"Sans Gloire! Sans Gloire!"*

Anastasia stood up tall on her back legs. *"Citoyens!*[54]" she called. "Welcome to the Free Warrens!" The roar became louder. There was more cheering, leavened with somersaulting *binks*. "Let us live like free peoples," shouted Anastasia. "Let us have music. And dancing. And *songs*." She held out her paws. "Where are our Rememberers? Our cantors?"

The bunnies looked around. Coriander sat up. "I'll go first."

"The bold and learned Coriander," called Anastasia. "Let us hear you, brother!"

---

[54] Citizens.

Coriander jumped up on the boulder. "This is from the Book of Kits." He lifted his voice, a warm baritone, and began a classic rabbit congregational hymn at a very slow pace, the lines punctuated by stamps. The musicians followed his lead, dropping into a slow tempo, scratching their claws across drum skin for the offbeat.

"When I was a little kitten,
My mother said to me,

Be careful darling child,
Be careful won't you, please?"

Coriander's eyes were closed. This was the rabbit music that he had been taught. The music he had always sung as a cantor. Anastasia looked out over the sea of upturned faces.

"For you see the world is ruled,
Ruled by those bigger than we,

And that's the way the world is made,
That's the way the world must be."

Anastasia sidled up next to Coriander and put her paw on his shoulder. "Good. Thank you, brother," she said quietly.

Then, as she felt all the eyes on her, she continued more loudly, "Thank you for reminding us of our roots."

Coriander looked surprised, and a little hurt at being interrupted, but he nodded his head and hopped down. Anastasia smoothed her golden jacket and looked around. She wanted something different. Her eye fell on Mabel, holding court in the middle of a fascinated group of young bucks, and she called out to her. "Sing me a song about how wonderful it is to be a rabbit."

Mabel came bounding toward her, the fairy foxglove around her ears glowing purple against her black and white fur. "Missed you at the pre-game, Loving Auntie," she said, hopping up onto the boulder. "Hope you're buzzed."

Anastasia leaned toward her. "Let's get this party started." Her eyes drifted out over all the eager faces, so hopeful. "I want a new happy song, not the same old *poor me*," she said, under her breath.

Mabel laughed and licked her forehead. "I read you, Loving Auntie," she whispered. Then, she turned to face the crowd. "Here's my interpretation of a few lines from the Book of Fluffy." She cocked back her head and started belting out a bright melody in a sprightly soprano, stamping along with her lyrics. The musicians looked startled for a moment, and then fell in closely behind her.

"Stamp for sweet leafies,
Stamp for the sun,
Stamp for warm burrows,
When the day is done."

A group of rabbits from Tumble Stone Warren, who clearly knew this song well, started doing a dance that involved a lot of stomping and tail-shaking. *Stamp, shakey-shakey-shake. Stamp, shakey-shakey-shake.* Coriander and some other *Sans Gloire* rabbits nearby picked up the moves and soon, a hundred rabbits were doing it, most of them noticeably tipsy.

"Stamp for your life,
Stamp for your love,
Stamp for the sun,
Shining down from above."

Holly and Yasmin were playfully bumping flanks, with Holly doing a good job holding her own with her three legs. Wendy clubbed Juniper with her substantial hip, and though Juniper looked surprised at first, she gamely bumped Wendy back, and soon they were doing the *shakey-shakey-shake* together. Even Death Rage and Exit Wound were bumping their tiny booties, which made their swords clash.

> *"Stamp for a lover,*
> *Stamp for a friend,*
> *Stamp for afternoons,*
> *That will never end."*

Mabel read the crowd right and started singing the song again from the top. The Warren *Orléans* rabbits really laid into their kick drum the second time around. The squirrel percussionists launched into an acrobatic frenzy of counterpoint. And when Mabel gave Throat Punch and Moody Loner the "take it" sign during the break, they leaped into a free-flowing call-and-response flute jam that went on for almost ten minutes.

By the time the third rendition was done, hundreds of mice and rabbits were dancing around the boulder, the tree branches vibrated with squirrels joining in, and even some curious songbirds were chiming in with a vigorous descant.

"Laissez les bon temps rouler![55]*"* called the leader of the Warren *Orléans* drum team. Suddenly, everyone was very tipsy. Most of these animals had never felt so free. Dirty apples were really for Blessed, because the happy dance of a prey animal who dropped her guard was likely to be short. But now, here, they were safe. And as Anastasia looked out over the dancing multitude, she was happy.

---

[55] Let the good times roll!

Mabel jumped down, and another bunny took her place. Then another. And another. It was late in the day when Anastasia leaped up onto the boulder again. She held up her paws for quiet, and the crowd slowly stilled.

"Friends," she said. "What we have done has never before been done in the history of the world." There was a huge cry of delight. "We are not hiding under the bushes any more." The band let loose with a sky-filling crescendo.

"We are happy," said Anastasia. There was a mighty whoop as hundreds of little hearts felt big for the very first time, and they let the world know it.

"We are powerful." Anastasia lifted her right paw skyward, and flicked out the Claw. At the sight of the pointed blade, gleaming in the late-afternoon sun, the crowd of mice, squirrels, and rabbits, little animals all, cheered so hard that they cried. A fierce elation swept through them like a summer storm.

Anastasia sheathed her blade, and spread her paws wide. The metal circlet on her head burned like fire in the blazing sunlight. And her golden coat was rich with majesty and love. All the animals caught their breaths in the silence, hanging on her words.

"And we are free." The cry of joy that greeted her was something no one had ever heard before. The throats of the animals were filled with something new and wondrous, a burning bright I-love-you mixed with a sob of ecstasy for

life. They embraced each other as the tears ran down their faces. Anastasia leaped down and entered the crowd, feeling their emotion wash over her in a storm of hope and yearning.

The kick drum began to sound a driving call that stirred the blood. The wild beat moved their souls, uniting them into a single swirling mass exulting in this moment. *We are free.* Whatever the morrow might bring, today was a very good day.

Thank you

Thank you so much for reading War Bunny! Please let me know what you think of it by leaving a review on amazon. com.

War Bunny is the first book in a series. The next book, *Summerday*, will be published in 2022. It picks up right where *War Bunny* ends.

Please join the email list at www.christopherstjohn. com to:

- Stay up-to-date on the latest *War Bunny* developments
- Get freebies and special deals

If you'd like to reach me with any questions, please email me at sansgloire@gmail.com.

Thanks again!
Christopher St. John

Acknowledgements

I would like to thank the animals who served as models for some of these characters. Rescue bunnies all, they've come to have a profound impact on my understanding of who counts as a "person." Anastasia and Freddie came from SaveABunny in Mill Valley, California. Love Bug and Wendy came from RabbitEARS in Oakland, California. Mabel was rescued from a California fur farm and lives with a friend.

Many thanks to my longtime friend and fellow writer, Mike Stevens. His insightful comments on the first draft were a milestone in the development of this book. Lynne Stevens also offered much warm encouragement.

I'd like to thank my sisters, Catherine McKenzie and Julia Singer Presar, who read early drafts and made many useful suggestions, as well as spending many hours talking through ideas with me.

I read new scenes aloud at weekly gatherings of the Animals in the Arts circle in Berkeley, California. As I listened to my artist and writer friends talk about what they hoped the story would be, I was inspired to shape the narrative in ways I had not thought of. Thanks and hugs to Diana

Navon, Leslie Goldberg, Michael Goldberg, Cassie King, Michelle Lang, Masha Aleskovski, and Deirdre Arima Duhan.

I would like to thank the beta readers I connected with on betabooks.com, who showed me what *War Bunny* looked like to someone seeing it for the first time. Their astute and honest feedback saved me from making some big mistakes, as well as enriching the story in countless ways. A heartfelt thank you to Teryl Mandel, Eileen L. Rubart, Athena Bailey, Hannah Nicklaus, Richard Davis, Sid Pits, Hyunmee Corlett, Adrian Frost, David Pruette, Brian Rawlings, Mark McQuown, Kat Anderson, Ann Gravity, Kim Brooks, Nicole Mandel, Rebecca Lane, Emily K., and Cee.

The team at Harvest Oak Press has been wonderful, and they've done all they can to make *War Bunny* the best it can be. Thanks for all your hard work!

And I must offer oodles of thanks to my wife, Gayle Paul, who this year, and every year, wins the Grand Slam Award for Being The Super Duperest Number One Very Tiptoppy Most Bestest Of All Da Bunniez.

Made in the USA
Middletown, DE
24 July 2021